A Rocky Divorce

A Rocky Series of Mysteries
Book One

By Matt Coleman

pandamoon
publishing

www.pandamoonpublishing.com

Jacket design and illustrations © Pandamoon Publishing
Art Direction by Don Kramer: Pandamoon Publishing
Editing by Zara Kramer, Rachel Schoenbauer, and Jessica Reino, Pandamoon Publishing

Pandamoon Publishing and the portrayal of a panda and a moon are registered trademarks of Pandamoon Publishing.

Library of Congress Cataloging-in-Publication Data is on file at the Library of Congress, Washington, DC

Edition: 1, version 1.00
ISBN 13: 978-1-950627-22-6

Reviews

"Matt Coleman's *A Rocky Divorce* has it all - a can't miss protagonist in the titular Rocky, razor-sharp prose, and a bonkers, gonzo feel that makes every page an adventure. Don't miss this one - Coleman's a name to watch." **—Alex Segura, acclaimed author of *Blackout* and *Dangerous Ends***

"*A Rocky Divorce* is a hilarious whodunnit with one of the more original amateur detectives you'll find. Rocky had me laughing, screaming, and wanting to know who the killer was. A truly awesome addition to the crime writing genre." **—Amina Akhtar, author of *#FashionVictim***

"LAUGH OUT LOUD FUNNY! Matt Coleman takes you on a rollercoaster ride with his first book in a new series. You will want to jump in and enjoy the ride. I can't wait for the next installment to see what Rocky is going to do next." **—The Write Review**

"Coleman's signature steady action pace is fully present, along with fantastic one-liners and well-rounded characters that would feel like clichés in less-skilled hands. *A Rocky Divorce* is a hilarious page-turner with a protagonist that you'll want to make your best friend, because you wouldn't want her for an enemy." **—Penni Jones, author of *Kricket***

* * *

Praise for *Juggling Kittens*

"Toss Tom Perotta, Raymond Chandler, and Hunter S. Thompson in the air, and you've got JUGGLING KITTENS: an electric, energized romp through the wilds of Ruddy Creek, Arkansas. When an outcast student goes missing, his doe-eyed middle school teacher takes it upon himself to find him. What ensues is a switchbacking chase from local character to back woods, churches to small town secrets. At once outlandish and heartfelt, hilarious and deeply macabre, this novel explodes with colorful, lively prose and crisp dialogue that will have you turning pages. A riveting, accomplished debut by a terrific new voice. Coleman's substantial talent is one to watch." —**Sara Lippmann, author of** *Doll Palace: Stories*

"It's sarcastic fun, and features an unsettling mystery. While [the] search for a missing student keeps the pages turning, Coleman's subtle exploration of rural life, education, relationships, parenthood, and America's response to 9/11 is the novel's true selling point." —**Daniel Ford,** *Writer's Bone*

"Juggling Kittens was absolutely fucking wonderful." —**David Joy, author of** *The Line That Held Us*

* * *

Praise for *Graffiti Creek*

"*Graffiti Creek* by Matt Coleman is a non-stop thrill ride that may be the best adventure/chase novel you read this year. From the opening pages, the action begins and keeps the reader on the edge of their seat all the way through to the climactic finale. However, Graffiti Creek is more than just an action adventure novel. Mr. Coleman takes particular care in bringing forth a nuanced cast of characters; each with a story to tell, each believable in their actions and motivations. *Graffiti Creek* is also deftly plotted with more twists and turns within the pages than one of Cary Trubody's many pulse-pounding acts of escape. Mr. Coleman has produced a first-rate thriller. And one that screams to be read in one sitting; those with heart conditions exempted, of course." — **Neil A White for Readers' Favorite**

"*Graffiti Creek* is stuffed to the covers with action, energy, and daring chase scenes - and also manages to demonstrate a good bit of heart along with its adrenaline." —**IndieReader**

"[A] book that, besides having a ton of heart and being superbly written, entertains constantly in that deep, brain-tingling way only great fiction can." —**Gabino Iglesias, Wonderland Book Award-winning author of** *Coyote Songs*

Dedication

To my wife, Samantha, and her ex-husband's mistress.
Without either of you two ladies this book would have never been possible.

A Rocky Divorce

Chapter 1

Raquel Champagnolle Arnold parked sideways across the driveway and chewed on a straw. The straw matched the baby blue of the monogram on her stainless-steel tumbler full of Diet 7-Up. She pulled for a drink but realized her distracted gnawing ruined the straw, so she dropped the cup back into its holder in her console and studied the scene before her. She parked before a quaint little house in a mediocre neighborhood. The house of an office assistant. Maybe a hairdresser. Raquel blocked in a jacked-up Chevy pickup—big and black and teetering on oversized, knobby tires. The man who purchased this truck overcompensated for things in his life. In fact, the same man bought the car pinning in the Silverado—Raquel's little black Lexus—in an effort to overcompensate for some of those things in his life. Raquel knew both of these to be facts. Because the truck parked in the hairdresser's driveway belonged to Chet Arnold. Her own husband.

A little bumper sticker on the shiny chrome displayed the *Rocky Horror* lips. Chet bought the sticker as a sort of tribute to Raquel, who had gone by Rocky all her life thanks to her father's love of the cult classic. When Chet first showed the decal to her, she answered his grunt of "sexy, huh?" with a riposte that the lips belonged to a transvestite. A sweet one, but still. Caustic wit served as one of the countless ways Rocky took the proverbial wind out of Chet's salacity. She realized it. And the awareness gave her a twinge of guilt, even now. The flirtations of a narcissistic asshole worked on a seventeen-year-old high school Rocky, but ten years later? She glanced from the lips to a pair of truck nuts and the twinge of guilt disappeared in an eye roll.

"Moron."

Rocky bounced out of her car, secured her Michael Kors bag in the crook of her arm, and nancied to the front porch. She stopped and straightened her dress. Pushed her sunglasses up into her dark, satiny hair. Then she took in her surroundings. The neighborhood was lower middle, bordering on poor, but safe. Along with too many windchimes, the narrow bungalow houses boasted hanging pots and daisy-shaped flags and all the trimmings of a neighborhood of older residents. The hairdresser tried to keep up with the manicured flower beds by putting out a few pansies and some ornamental rocks. A weak attempt at best. Pegging the hairdresser as young and stupid, an empty space in her sickly rows of flowers advertised the lack of a security sign. Rocky eyed the rocks and found one a little glossier than the rest. She toed the synthetic cobblestone and it flipped over without any trouble, so she knelt and opened a false bottom, fished out a key, and tossed the fake rock into the front yard.

The front door opened with a quiet sigh. An overwhelming blend of plug-in air freshener and litter box fumes hit Rocky as she walked into the living room. She turned her nose up at the blue plastic box in the corner surrounded by a disgusting array of gravelly litter kicked out all over the floor. The decorative style of the living room screamed eclectic, to put it nicer than Rocky would describe the mess of a space. There were four different grains of wood between the coffee table, media stand, and bookcases, alone. A hideous floral pattern poked out from underneath a tan slipcover battling to stay in place on the couch. These furniture choices belonged to a person used to saying, *No, Grandma, don't put that on the curb. I can use it.*

Rocky wanted to stroll on into the kitchen and just keep right on dressing down the whole set-up in an inner monologue, but faint moaning coming from the back of the house distracted her. She recognized the sound all too well. A pained, rhythmic grunt—imagine a caveman playing tennis with a sore knee. The instinctive shudder up her spine coincided with the thought of sex for at least the last two years or so. The other sound—the feigned throes of passion, a porn star imitation in lieu of any threat of actual orgasm…well, she knew that sound pretty well, too.

She clucked her tongue and strolled back toward the open bedroom door, plucking a vase off a low bookshelf on her way. As she rounded the corner, she recognized the hairy backside of Chet, draped over the bent form of a blonde, thrusting into her with all the grace of a seasick dock worker. Although Chet was a bit doughy, the blonde sported a muscular back and slender ass, like maybe someone he met at the gym. The hairdresser theory fell apart, however. A stark hombre—like your drunk aunt would give you when you slept over at her trailer—flopped around with the motion. But shitty hairdresser remained a viable option.

Rocky palmed the vase and chunked it hard at Chet's head, connecting with a clunk and sending the vase bouncing off the wall and to the floor. He swore and jump-turned, covering his crotch. Rocky made the face of someone who had just been served spoiled fish. "Plastic? Who the fuck puts out a plastic vase in your living room?"

Chet shook his head in disbelief. "Rocky? What the fuck? How'd you get in here?"

Rocky shrugged. "Well, I somehow managed to crack your girlfriend's top-notch security system. The better question is how'd you get in there? Could you even feel anything, sweetie? If you want to finish, Chet, go ahead. What's ten more seconds?"

Chet started fighting with a pair of khakis from the floor, mumbling, "Jesus, Rocky. You're so stupid."

Rocky flew into a rage, grabbing pictures off the wall and throwing them. "I'm stupid? Me? You parked your ginormous truck in front of your girlfriend's fuck pad!"

A picture of an older couple shattered over Chet's head sending glass all over the bed. The shitty hairdresser shot up to avoid flying shards, revealing a pregnant belly.

Rocky's eyes turned from almonds into big, hazel saucers. "She's pregnant?!?"

Chet waved his hands in front of him, struggling to put on a pale green polo. "It's not what you think."

Rocky laughed. "I think you're fucking a pregnant girl."

The shitty hairdresser squeaked, "It's not his."

Rocky shot her a look. "Shut the fuck up. You don't get to talk unless you're asking for directions to the abortion clinic."

Chet took a step toward Rocky. "She's telling the truth. It's not mine."

Rocky oscillated back and forth between them. "So you mean…" She shook her head in twittery little jerks. "You mean you just *want* to fuck a pregnant girl?"

Chet cocked his head. "Baby, you know I have some fetishes."

The shitty hairdresser nodded. "It's more common than you think."

Rocky pointed a finger at her. "Shut the fuck up, hairdresser." She gave her a disgusted shudder. "And fucking wax, for Christ's sake. What are you, a 1970s centerfold?"

The shitty hairdresser covered herself and stared back, confused. "I'm a waitress."

Rocky threw her head back and laughed. "Of course you are." She threw a small jewelry box into Chet's stomach and spun on her heels to storm back down the hallway.

He caught up with her in the living room and grabbed her arm. She spun out of his grip and he threw his hands up in apology. "I'm sorry. I'm sorry. I won't touch you. But, baby, just hear me out. Please."

Rocky raised her eyebrows.

Chet nodded with the gentle motion of a man trying to get a leash on a mean stray dog. "This. All this," he motioned back toward the shitty hairdresser-turned-waitress. "This means nothing. Less than nothing. I love you, baby. You're everything to me. It's just—" He paused, waiting for her to cut him off. But she didn't. Rocky always gave a person plenty of kindling with which to build their own effigies. "It's just we both know you haven't been too sexual as of late. And I get that. I mean, you put on a couple of pounds and it's hard to feel sexual. I understand. But, baby, I have needs. I've tried to get you to help me with some of my sexual proclivities. And you've never been willing. I feel like you almost wanted me to go looking for it somewhere else. When's the last time we even had sex? The time you passed out drunk after my office party. You weren't even awake. I don't think it counts. And that was over a month ago. I can't go so long. You have to understand that, right?"

Rocky gave one calm nod. Her lips tight. "So let me get this straight. The reason you made the choice to fuck a pregnant waitress is because I am too fat and won't participate in threeways with you. Is this accurate?"

Chet rolled his eyes in exasperated disgust.

"And you decided to tell me this in the living room of your girlfriend while she gets dressed in the back room. And to do so using the word *proclivities*, which you cannot possibly know how to spell or use in any sentence other than the one you just said."

Chet shook his head in angry jerks. "Hey. You came here on your own. I didn't ask you to come here. You made a choice. And do you know how many opportunities to cheat I've had? How many times I've been faithful to you? I'm one of the faithfullest people I know."

Rocky smiled. "And we're back."

Chet's forehead wrinkled in confusion. "Why do you have to make a joke about everything? You're so stupid."

Rocky grinned. "Chet. I want a divorce. No jokes."

His cheeks and eyes dropped with genuine hurt. "Baby, no. Wait. I love you. Give me another chance. Please."

"You've had chances, Chet. This is the last one. I want a divorce. And I am going to take fucking everything."

Rocky turned to storm out with dramatic flair. She stopped at the sound of Chet chuckling to himself, and she whipped around. "What the fuck are you laughing at?"

Chet rubbed his chin and shook his head. "What are you going to take, Rock?"

She shrugged. "Everything. The land—"

"Is in my dad's name."

She paused. "The—the house."

"My name. My dad co-signed. I can switch the deed over to him by morning."

Rocky started to pant, in spite of herself.

Chet smiled. "You have no fucking clue about anything we own. You've been perfectly content to shop and prance around in your fancy fucking car and let me take care of every little thing in your life. And now what? Now you think you can live all on your own?" He laughed. "Rocky, you couldn't make a pile of your own shit without help."

Rocky shrunk away and out the door. She hobbled to her car and sat down hard in the driver's seat. She was not one to cry. Ever. About anything. But she could feel the sting in her eyes. Not about Chet. He could fuck whomever he wanted to fuck. In all honesty, part of her felt relieved. Infidelity gave her a reason. Something tangible to put on a divorce filing. Anything sounded better than "I grew up and realized he isn't my person." But he was right. She had allowed this. Not just the affair, which she halfway allowed by being oblivious to him for half their marriage. She didn't like being fooled, and it didn't happen often. But she had let the rest happen, too. Her knowledge of their business dealings amounted to a cursory glance at the checking account and a yearly signing of tax returns she never read. Investments. Savings. Retirement. Land. House. Vehicles. She was clueless. Learned helplessness. Willing, learned helplessness. And now here she was: soon to be divorced and walking away with nothing. She had been duped by a complete fucking idiot.

She got back out of the car and stormed to the door. She whipped it open and found the two of them sitting and talking in hushed tones on the couch. They barely even registered shock when the door flew open. They did show some puzzlement though when she walked over and picked up the cat box by the handle on top. The clasps on the edges sagged, heavier than she expected, but she was able to carry the box out the door. Rocky hoisted the straining plastic up to the open window of Chet's truck and pushed the whole thing over and in. The lid made a loud thunk and litter spilled out in a rattling whoosh all over the seat and floor. She turned back, brushing off her hands to find them both standing on the porch, staring in stunned silence. Rocky motioned behind her with a jerk of her head. "I made a pile of that shit all by myself." She left them standing in the same spot as she drove away.

Chapter 2

One month and three days after walking in on her husband boning a pregnant waitress, Rocky severed the Arnold from Raquel Champagnolle. The official divorce occurred on the Monday after her final day of school. During her first six years teaching first grade, Rocky picked up two campus Teacher of the Year awards. Rumors told Rocky she might be named the district Teacher of the Year, but the kind (read: judgmental) Southerners of Texarkana Arkansas Consolidated School District couldn't nail down which family to invite to the ceremony. So they made a safer choice by selecting a single P.E. teacher. Rocky theorized they will take the honor back as soon as they figure out the P.E. teacher is a lesbian.

Chet was right about one thing. She didn't get shit. Rocky's lawyer discovered Chet kept most of what he had in his dad's name. With the state of Arkansas being a 50/50 state, she did get her Lexus and some cash out of savings, some of which went to pay her lawyer. But at least the court date fell during the summer, so she wore her shortest, sheerest summer dress. Even the judge glared a little too hard and flashed Chet an "I'm sorry for your loss" cock of the head.

Numerous friends offered to take Rocky out for a "Freedom Party." After living with her parents for a month, Rocky accepted the offers with ease. All of them. First, Martha Collins, a friend from the first school where Rocky taught who served as witness in court, treated Rocky to Eggs Benedict and mimosas at a little place downtown called Martin's. The dress continued to work wonders. The bartender at Martin's told Rocky he couldn't decide which looked more beautiful, her face or her ass. She informed the gentleman he had seen all he was going to see of either and demanded he make her pay for her drinks.

After a four-mimosa brunch, they met up with another former coworker for a three-hour bout of shopping. Living with her parents at least meant her whole paycheck could go toward new dresses if she wanted. And after a fresh divorce and a little day-drinking, she kind of wanted new dresses.

But a call from her cousin, Jennifer, stopped her. After a moment of phone-fumbling silence, Jennifer shouted, "Rocky? Are you okay?"

Rocky slurred, "I'm great, Jen. Grrreat."

Jen sighed into the phone. "Yeah. Well, I was thinking about taking you to a late lunch. Would you go to lunch with me?"

"I would. But I've already had drunch."

Jen paused. "Did you say drunch?"

"Yeah. Like brunch. But drunker."

Jen grumbled, "Okay. I'm coming to get you. Where are you?"

Thirty minutes later, Rocky half dozed against the passenger-side window of Jen's car as they drove to Rocky's dad's furniture shop. Frank Champagnolle had been running Champagnolle Mattress and Furniture since he turned seventeen. And the way he saw it, he might be manning the business until he hit ninety-seven. Only child Rocky never showed any interest in taking over, and Frank recognized Chet as a douchebag from day one. Since Jen moved back to Texarkana, he at least garnered some help out of one Champagnolle. She did some part-time interior design work for him. Opened up the business to a whole new level of clientele.

Frank all but begged Rocky to let him take her to the courthouse. But as soon as she got her court date, Rocky withdrew about half the money Chet set aside for the boob job he begged her to get. And she spent every penny on a Carolina Herrera dress. A dress with one purpose. A purpose you didn't much want your father there to see. When she picked out the flared shirtdress, she described the little black number to Jen as what Jackie Onassis would wear to make Jack regret fucking Marilyn. And if the way Rocky twirled to make the hem dance up was any judge, the plan would've worked. Ironically, undoing a couple of extra buttons made her boobs really pop. Her dad walked in on her drunkenly admiring them as she sprawled out on a leopard-print chaise lounger in his shop.

"Sweetheart, I'm still working on that one."

Rocky struggled to get up while looking back at the unpinned fabric like she sat in wet paint. "Didn't you just finish one like this? For the lawyer woman?"

Frank laughed. "Yep. Cat scratched the back all to hell. Ruined it."

"Fuck all. How awful."

Frank pointed at the chaise lounger. "Not for me. She's paying for a replacement."

Jen came barreling through with a handful of various fabrics. "And tell her why you need the extra business right now, Uncle Frank."

Frank rubbed at his forehead. "How was court, sweetheart? You haven't even told me how it went."

Rocky shook her head. "Um, no. Dad, tell me what she's talking about."

Frank waved her off. "No, honey. You first."

Rocky rolled her eyes. "Fine. It was fine. Now, what is she talking about?"

Jen stood between them and laughed through her nose. "Unbelievable. You are both going to stand there changing the subject to avoid talking about your own bullshit." She addressed Frank, "Court went as expected. She told me on the drive over. Chet, the asshole, completed his grand theft of your daughter's worldly possessions. But she doesn't have to ever touch him again, so…pretty much a win-win. She went in there looking like this and got somewhere around four marriage proposals before the ink dried." She spun around to Rocky, eye to eye, both of them standing no more than five feet (now that Rocky stood barefoot—heels kicked off in Jen's car). "Your father has been robbed. Twice."

Rocky stared Frank down like he had robbed himself. "What?"

Frank held his hands up, palms out. "Now, Rocky. It was no big deal." He scowled at Jen. "You make it sound like a big deal."

Jen and Rocky replied in unison, respectively matter-of-fact and incredulous, "You got robbed."

Frank shrugged and started messing with a leg of the chaise lounger. "I know, I know. And I should be more pissed than I am. I get it. But it could have been a lot worse."

Rocky made a sour face at Jen, but Jen nodded. "He's right. They took a cash box from up front both times. Petty cash. They didn't bother walking into the back at all."

Frank nodded along with her. "It was one of those deals where they could've had twice as much as they got. Ignored the computers, my television. Hell, the safe got left open one of those nights."

Rocky crossed her arms. "And how much did they get?"

Frank hung his head in silence until Jen answered, "Five thousand, give or take."

Rocky laughed. "Take. I think take is exactly what happened."

Frank waved her off. "It wasn't the money as much as the property damage. Broke a damn window both times. And this last time they smashed the place up a little."

Rocky walked to the door and glanced out into the front lobby to see some evidence of repairs. "I assume you've called the cops?"

Frank nodded. "Yep. They even found my cash box the first time. Empty and sitting in a Shreveport casino parking lot."

Rocky pleaded toward the ceiling, "Great."

Frank laughed. "Yeah. They don't hold out much hope of getting the money back. They did print the box, but they couldn't get a good one."

Jen slammed down a fabric sample. "But we know who did it."

Frank nodded, and Rocky looked back and forth between them with a questioning in her eyes until Frank spoke up. "We had this delivery guy. Used to hang out flirting with Rachel up at the front desk. He saw her go to the cash box plenty of times. Knew right where it sat. But he wouldn't know about any of the stuff back here. I even had a conversation with him once about going to the boats down there in Shreveport. It fits."

Rocky rubbed her hands together, thinking. "So? Have you told anyone this?"

Jen nodded. "He told the cops. They talked to his employer and the guy got fired. That's why we think he came back and trashed the place."

Rocky pulled her phone out. "What's this guy's name?"

Frank hesitated but relented. "Jeremy Buckwalter."

Rocky tapped away at the phone and made a disgusted face. "Buckwalter? Jesus. I almost hope he gets away with it now. He's suffered enough."

After a few minutes of tapping and scrolling, Rocky looked at Jen. "Is Rachel here today?"

Jen nodded toward the front. "Yeah. She's out there."

Rocky bounced her way into the front lobby and called out to a bored girl slouching at the front desk. "Hey, Rache!"

The girl startled alert and straightened up. She was pretty, but country girl in the city pretty. She wore a touch too much makeup. And her hair highlights stood out a little too pronounced. A shimmer of glitter sparkled from the cleavage of her tanning bed dark skin. Next to someone like Rocky, even at a good five years younger, a girl like Rachel was trying too hard. Like her knock-off Britney Spears, circa 1999, look would be all she had going for her until the freshness faded with a few more years of age. While Rocky rolled out of bed in the guise of a 1950s Hollywood starlet, and her looks would remain the least interesting thing about her for all her life. Rachel dropped her *Us Weekly* and smiled. "Hey, Rocky. How's it going?"

Rocky patted the desk between them and shouted, "She did it!"

Rachel scrunched up her face but flushed and began to tremble at the chin. Jen and Frank eased around the corner to gape wide-eyed at Rocky, who swiveled toward them, examining her nails. She jerked a thumb over her shoulder. "See those sunglasses on her head? Those are Burberry. The purse? Coach. Those aren't knock-offs, either. They're real. This girl makes minimum wage and grew up with a single mom who's a bookkeeper."

Rachel squeaked, "Accountant."

Rocky rolled her eyes and glanced back. "Bookkeeper." She turned back toward Frank and Jen. "Until tonight, I had only ever seen her carrying purses from Target. Her purse tonight is $800 easy. And those glasses were another $200. You are staring at one-fifth of the contents of your cash boxes."

Rachel tried stammering but couldn't find the words.

Rocky pushed up from her spot leaning against the counter and patted Frank on the arm. "Rachel and Jeremy were doing more than flirting. They hooked up. Maybe even dated a little. But he did something to piss her off. She is cutting him out of all social media, but he isn't showing the same sense of urgency. He's indifferent. She wanted to do something to hurt him and she reached for the one thing she could think of."

Frank nodded. "My cash boxes?"

Rocky nodded. "Simple frame job, Dad."

Jen shook her head in amazement. "Ten minutes."

Rocky glanced at a gaudy, rose-gold watch. "Five."

Jen rolled her eyes. "Does that watch even work?"

Rocky inspected the clock hands, squinting. "I don't know. Is it 9:35?" She made her way toward the back. "I'm going to take a nap while y'all deal with this."

Frank's eyes glassed over as he stared at Rachel and patted Rocky on her way by. "You can use the chaise lounger, sweetheart."

"Already planning to, Frank. Already planning to."

Chapter 3

Rachel paid Frank back about two-thirds of the money she took. To Rocky's disgust, her father's big heart prevented him from firing the girl. "God, I'm glad you didn't pass that on," she told him. To which he replied, "I tried, Sweetheart. My compassion was no match for your mother's vindictiveness." Quite true. Rocky tormented young Rachel for three days before the girl quit in the hysterics of a tearful exit.

After another handful of days during which Rocky binge watched Netflix shows and ate hundred calorie ice cream bars, Jen signed them both up to join the Junior League. In a painstaking series of texts, Jen explained to Rocky how much membership could help both of them (read: Jen) meet new friends and find something to do other than holing up in their house or torturing young girls (read: Rocky). Although Jen filled out all the paperwork for her, Rocky never gave an explicit *no*. She even unblocked Jen's number on her phone after a day and a half. Just as soon as she finished the last episode of *Hart of Dixie*.

The day of their first Junior League meeting, Jen pulled up to her aunt and uncle's house to pick up Rocky an hour early. And then spent fifteen minutes honking, calling, and ringing the doorbell before Rocky exploded in a ceremonious stomp out the front door. "You better be glad this gave me an excuse to buy a new dress," Rocky snarked as she huffed into the car.

Jen winced. "You look gorgeous. Thank you for doing this."

Rocky glared at her.

"Rocky, you know I can't do things like this by myself. And you're such the life of the party. I don't know why you hate going out. You're kind of the perfect socialite."

Rocky started ticking things off on her fingers, "I'm not blonde. I weigh more than 110 pounds. I am not married to a doctor. If I were married to a doctor, I wouldn't quit my job to dress his kids in cute outfits and take yoga classes."

Jen rolled her eyes. "You know you would dress your kids in cute outfits."

"Yeah. But they would be *my* kids. Not his. And I wouldn't fucking yoga."

Jen laughed, but retorted, "They aren't all like that. There is an element of the pampered kept wife, sure. But there are plenty of nice girls in the Junior League, Rocky. They do good work."

Rocky mumbled, "They've had good work done."

The Junior League initiation event, dubbed their annual "Wine and Sign," took place in the backroom of a little cafe in a wealthier part of Texarkana. The new class would be signing their commitments. The old guard provided the wine. The big mixer gave everyone an excuse to get day drunk on a Saturday afternoon, but still included the rundown of responsibilities of a first-year member and the general goals for the year. Jen and Rocky spent their first ten minutes slinking around to the cash bar to down a couple of lonely vodka spritzers before having to talk to anyone. They returned pleasantries with a few top-heavy blondes who always introduced themselves with a "Hey, girls! How are y'all doing? I'm Missy (name ending in *-y*) Murphy (alliterative middle/maiden name) Day (always three names, with a punchy last name—could catch eyes on a yard sign for school board someday). So glad to see you here." Jen would reply with a gracious *thank you* or *so glad to be here.* Rocky would reply with something along the lines of, "Thanks so much. Can I call you Missay Murphay Day? It's way more fun to say."

When things settled down, Jen and Rocky were seated in the front row of a block of chairs in the back room. The recruits took up about fourteen chairs in the front two rows. Before them sat a table with three chairs for the Junior League president and her two highest ranking officers. The scene resembled a press conference. Rocky even held up her phone at one point like a recorder and pantomimed asking a question. Jen slapped her arm down before anyone noticed.

The president was Brittney Binet Bridges. A little social media stalking revealed B Cubed to be a horseback riding aficionado. Which took Rocky a little by surprise. She held her phone over to Jen and commented, too loud, "For fuck's sake. Would you look at that? I was scanning pictures for her Sweet Valley twin. And what did I find? Fucking Saddle Club. I'm usually not so far off."

Jen elbowed her. "Shut. Up."

Rocky scrolled through pictures. "You think she's a Carole? A Stevie? Ah." She held the phone over for Jen to see again. "Lisa. All the way."

Jen laughed a little in spite of herself. "Please, Rocky."

Brittney Binet Bridges didn't seem to notice any of Rocky's comments. She tapped her wine glass with a salad fork and flashed the cocked-head smile of a former pageant queen. "I'm gonna go ahead and call this meeting to order, girls. First order of business is to review last month's minutes. Do any of y'all see any need for revisions or additions?" She raised her eyebrows as she scanned the faces before her—all of which matched her facial expression with eerie precision.

Rocky glanced behind her and marveled, "What fresh hell is this?"

Britney Binet Bridges continued, "Hearing none, do I have a motion?"

The girl to her left closed her eyes and placed a hand on Britney Binet Bridges' forearm. "I move we approve those minutes, hon."

Brittney Binet Bridges gave her a rubber-stamp smile. "I have a motion. Do I have a second?"

The girl on her right repeated the same creepy-ass gesture and said, "I second, Miss B."

Rocky looked to Jen and mouthed, "Miss B?"

Brittney Binet Bridges tapped her salad fork down on the table. "I have a motion and a second. Last month's minutes are approved. Moving on to new business. Let's all take a moment and recognize our new member class. Girls?"

Everyone tapped their gaudy wedding rings on their wine glasses in a chorus of tinkling approval. Like someone turned a fan on in a wind chime store. Rocky leaned over to Jen, "What do you use if you're single?"

Jen shushed her.

"Ohhh. Never mind. They don't give wine glasses to single girls. Just hand you the bottle."

Brittney Binet Bridges held a hand up for silence. (Rocky waved back at her. She didn't notice.) "Thank you, girls. This is always an exciting time. So much hope and potential. And I expect great things out of this class of girls."

Rocky spoke out of the side of her mouth. "But if we disappoint her, it's off to the glue factory."

Jen pleaded with her eyes.

"I hope I get put out to stud when this is over. Wouldn't that be fun?"

Brittney Binet Bridges explained that each new class bore the responsibility of coming up with a new fundraiser. And this year would prove vital for the League. "Never been as important, girls. We've had new class fundraisers turn into permanent League fixtures. Our 'Cots for Tots' campaign was a new member idea."

There were reverent murmurs from the crowd. Rocky eyed Jen. "Please tell me that was an effort to fashion proportionate bedding for little people."

"Other new member ideas included 'Feedy the Needy,' 'Socks on Pocks,' and 'Caps for Chaps.'"

During a smattering of applause, Rocky pointed. "That one. I want to make hats for early century newsboys. Let's volunteer, Jen."

Brittney Binet Bridges continued, "And, girls, we need this year's effort to be our best yet. I hate to even say it out loud, but, girls, we're being passed up."

There were outcries of *No* and *Don't put it in the universe*. Rocky took the opportunity to toss out a "Burn it all down and let Satan reclaim the souls."

Brittney Binet Bridges held a hand up in a testifying pose and shook her head. "I know. I know, girls. Terrible. But true. We have seen charitable organizations in Texarkana take great strides. The United Way has its own Division III bowl game now. And Easter Seals is sponsoring the Special Olympics. They've turned a little feel-good field day into a huge spectacle. A real event. People went in droves last year. They set up a crafts table with a bartender and everybody dressed up. It was like the Kentucky Derby with handicaps instead of horses. I want us to take back the throne as the preeminent charity organization in this town. And it is up to you—our newest members—to make that happen."

The Queen BBB rode the reaction she got from her call to action straight into an inauguration ceremony. All the new members stood and raised their right hands and swore to uphold the values of the Junior League of Texarkana, USA. Rocky added a very loud "Amen" to the tail end of the recited vows. Brittney Binet Bridges seemed to like it. The meeting closed and the staff poured the wine. Junior Leaguers exploded into their natural postures: wine glass in a cocked wrist, free hand alternating between hair and conversation and hip, voices laughing and gasping and trilling through one anecdote after another.

Jen and Rocky tried to stick together, but Junior Leaguers worked like experienced jungle hunters. They could separate you from your pack with ease. Get you alone. Work you over until your bones were licked clean. Jen accused Rocky of taking the analogy a bit too far, but aggrandizing seemed apropos for the occasion.

One gaggle of blondes cornered Rocky next to the finger sandwiches and asked her about the absence of a ring on her finger.

Blonde 1: "So, girl, you know me, I couldn't help but notice." She waggled her ring finger.

Rocky shook her head. "Well, actually, I don't know you. But I noticed you have fingers, too. I'm not going to lie; I didn't figure on it taking you quite this long to discover them for yourself. But witnessing the process does make me feel like I know you better than I'm giving myself credit for."

Blonde 2: "Oh, girl. You are too funny. You know what she means. Give us the scoop. Have you not found Mr. Right? Or did Mr. Right turn into Mr. Wrong."

Rocky nodded. "How cute. Did you make that up?"

Blonde 2 shook her head in confusion.

16

Rocky patted her arm. "Don't hurt yourself. I'm divorced. If this was your circuitous way of asking a very simple question, then, yes. I am recently divorced."

They both donned their best pity faces. In unison they asked, "What happened, honey?"

Rocky smiled huge. "Wow. Do y'all practice? That was so good. Oh, it's a cliché, to be honest."

Blonde 1 grimaced. "Cheated?"

Rocky made a sour face and shook her head. "Inverted penis." She mimed pushing on a person's stomach. "Had to shove a thumb pretty hard into his belly button just to get it to pop out when we wanted to have sex."

Their shocked faces were met with Jen stepping in to say, "He cheated on her, yes. With a waitress and plenty of other women. She just can't give a straight answer. Now, if I can borrow her for a moment?"

Jen dragged a giggling Rocky over to a different group of Leaguers, not all blonde this time. Rocky could tell Jen wanted her to hear something, but she entered mid-conversation. An older Leaguer—one of the sustainers—recounted some recent happening, judging from how the story upset her.

"I felt so invaded. I mean, he could have touched anything. I can't go to sleep in my own house without being terrified." She put off a little more hippy-dippy vibe than the normal crowd. She smelled a little like patchouli and dressed more granola than the younger, blonder set. She was in her fifties and the only sign of wealth sparkled in the form of high-priced jewelry on a few fingers and her earlobes.

The crowd around her gave her accommodating gasps and patted at her back. Someone asked, "Could you tell what he wanted?"

She looked to the ceiling and rolled her head around, lost. "I have no idea. He messed with a few things, but he never asked for anything. He just asked me not to move. He was even polite about it, to be honest. He said, 'Pardon me,' for God's sake. Kept asking when Roger would be home."

Jen held a hand over her mouth and kept eyeing Rocky. She gave her a nudge with a shoulder.

Rocky rolled her eyes and stepped forward. "He 'messed with a few things?' Like what?"

The woman breathed into her trembling hands and thought. "I don't know. Pictures mostly."

Rocky frowned. "Pictures? Of what?"

"Nothing of note. Family pictures."

Jen gave Rocky the big eyes.

Rocky joined the "back pat club" and added, "Sounds horrible. I'm so sorry." Then she started away.

Jen hurried to catch up. "What are you doing? You can do your thing. Do your thing and get us in good with these people."

Rocky twisted her lips to the side. "Nah."

Jen laughed. "Nah? Did you just fucking 'nah' me?"

Rocky kept walking toward the table with the sign-up sheets for new member committees. "I'm not interested."

"You're thinking something. I can tell. Something about those pictures."

Rocky shook her head and studied the committee titles. "I can't do," she curled her top lip and made air quotation marks, "'my thing' if I'm not interested. Did you sign up?"

Jen waved at the tables. "Yeah. Decorations. How can you not be interested? You didn't even hear the whole story. Three Junior League members have been victims of home invasion robberies. Three! That is interesting."

"Not robberies."

"What?"

"Not robberies. She didn't say he took anything. She said he messed with stuff. Probably the same at all three. I can't do decorations. What should I sign up for?"

Jen flailed her hands in the air. "See? You're interested. You could make us heroes in this bitch."

Rocky turned, pen in hand, to respond and found Brittney Binet Bridges standing right behind Jen. BBB smiled and placed a hand at Jen's back. "Well, we love heroes around here. What have we signed up for, girls?"

Rocky returned the cartoonish smile. "I absolutely cannot decide. My dear cousin is aces at decorating, but I'm clumsier than a puppy in a sex swing. What do you think I should do?"

Brittney Binet Bridges sneered at her. "Oh, you seem like an idea girl to me."

Rocky scanned the sheets until she found one labeled 'Ideas.' She scribbled a signature down below the other three and dropped the pen, glancing around the room before facing Brittney Binet Bridges again. "I think you're right. And don't you worry. We are going to come up with something so good no one would ever dream it came from you girls."

Chapter 4

The Ideas Subcommittee served as the proverbial first domino. Without an idea, all the other subcommittees had fuck all to do. Rocky always rose into a role of an accidental leader. She and three other Leaguers signed up, and the others each flashed the doe eyes and pouty mouth of someone whose "ideas" generally involved makeup. They agreed to meet at a Books-a-Million (Rocky's idea). One of the blondes needed directions, which consisted of "beside the mall." Each of the ladies agreed to come armed with an idea of her own, and then the subcommittee would pick the best one. Rocky arrived last and empty-handed to find three perky blondes sitting primly in front of their monogrammed journals.

Rocky decided to go first. She planned to freestyle. Not her best plan, but she hadn't committed much time to it. She placed her hands on a knee and crossed her legs, paying careful attention to her posture. "Well, ladies, my idea is called 'Ticket to Ride.' I propose we help our local homeless population."

They all clapped out soft patters and hummed in agreement.

"So here's what we do: we raise money for some mid-priced luggage, with, of course, the Junior League monogram."

"Of course."

"Of course."

"Of course."

"Of course. And then we help the homeless pack their belongings and we give them a ticket, which we also raise the money for, to any town of their choice. Just send them on their way."

Pensive nods.

Two of the next three ideas were even worse. The first blonde sat up on the edge of her seat and cleared her throat in what could only be described as somehow delicately. "What does the Junior League need more than anything?"

The other three team members answered with "funding," "support," and "dicks" in chorus.

She fluttered a little but shook them all off. "No. Girls, we need future Junior Leaguers."

Rocky closed her eyes and nodded. "Yes. Perfect."

The first blonde waggled her head at her in agreement. "Listen, girl. My idea is called 'L. I. T. U. P.'" She cast the words in the air with her hands as she talked. "Leaguer In Training for the UnderPrivileged."

Rocky waved her hands in the air over the invisible words. "Brilliant."

"So you see, we take underprivileged children and we put them through what amounts to a basic cotillion class. We teach them proper etiquette, ballroom dancing, fashion tips, makeup tips, all the important stuff. And when they come out, you know what they'll be?"

"Cultured?"

"Sophisticated?"

"Insufferable?"

She bit her lip and shook her head. "Junior League material."

Rocky giggled along with the high praise she received from the other two. When the second blonde took the metaphorical stage, Rocky got to hear all about the girl's sister who sells these wonderful monogrammed blankets. Before she could even finish the sentence about "finding out the initials of homeless people," the first blonde interrupted with a gentle reminder they couldn't buy products from relatives for fundraisers.

Rocky pouted, "Such a great idea, too."

When the third blonde shifted in her seat, Rocky cocked her head with the giddy excitement of an audience at a Vaudeville show. The girl settled in and started, "Well, I have this sorority sister who works for CASA. They're, like, these Court Assigned Super Assistants."

Rocky nodded. "Court Appointed Special Advocates."

"Right. Well, she told us the other night about how these kids get taken into foster care and everything. And they put all their stuff in a trash bag. Like garbage. Even the rich kids; it doesn't matter."

Another blonde gasped. "All their stuff in trash bags? How awful."

The blonde with the floor shook her head. "No, girl. One trash bag. That's it."

The other cocked her head. "Nuh-uh."

Rocky sighed. "She's right. It happens at school sometimes. They get one black trash bag for everything they own." She swallowed. "It is awful."

The third blonde continued, "So I think we should put together toiletry bags and little satchels or backpacks ready to go for anyone who gets taken to foster care or the battered women's shelter or anything."

Rocky mumbled under her breath, "Fuck me." Then she held her head up and flailed her arms out. "An actual good idea." Her three team members watched her with a mild surprise. She shrugged. "I know. I've got nothing snarky to say. Those kids get uprooted in the middle of the night sometimes. And they are left to carry their shit around in a garbage bag. It's demoralizing and inhumane. If this is the kind of shit we're going to do, then sign me up."

One girl submitted a mild argument for underprivileged cotillion classes, but the dialogue didn't last long. Rocky swayed the decision without too much effort. They spent the next hour or so putting together a presentation to give to a group of the wealthier sustainers from whom they hoped to secure some seed money. They were scheduled to go before the sustainers, along with the Junior League Board of Directors, the following week.

* * *

Rocky volunteered to speak for the group. She spent three nights working on her notes and prepping. Jen's smug expression earned more than one "Yeah, I care a little. You can fuck right off about it, too."

The day of the proposal to the board merited another new dress—subtle floral pattern and flowy. The League met in the backroom of an old downtown building converted to house the local arts council. The room stretched out large and elegant, like a ballroom. The ceilings reached a good thirty feet high, with ornate molding and the cracked marbling of ceiling panels resulting from decades of age. Everything was a deep burgundy traced and brushed with bronze like dust on an old piano. One wall contained five windows which faced out onto the streets of downtown Texarkana. They were long, slender windows about the width of a small person, with the farthest to the left stretching only halfway to accommodate the rattling air conditioning unit. Taken in together, the windows formed a hand— fingers outstretched and ready to clasp down on the room and everyone in it. Rocky's dress was a navy with merlot and gold flowers. The blending colors made her both match the room and stand out as a perfect complement to her surroundings, a room boasting far too many pantsuits. And gaucho pants flopping around like so much sartorial failure.

Although populated with many of the same faces, setup differed from the Wine and Sign. League organizers replaced the press conference table with a curved row of velvety armchairs. Brittney Binet Bridges sat in one, but all other occupants were older, anywhere from early forties to eighties. The obvious matriarch took center stage in the room. Her coiffed hair curled and morphed in color like a storm cloud—not quite gray or black. And she wore big tinted glasses with neon green frames. Her clothing and makeup flourished unapologetic. Everything flashed bright but reeked of money. Her outfit consisted of a slender green dress matched to her frames, with white striping just above the hem. She sat with crossed legs, wine glass in one hand, unlit cigarette in the other. She didn't smile. One should never ask her to do so. Rocky struggled to place her age, but the best guess fell somewhere deep within the AARP range—between 60 and 80. She proffered all the stature of a cultural dictator in the last years of a career running a fashion magazine.

After enjoying a moment of belonging in the room, Rocky leaned over to Jen and asked, "Who in the good fuck is the marvelous woman in the middle?"

Jen pursed her lips. "That, my dear, is Waverly St. Laurent. She's what money looks like when it grows up."

Before Rocky even had time to reply, Brittney Binet Bridges' two side pieces from the first meeting started ushering everyone to a seat. The meeting as a whole felt less formalized. Everything seemed to be catered toward the older ladies in the armchairs and tailored for Waverly St. Laurent. The room forced a palpable deference to the lady in green.

A brusque woman with a Janet Reno hair-do did most of the talking at first. She explained the time-honored tradition of the delivery of ideas to the board and the sustainers. After a nod to Brittney Binet Bridges and a brief introduction, Rocky stood before the row of ladies with her hands clasped before her waist in what she thought of as her charming pose.

"Thank you so much for having us, ladies. We are honored to be able to share this fabulous idea with you all." Her eyes scanned back and forth once, but then remained locked in on Waverly St. Laurent. "If I may, allow me to paint you a bit of a portrait. Imagine a young lady, not unlike any of you at a tender age of eight, maybe nine. She still loves her favorite dolls. Not all of them, mind you. She's no baby. But she will still pull out those two favorites to brush their hair every night before bed. Our little girl, she's growing up. Has a little case of makeup she'll play with when no one's watching. Her favorite books are lined up on her little nightstand, so she can read them again and again." Rocky ducked her head. "But our little darling's parents—well, they aren't in a good place. Her daddy, he's a drinker. And a mean one. He knocks her momma around every third night or so. Even backhanded our little angel once in a fit. Well, the momma screws up the courage to leave this sorry, no-good, drunk. She calls the Battered Women's Shelter, and they send transport and a police escort while the daddy's at work. In order to avoid a disturbance, the escorts can only afford to offer a few precious minutes. And the little girl, our little angel, she's forced to throw any of her worldly possessions she cares to take into one black garbage bag. The dolls are too big. The books' edges would rip the bag. She forgets about her makeup kit. She takes one wistful glance back out of the car she's in and hugs her black trash bag close, wondering whether she'll ever see any of her things again."

Waverly St. Laurent leaned forward and peered over her glasses. "You got a project in all your story, Missy? Some of us would like to get to the snacks." She eyed Rocky up and down. "I can tell you would, too. Let's move it along."

Rocky blanched. Her mouth became a thin red line. Her head cocked back, almost like a coiled snake. She spoke in slow deliberate sentences. "Yes, ma'am. I would be more than happy to do so." She ran through the particulars in a monotone, but she didn't miss a detail.

When Rocky finished, Waverly St. Laurent stood with an air of ceremony and pulled a check from her purse. "Here you go, Brittney. Sounds good. I'll cover the costs."

Everyone clapped excitedly. Everyone, except Rocky.

Chapter 5

Rocky sulked the whole drive home. She stared out the window with her arms crossed as Jen tried to talk to her. With limited success.

"Everybody is talking about these home invasions."

Rocky grunted, "Uh huh."

"Did I tell you there were three of them? Yeah. All Junior League sustainers. Pretty weird, huh?"

Rocky chewed at a thumbnail. "What the fuck did she mean? 'I can tell you would, too.' The fuck's that supposed to mean? Huh?"

Jen sighed. "She was incredibly rude. I'm sorry that happened, Rocky. But, hey. You got funded. That's the important thing."

Rocky rolled her eyes. "I don't want her money. I'd rather do a fundraiser."

Jen laughed. "Waverly St. Laurent wrote a $10,000 check. What fundraiser do you expect to do?"

Rocky mumbled, "A good one."

Jen gave her a patronizing smile. "You know you aren't good at that sort of thing, Rocky. When we were in Girl Scouts your dad had to buy all your cookies because you wouldn't even try to sell them. He gained thirty pounds." She sniffed and scratched at her neck. "But I happen to know what you are good at."

Rocky leaned her head back on the neck rest. "Jesus, Jen."

"There's no way it would be any harder than figuring out who took your dad's cash box. And solving this mystery would be such a huge win for us, Rocky. If you could do your thing and find who is breaking into these ladies' homes, we would be Junior League royalty."

"Solving this…" Rocky trailed off into a sigh. "Jesus, Jen. I can't just roll up into the Junior League like fucking Jessica Fletcher."

Jen pulled into Rocky's parents' driveway and hit the door locks so Rocky couldn't jump out. "Promise me you'll at least think about those break-ins."

Rocky hung her head. "Why?"

"Because if you think about them, you'll end up wanting to figure out what's going on. You can't help yourself."

"Goodnight, Jen."

Jen unlocked the doors. "I'm taking that as a yes."

When she got inside, Rocky found her mother sitting at the kitchen table in front of a magazine. When Rocky had been in high school, her mother had been a smoker. She could see the burning red ember from her car. But since she'd moved back home post-divorce, her mother's insistence on waiting up for her always came with a bit of a jump-scare.

Rocky put a hand to her chest. "Shit, mom. You look like a damn ghost sitting there in the dark."

Her mother laughed at her but defended herself. "I'm just reading a magazine, Raquel. You know I can't go to bed unless you're home."

Rocky filled a glass with water. "Doesn't make it less weird. But I appreciate the gesture, I suppose."

"How was your meeting? I see they haven't dyed your hair yet."

"Nah. I'm sure you don't go blonde until you're a full member. I'm still a pledge."

Her mother rolled her eyes behind the magazine. "Sounds like a damn sorority."

"You encouraged this, remember?" Rocky raised her eyebrows at her mother. "You jumped all over the idea when Jen first mentioned us joining."

Her mother nodded. "Well, you need to get back out there, Raquel. You need to meet people. You've lived a socially sheltered life. And here you are. Almost thirty and single. I love you, sweetheart, but you married the first man you slept with."

Rocky shrugged. "Yeah. What's wrong with that?"

Her mother peered over the magazine. "You always throw away the first pancake, Raquel." She returned to her article. "And you did, I suppose. Only took you twelve years."

"Well, I'm not sure how the Junior League is going to help with meeting people or, for that matter, my self-confidence. An old lady called me fat tonight."

Her mother slammed the magazine down on the table. "What?"

Rocky shrugged and nodded. "Yeah. In not so many words. Said she could tell I was ready to get to the snack table. After eyeing me up and down."

"The bitch. I ought to go to the next meeting with you. See if she says shit then." Her mother looked her up and down. "I mean, I can say it. But some crusty old bitch? No way."

Rocky's face soured. "Say what?"

Her mother teetered her head back and forth. "Your dress is a little …"

"A little what?"

"It could be mistaken for maternity wear."

Rocky sighed. "I'm going to bed."

"I'm not trying to hurt your feelings. I've got some exercise DVDs you can use. And if you lose a little weight, I'll even take you shopping."

"Goodnight, Mother."

Rocky stormed into her bedroom in the manner reserved for post-conversation with her mother. In all the world, no one loved Raquel Champagnolle more than her mother. But if anyone showed love more awkwardly than Rocky, it was her mother. Darrelene Champagnolle both put Rocky on a pedestal and made her personal mission in life to knock her down off of it every time she struck too proud a pose. Rocky scanned the room, which her mother kept in pristine museum control for the six years since Rocky moved out. She muttered to herself, "Like a goddamn teenager." The anger toward her mother faded a touch with the sight of the Racquel Champagnolle Shrine her mother created. But her Waverly St. Laurent hate raged on as strong as ever.

Rocky slipped out of her dress and found a tank top to pair with some sleep shorts. She collapsed on her bed and pulled up Google on her phone. Finding information didn't take long. Waverly St. Laurent exploded all over her phone. There were any number of results to pick from. However, the first three pages were all nothing more than Waverly and Dr. Baudouin St. Laurent at various events or donating ridiculous amounts of money to one charity or the other.

Somewhere around the fifth page of results, one caught her eye. Not so much because of the title ("Coping, Thirty Years Later"), but more because of the source. The article appeared four or five years back in *Arkansas Monthly*, a pretty prestigious magazine—one of Arkansas' only claims to fame. When she clicked on the link, Rocky found a stately photo of Dr. and Mrs. Baudouin (or "Bo") St. Laurent posed in the gaudy living room of their mansion. Waverly sat in an armchair not unlike the one from the meeting, and Bo stood solemn behind her, one hand resting on her shoulder in a stereotypical pose. Waverly was decked out in a bright pink dress and more jewelry than seemed appropriate. Three fingers rested on her husband's hand. In her other hand, she held a tinted pair of pink frames which she likely had been convinced to remove for the picture. Neither smiled. Waverly squinted almost to the point of closing her eyes.

Rocky—one of her many talents being the ability to read with exceptional speed—devoured the article in a few minutes. And came out with more questions than answers, as the saying goes. The article followed up on another article published in the magazine some thirty years prior. Most of the anniversary piece seemed to be fluff, in Rocky's opinion. The writer documented Bo's rise to prominence as one of only a couple of brain surgeons in Texarkana and touted Waverly's charity work. There were paragraphs dedicated to the phoniest-sounding love story ever told. Bo plays golf. Waverly paints. They both enjoy Saturday afternoon movies and Sunday brunch. Nowhere did the reporter answer a burning question the article itself created:

What the fuck happened to Jason?

Bo and Waverly St. Laurent adopted Jason later in life, after years of unsuccessful attempts to conceive. Well into their thirties, they took in Baby Jason and set him up to be the sole heir to a couple of old money families. The St. Laurents relocated from somewhere in Louisiana to buy up half the land in Texarkana. Bo, in addition to being a brain surgeon, sat on a good third of the St. Laurent land development fortune. And Waverly, in her own right, hailed from the Texarkana-famous Brighton family. Although unclear as to just how much of the Brighton hotel money she inherited, all signs pointed to more than enough. Between the two of them, they owned a couple of apartment complexes, most of the hotels, and both major funeral homes in Texarkana. In short, wherever you lay your head—alive or dead—you stood about a fifty-fifty chance of paying the St. Laurents to lay it there.

And the world bent over for the St. Laurents in those days. Until 1985. That fall, Jason St. Laurent rode his bicycle away from school. He was eight-going-on-nine, and the elementary school where he attended fourth grade was only a few blocks from the St. Laurent home. He left school as scheduled around 3:00 in the afternoon, he spoke to a few friends before leaving, and his nanny contacted the school at 4:30 worried because he never arrived home. Between 3:00 and 4:30, Jason St. Laurent came into contact with an unknown person or persons known locally as the Rye Mother. The writer of the article, in an obvious nod of respect to the family, only gave a one sentence summation of the killer: "Jason became the last known victim of the notorious Texarkana serial killer labeled by the press as the Rye Mother, the believed perpetrator of five child abductions and murders during the early-mid 1980s." The topic shifted to the sorrow of burying a child when only a "few charred remains were found." In the article, Waverly claimed to have "laid him to rest in her head, in her own way."

Rocky scoured the Internet for any other information about Jason St. Laurent or the Rye Mother killings from the 80s. She had, of course, heard of the Rye Mother stories. They turned into one big boogeyman tale. In school, her classmates were always wanting to do their research projects over the Rye Mother. Rocky found the stories all too morbid. The scattered, creepy websites focusing on a variety of grisly, unsolved crimes were some of the first details she had ever gotten on the topic. According to every narrative, the Rye Mother case consisted of a string of five child abductions between the years of 1981 and 1985 in the Texarkana area. All five had been taken from wooded areas, and all five had been dismembered and burned. Authorities found a small pile of burned remains—partial remains—next to a tiny bouquet of cornflowers in each case. Jason got mentioned on a few of the sites, but the details were minimal. Jason became the fifth and final known victim. And while his window of disappearance spanned more time than most victims, Jason spent far less time missing. In each of the other cases, the boy—always a boy—went missing in early October and turned up dead about a month later. In Jason's case, his remains were found in the trademark fashion within a week or so. No explanation offered other than some crackpot theories on message boards. Rocky continued to read the same slipshod versions of the incident over and over until she fell asleep with her phone on her chest.

The next morning was a Sunday, which meant Frank always let Rocky and her mom sleep until around 10:00, at which point he would show up with breakfast from McDonald's. At age nine or twenty-nine, Rocky couldn't help but wake up excited at the smell of shitty pancakes in Styrofoam containers. Something about those pancakes and sausages tasted like childhood.

She slipped on some pajama pants and went, rubbing her eyes, into the kitchen. As she fixed herself some juice, her dad greeted her with, "So your mom tells me somebody pissed you off at your meeting last night."

Rocky didn't turn but waved him off. "It was nothing. I overreacted, I guess."

She could hear him return to his paper, laughing under his breath.

Something about his giggle changed her mind, and she spun around. Leaning against the counter and sipping at her juice, she narrowed her eyes. "What do you know about Waverly St. Laurent?"

Her dad looked from her to the paper and back again. "Did you read this?"

Rocky shook her head. "Read what?"

Frank fished for the front page and handed the folded newspaper to her. "This."

Rocky flipped it over to find a giant picture of Waverly St. Laurent in a housecoat and those ridiculous tinted glasses being led away by police. She almost dropped her juice. "The fuck is this?"

Frank scrutinized her, puzzled. "You mean you hadn't seen this? Waverly St. Laurent shot her husband last night. She thought it was one of those deals lately with the home invasions. Mistook him for a burglar, so she says."

Chapter 6

After spending her Sunday zombified by the news about Waverly St. Laurent, Rocky wanted to spend her whole Monday in bed. At least until her Junior League fundraising meeting at 3:00. Jen however, subscribed to far different ideas. She barraged Rocky with a text campaign for them to keep a lunch date Jen made on their behalf. Rocky held strong until mid-morning, when the rumbling in her stomach began to overshadow the buzzing of her phone.

When Jen pulled up in Rocky's parents' driveway, the smile on her face made Rocky almost gag. "Stop smiling, would you?" She flopped her Frye hobo bag into the floorboard and adjusted her flouncy dress as she settled into the passenger seat. Rocky turned her oversized sunglasses toward Jen and snarled. "I was hungry. Don't gloat."

"Not gloating. Just smiling." Jen tittered as she threw the car into drive and circled around toward the road.

"Well, you look like a simpleton." Rocky reclined her seat back and closed her eyes behind the sunglasses. "Who are we meeting?"

"Dorothy Dingledowd."

Rocky laughed. "What the fuck? Dorothy Dingledowd is not a real person. That's the name of a Dickens character in some story about midwives."

"I think she goes by Dot."

Rocky shook her head without raising her head or opening her eyes. "No one goes by Dot, Jen. Cartoon mice don't even do it anymore. I think there was an uprising."

"Rocky," Jen cut her eyes at her passenger, "can you please try to be nice? Please? Ms. Dingledowd is a sustainer. She helps fund a lot of these projects."

"Yeah. About that. Why are we even still having this meeting? Didn't the honorable Miss Shotgun Divorce St. Laurent fund the whole thing?"

Jen raised an eyebrow. "No one's sure what happens with her donation now. Obviously, recent events could affect the timeline, at the very least. Besides, each new member class is responsible for a fundraiser to go along with their service project. So even if we get funded, we still have to plan a fundraiser."

"Did you hear that?" Rocky leaned toward Jen. "My cynicism groaned. My inner snark couldn't even be bothered to comment. She was just like, 'Ugh, you guys. I'm going back to sleep.'"

"That was your stomach." She punched Rocky's shoulder. "Come on. You can't spell fundraiser without F-U-N."

Rocky rubbed at her shoulder and pouted. "I stopped listening after F-U."

Rocky ate almost every meal at local eateries, a habit she picked up from her father. Chains and fast food restaurants deluged Texarkana, but Raquel Champagnolle did not eat at Chili's. So Jen drove them across town to a locally owned restaurant called Steel and Stone. As they pulled into the parking lot, Rocky croaked out, "We drove all the way across town. This better be Steel and Stone." She sat up and peered over her glasses. "Okay. I want to eat—"

"On the patio," Jen interrupted. "I know. I told her. Now come on. We're late."

During Rocky's eleventh grade year, she charmed her way into a position as a student aid in the counselor's office. Her goal, which she achieved, was to access her schedule for her senior year of high school and leave first period blank. Rocky never made it on time. To anything.

Once inside, the hostess informed Jen that she had seated the party they were meeting on the patio. Rocky pushed her sunglasses into her hair as they weaved their way behind the spry sixteen-year-old guiding them to their table. As they stepped on the patio, really more of a partially covered deck, Rocky laughed audibly. Jen elbowed her in the stomach, to which Rocky replied, "What? Jesus. Look at her, Jen. I take back my previous objections. This woman is totally a Dot."

Dorothy "Dot" Dingledowd wore a pair of reading glasses hanging onto her nose for dear life. As they started her way, she flipped them down to hang by their bejeweled string around her neck and pulled the thick-lensed John-Lennon-round glasses down out of her hair to get a better eyeful of Rocky and Jen. She wore her hair, her most composed feature, in a neat bob. One, Rocky thought, not unlike what one would imagine a cartoon mouse might ask for were she to be granted a head of hair and a fifteen-dollar gift certificate to Supercuts. Even in the heat of the summer, she wore loose, flowy, and layered clothing. While Rocky wore a silky summer dress and Jen a stylish pair of cuffed shorts with a striped top, Dot sported a cardigan...over a cardigan. She wore an ankle-length dress-of-many-colors and Croc sandals.

Jen gave a broad smile and greeted Dot for them both, "Ms. Dingledowd, so nice to see you again. Thanks for meeting with us."

"Call me Dot, please. And thank you. I never socialize. If I'm not careful, I could let myself turn into a recluse. I appreciate a reason to meet someone." She turned to Rocky. "You must be Raquel."

Rocky flashed her people smile, flipping the cynical switch into the off position and going full-tilt social butterfly. "Yes, ma'am. Jen here has told me all about you. So interesting."

Jen cut her eyes at Rocky as they all settled at the table. Dot fluttered her eyes and grinned. "Oh? Like what?"

"Well," Rocky placed her fingers on her bare chest in a delicate strum between the collarbones, "I so wish I had learned an instrument. I always love to meet someone who is musically inclined. Especially a pianist. I am filled with such a delightful mixture of envy and wonder."

Dot blushed. "So sweet of you to say. I'm not sure I consider myself a true pianist. I dabble, I suppose." She frowned at Jen. "I wasn't aware you knew."

Jen shrugged.

"Oh, modesty." Rocky laughed and shook her head. "I would imagine you would also refer to yourself as a bird *watcher*." She squinted one eye. "But our Granny used to tell us the difference between being a bird watcher and being a true birder."

Dot's eyes grew wide and she looked back and forth between the two Champagnolle girls.

Jen swallowed a lump in her throat, but Rocky never broke stride. "Our Granny used to keep us enthralled for hours rattling off names of rare birds she spotted right here in Arkansas."

Dot nodded, bristling with enthusiasm. "Oh, yes. You would be amazed at the birds I've seen. People think we're a state full of mockingbirds and blue jays, but let me tell you, one trip up to—"

Rocky completed Dot's sentence along with her, nodding and pointing, "Eureka Springs."

They both chortled, and Jen joined in with shaky, nervous, breathy laughs. Dot reached over and patted Rocky's hand, adding, "You ladies order us some wine." She flashed a mischievous smirk. "I can tell we're going to have a fun lunch." She rose, folding a napkin into her chair. "I'm going to run to the restroom. I will be right back."

As soon as she left, Jen leaned into Rocky. "What the hell was that?"

Rocky touched up her lipstick in a compact mirror. "Oh, calm down. This is softball."

"Birding?"

Rocky cocked her head. "Okay. The birding was part lucky guess. I mean, look at her."

"I shouldn't still be asking." Jen sighed. "Enlighten me. Please."

Snapping the compact closed, Rocky nodded toward Dot's phone, sitting face up on the table. "Her lock screen is a quote. I noticed when we first sat down. I assume she checked the time with the compulsive nature of a grown woman with few friends. The quote read, 'Simplicity is the final achievement.' Francis Chopin, I believe. The quote, combined with her slender fingers and the musical notes adorning *one* of her *two* cardigans—Jesus, Jen, two—said to me this woman fancies herself an amateur pianist." She began studying the wine list.

Jen slapped the laminated menu down to the table. "Birding! Please."

"Oh. Sorry. Yes, the birding. Well, she wears two pairs of glasses. Not bifocals. Other than just being weird as fuck, I'm assuming there is a logical reason. Most likely, she has trouble peering through a set of binoculars with bifocals on. And her haphazard style of dress, besides being sad and homely, is pieced together like a traveler of the state. The Croc sandals—Lord help her poor little heart—are not your typical Croc, purchased wherever shitty footwear is sold. They only sell those in an actual Croc store, like the one in Hot Springs. If I remember right, which I do, the only place you can buy a tie-dyed dress made out of strips of patchouli-soaked fabric discarded by hobos is at—"

Jen nodded, remembering, "—the Jonquil Festival. The crazy couple with the booth who played nothing but Grateful Dead."

"And the reading glasses string? Those beads? The only place I've ever seen anything like those was the creepy guy with the monocle in—"

Jen chuckled along as she spoke. And they said it together, "Eureka Springs."

Rocky nodded. "So, lucky guess, sure. But each of those spots? The have the nature draw. They pull in bird watchers from all over. And look at her. Come on."

A waitress hovered over Jen's shoulder, which led Rocky to pick the wine list back up and rattle off a couple of sweet white wines. When Dot returned, they all drank and talked, with Jen allowing Rocky to take the lead through pretending to find piano concertos and birding stories interesting. Rocky ordered a grilled flatbread sandwich that she smelled more than ate—she loved the way a smoky aroma paired with a crisp white wine. She breathed into her glass, letting the scents mix, as Dot said, "I'm so glad I donated some money for your community outreach. You seem like such big-hearted young ladies." She smiled into the distance. "You remind me of myself ten…or fifteen years ago."

Rocky cut her eyes at Jen, who sipped at an empty glass and avoided eye contact. "You—you *already* donated?"

"Oh yes, dear." Dot nodded. "Jen told me all about your project. Wonderful cause. I couldn't give you enough to fund the whole thing, but it should help."

"It does. Tremendously." Jen patted the table and smiled. "And I know how hard of a time you've had. So I can't tell you how much we appreciate you."

Rocky cut her eyes back and forth between the two. Jen twirled a French fry and shook her head. "So terrible. Have the police gotten any leads?"

Rocky pursed her lips and kicked Jen under the table.

"No. I'm afraid not." Dot hung her head. "And poor Waverly." She looked up, wide-eyed. "We're all living in fear."

Jen nodded, frowning. "You're so right. Something," she glared at Rocky, "must be done. Soon."

"I agree. Before we see another tragic turn." Dot put a hand to her cheek. "The irony is, I don't even think this…this man, the home invader, is dangerous."

Rocky rolled her eyes hard at Jen and poured herself more wine. Jen wrinkled her nose at Rocky and prodded Dot, "What do you mean? I hate to ask, but what happened? If you don't mind sharing, I mean."

Dot shuddered, but her eyes took on the twinkle of someone sitting on a story they've been dying to tell. "Well, I was home alone. David was on call, and he had run up to check on a patient." She blinked at them both. "My husband is a doctor."

"Yeah, we'd made the deductive leap, thanks." Rocky drained the last of a bottle and whirled it at the waitress for another. Jen punched Rocky's leg under the table, which caused Rocky to titter at her like a frightened meerkat. But she relented and forced out a sober, "I mean, this isn't about your husband, Dot. Our only concern is how this calamity affected you."

Dot squinted at her and nodded. "You're right, Raquel. You're absolutely right. I was terrified. And alone. The young man stormed through the downstairs living room."

"Did you get a look at him?" Jen asked.

Rocky wobbled over the table. "You say that as if you have an upstairs living room."

"Yes. We do."

"Huh."

Jen nudged Rocky's arm, causing her to almost hit her head on her plate.

Dot continued, "He wore a mask and a ball cap—plain, black, dingy. So, no, I couldn't see his face at all. White man, average height. Had on an army green field jacket. It was lightweight, but he must have been burning up. He rummaged around, picking up things and tossing them like a savage."

"Horrible." Jen clucked her tongue.

"What kinds of things?"

Dot looked at Rocky's confused grimace and shook her head. "I don't know. Family photos, keepsakes. Searching for valuables, I presume."

"Did you go downstairs?" Jen showed genuine concern. "Do you own a gun?"

Dot and Rocky answered in unison, "No." Rocky coupled her answer with a tipsy chuckle. Jen kicked her under the table. Rocky responded with an up and down wave of her hand in Dot's direction.

Fortunately, Dot closed her eyes when she answered and shook her head with them still squeezed shut. "No, no, no. We detest violence. I did call down to him, though. I asked him, very politely, to leave."

Rocky opened her mouth and Jen shoved a fry into it.

Dot continued, "He was so polite. As soon as he spoke, I must say, I felt no fear. I'm not suggesting he shouldn't be arrested, but I do not believe he intends to hurt anyone."

"What'd he take?" Rocky chewed at the fry and motioned with a smile for the approaching waitress to fill her glass.

"My son's Adderall. Out of my purse."

"That's it?"

Jen reached across for Dot. "Your poor son. Can you get more medicine?"

Dot waved off the concern. "Oh, sure. David can get a prescription refill. I just tell him when we need more. The bottle was practically empty anyway."

By the end of the third bottle, Jen helped Rocky stumble to the car. Jen chided her for over-drinking but was too excited about what they gleaned from the robbery story to stay mad. In the car, while Rocky leaned back with her sunglasses pressed tight against her face, Jen bounced in her seat. "So what do you think?"

"I think she should stop being such a damn Democrat and buy a gun to protect her family."

"Rocky, you're a Democrat."

Rocky shot a finger into the air. "I am not. I'm a social progressive."

"What's the difference?"

"My purse has more guns than a Democrat and less money than a Republican."

Jen sighed. "I know you picked up on something."

"Picked up on the check," Rocky mumbled. "I thought richie-doctor's-wife was paying. I would have stopped at two bottles."

"You know, her husband—"

Rocky interrupted her, "Ssstop right there. I don' wanna hear about her husband. All these women so per-occupied with their husbands. We are women. Capable women. We don' need men to prop us up anymore."

"Okay, before you burn your bra, run in here with me for a second." Jen nodded toward a house. She only drove a short ways before whipping into a driveway of a two-story Colonial house in an older neighborhood on the Texas side of Texarkana.

Rocky stumbled out of the car, retorting, "Joke's on you, wise ass. I'm not wearing a bra." She peered over her sunglasses. "Where are we?"

Jen strode up the front walk to the door. "Elaine Maplethorpe's house."

Rocky tilted her glasses so they rested crooked on her face. She closed one eye and took in her surroundings. Spinning and shimmering pinwheels on stakes filled the yard. An artificial tree made out of colored glass bottles stood on one side. A triangular rainbow flag hung from the front porch. Rocky did her meerkat impression again. "Where are we?"

Trotting to catch up, Rocky reached Jen as Elaine Maplethorpe answered the doorbell. Elaine flung open her front door with a dramatic flair. She could have been anywhere between fifty and seventy, with silvery hair flowing down past her breasts. Mixed among the long white strands of hair were colorful feathers. She wore a puffy orange shirt with purple stitching. Her purple dress crinkled and bunched at her bare feet. She wore several toe rings and countless other pieces of jewelry—bracelets and necklaces and rings. A fog of incense followed her to the door, and she held her hands up into the mist as if she held it indoors.

When Elaine saw Jen, she squealed. Jen returned the squeal in a lower decibel. Elaine pulled her into a tight hug, saying through gritted teeth, "Jennifer, Jennifer, Jennifer. I am so happy to see you at my home." She released her and stepped back with wide eyes. "What am I doing? Come in. Please. Come in and let me fix you a drink." Elaine whirled and disappeared into the fog.

Jen turned to Rocky and motioned inside with her head. Rocky pointed into the house. "You know this fortune teller?"

Jen responded by entering the house, forcing Rocky to continue following at her heels. Inside, Elaine invited them to sit on her colorful floral couch while she retrieved some tea from the kitchen. Stones and crystals and tapestries littered the dark house.

Elaine returned with a tray of tea, steaming with a faint trail of jasmine-scented smoke. She poured them each a cup, apologizing, "It's a little weak. I'm so sorry. Would you like sugar? How do you take your tea?"

"Cold and sweet. I don't like hot liquids." Jen elbowed Rocky, knocking off the sneer Rocky gave to the cup offered her. "I mean, this is perfect, thank you. I like my tea like I like my men. Transparent, bitter, and disappointing."

Elaine smiled. "You must be Rocky. I've heard about you."

Rocky pretended to take a sip and set the cup back down, raising her eyebrows in a non-verbal complement of thanks.

After Elaine poured Jen a cup, to which Jen added several spoons of sugar, they settled into small talk for a moment before Elaine sprang up. "Oh, Jennifer! Let me get you a check before I forget."

Rocky turned to Jen as Elaine scrambled off and mouthed, "Check?"

Jen nodded, and Elaine came back into the room writing in a checkbook. "I can only donate a thousand, but every little bit helps. Such a wonderful cause."

"Oh, this is more than generous. Yes. Thank you so much, Elaine," Jen nodded and accepted the check with a bowed head. "And here with," she paused, eyeing Rocky, "everything you've been through."

Chapter 7

Elaine Maplethorpe recounted her harrowing tale of falling victim to the home invader. "My Beverly was at work, so I was home alone. Defenseless."

Rocky busied herself examining a set of crystals on the side table. She held one into the light and closed one eye. "You could've cast a spell, I suppose."

"Rocky," Jen chided.

"No, no," Elaine held a hand out and shook her head. "She's right. I was ill prepared."

Rocky glanced over to Jen and raised her eyebrows in boast.

Elaine continued, "The funny thing is, he didn't take one item. Not one."

"Yep." Rocky swirled a hand around in the air. "Looked at some pictures and blah, blah, blah."

"Pictures?" Elaine shook her head. "No, I don't recall him looking at pictures." She laughed and waved a hand around the living room. "I'm afraid we don't own many of those. We tend to be more temporal, by nature. Photographs are so fleeting and meaningless. We should all live in the moment. Breathe in life rather than merely—"

Rocky sat up and blinked to focus on Elaine's face. "Yeah. I get it. Viewing everything through a little whatever. Tell me again? He didn't look at any pictures? None?"

Elaine shook her head more emphatically. "No."

"What did he do?"

"He came in," Elaine stared off, remembering, "asked a few questions, and left."

Rocky closed her eyes and pursed her lips. "No. Exactly. *What* did he ask? What did he hold when he asked it? Did he pick anything up? Knock anything over?"

Elaine nodded "Hold. Yes. He was holding something." She rose and walked over to a bookshelf. Picking up a vase emblazoned with a rainbow-colored equality sign, she turned back toward Rocky. "He was holding this. He had it in his hand when we first encountered one another."

"But he didn't break it, smash it?"

"No. He placed it back on the shelf where he found it. I had some fresh flowers in there at the time, and they fell out, but other than—"

Rocky frowned. "What did he ask? You said 'asked a few questions.'"

Elaine shrugged. "He asked if I was alone, and I told him I was. I guess I should have lied."

"Asked how? What did he say? His exact words. And how did he say them? What was his reaction?" Rocky flailed her hands out impatiently.

Elaine set the vase back and moved back around to an armchair facing the couch, where Jen and Rocky sat. She thought back, "He asked if my husband was home. And—"

Rocky held a hand up for her to stop. "What was your *precise* answer? Word for word."

Elaine nodded and added with concentration, "I said my Beverly would be returning any moment."

Rocky paused her and said, "And his reaction? Think. What did he do?"

"Well," Elaine craned her eyes toward her furrowed eyebrows, "he looked down at the vase, set it back where he found it, and he," she smiled, "he apologized."

Jen laughed under her breath. "Apologized?"

"Yes. 'Pardon me for having bothered you,' he said." Elaine flopped her hands into her lap. "And he left." Elaine cocked her head at Rocky. "You appear to be sobering up, dear." She grinned, flitting her eyes back and forth between Jen and Rocky. "I think you girls would enjoy some brownies."

After she sprung to her feet and danced out of the room into the kitchen, Jen bounced in her seat, slapping Rocky on the leg. "I knew it! I knew you'd come around! You can't resist. You're doing your thing, aren't you?"

Rocky pushed her away and recoiled. "Ouch! Stop hitting me! I'm not doing anything. I was making conversation."

"Bullshit! You're about to solve the case."

"Can you please stop using the word *case*?"

Jen snaked her neck back and forth rhythmically. "Nope. You are on the case. You want to solve the case."

Rocky rolled her eyes. "No. I *want* to eat some brownies."

Jen made a sour face. "Oh, no. Don't eat the brownies."

"Why the hell not? Are you about to fat shame me? You whore."

Jen shook her head. "No, no. I don't care about your calorie count, Rocky. Elaine's brownies? Well, they will be...*brownies*. If you know what I mean."

"You just said brownies will be brownies. English language learners would know what you mean, Jen." Rocky collapsed back into the couch and her eyes grew wide. "Oh! Oh, you mean pot, don't you?"

"Shh."

Rocky frowned. "Why? She's in there folding it into baked goods and I can't say the word?"

"Just don't eat a brownie."

"Oh, I'm eating a brownie."

"Rocky, please. No brownies."

"I said one, but now you pluralized it. So I'm eating two. Maybe three."

Elaine returned with a plate of ten or twelve brownies stacked in a pyramid. Rocky snatched one up before the plate hit the coffee table and took a heaping bite while glaring at Jen, who tried to decline for the both of them. Elaine laughed off Jen's polite refusal and helped Rocky polish off half the plate. As 3:00 rushed up on them, Rocky and Elaine cackled their way through recounting their respective lists of the ten dumbest moments on *Charmed*. They both worked to ignore Jen, who stood at the door tapping her foot, until Jen physically drug Rocky to the car.

Rocky sat in the passenger seat pushing the pads of her fingers together and studying the sensation through her sunglasses as Jen derided her in silence and drove. Holding both middle fingers up to Jen's face, Rocky broke the silence by asking, "Which of these is more squishy?"

"You're high."

"Am I?" Rocky curled her lip. "I think there was," she lowered her voice to a whisper, "pot in those brownies."

"Rocky, our fundraiser meeting is in," Jen glanced at the clock in the dashboard, "ten minutes ago."

"These women can wait. They've been waiting all their lives."

Jen scrunched her face up. "For what?" Rocky pushed a finger in the air, and Jen rolled her eyes, adding, "Don't say—"

They said in unison, "To be liberated."

Rocky nodded and pointed back toward Elaine's house. "Your lesbian gypsy friend is onto something."

Jen laughed. "Well—"

"No," Rocky snapped at her. "No, Jen. Don't you dare disparage that beautiful warlock's way of life."

Jen rolled her eyes. "She is not a witch."

"I didn't say witch, did I? Because women can be warlocks. They can be anything."

"Are you going to be high in this meeting? Because you can't be high in a Junior League meeting."

Rocky blew a faltering raspberry toward Jen. "I can be anything, Jen." She waggled her fingers. "Anything."

"At least you're starting to be a detective, like I asked."

"What do you mean?"

"I mean you. Back there. You're in it now. You got all interested."

Rocky blew another raspberry. "I am not interested in some snooty women getting scared by the world's politest robber."

"Home invader."

"Home Invader is a horrible name." Rocky stuck her tongue out. "We need a better name. Is he British? I've been imagining him British." She took on a bad English accent. "So sorry, madam. Bit of a bother, I'm afraid. Don't mind me. I'll bugger off. Cheerio."

"He's not British."

Rocky's eyes grew wide. "The Hi-Ho Cheerio Killer!"

"He hasn't killed anyone."

"The Punctilious Pilferer. The Courteous Crook. The Genteel who Steals."

Jen laughed, but retorted, "He doesn't steal either."

"You are so bad at naming. You are killing my buzz."

"Good!"

Rocky stared out the window. "You know what does interest me?"

Jen sighed. "What?"

"Waverly St. Laurent."

"Jesus, Rocky. Let it go. Yes. She was a bitch to you, but—"

"Did you know her son was," Rocky whipped around dramatically, "murdered?"

Jen rolled her eyes. "Yes. I did. Along with everyone else in Texarkana. How do you miss these things?"

Rocky frowned. "It didn't affect me. Until now."

"It still doesn't affect you."

"She affects me. Like a rash. Or a boil."

"Let it rest, Rocky."

"She killed her husband. And ate her son."

Jen laughed. "She did not eat her son."

"Dismemberment is the only rational explanation. They only found part of him. And the part they found was, like, burned. The burned part. The part she didn't eat. She's obviously the Rye Mother. And her husband was about to turn her in. Or maybe he's the Rye Mother. And she covered for him. But her anger raged inside of her for two decades until the rage boiled over," Rocky made the sound effects with her mouth of a shotgun being cocked and fired, "with the blast of a shotgun."

"Can you just figure out the home invasions? They even connect, Rocky."

Rocky took on her English accent again. "Bollocks, Jennifer, old sport."

"What do you mean? Waverly St. Laurent was so terrorized by the thought—"

"Bullshit. She wanted to divorce her husband. He had a prenuptial agreement or something or a hundred-million-dollar life insurance policy or a twenty-year-old girlfriend. And so she divorced him with a shotgun instead of a lawyer. Our Neighborly Knave has nothing to do with Waverly St. Laurent, and I can—"

Jen whipped around with a massive smile. "And you can what?"

Rocky ducked her chin into her chest and pouted, "Nothing. I can nothing."

"No, no. You can prove it! You were about to say you can prove it!"

"Maybe."

Jen howled with laughter as they pulled into the Holiday Inn parking lot. One of the new members did public relations and event planning for several local hotels, so she booked a conference room for their meeting.

Rocky still sulked as they walked in almost thirty minutes late. The seven new members in attendance were sputtering to fill silence and spinning their wheels around a series of erased ideas on a dry erase board. Jen poured herself into an apology for being late as Rocky slouched into a seat and left her sunglasses on. Within minutes, Rocky fell asleep and spent her first half hour being shoved off Jen's shoulder.

Once Rocky woke up, she managed to catch the last of a conversation about organizing a bake sale. Several of the girls groaned at the idea, but Rocky perked up, "We could sell brownies."

Jen elbowed her hard in the side, but Rocky continued, pushing her glasses up into her hair. "I happen to know for a fact Elaine Maplethorpe makes wonderful brownies."

One girl made a face and asked, "Isn't she a witch?"

Jen and Rocky both answered, "No," but Rocky added, "She's a warlock."

Jen ducked her head. "We are not traveling down this path, Rock."

Rocky stood up. "When our Granny was in a nursing home, dying a slow death from Glaucoma—"

Jen shook her head. "Never happened. You can't die from Glaucoma."

"We, Jennifer and I, we watched in horror as she suffered. In pain. Unable to receive the natural balm provided by Our Father, her Creator."

Jen mumbled, "Please stop this."

A girl with a scrutinizing glare and eyes a little more clever than most, spoke up from the back of the group. "Are you talking about pot brownies?"

Rocky held her arms out in her patented innocent shyster pose. "I'm talking about giving the people what they want."

Most of the group laughed. Some with the loud bark of social discomfort. Rocky cocked her head. "Oh, I'm not joking."

Several raised their eyebrows and asked, "What?"

Rocky nodded. "Think about it. We are operating within the biggest blind spot of all time. We are a bunch of harmless girls. We are viewed as bored housewives trying to do good. Nothing—absolutely nothing would play more into the fantasy our male-driven community wants to believe than us selling baked goods. It's perfect. All we do is find the right target audience and set a reasonable price point."

A couple of ladies stood and started into sermonizing why they wouldn't stand for this type of talk, but the cynic in the back spoke over them. "She's not wrong."

Everyone turned to ogle her with varied expressions. "She's not. In fact, it's brilliant. Three of my grandparents wasted away in nursing homes. My uncle died of cancer. My mom takes monthly chemo. Any and all of them would take some relief from the pain and illness associated with treatment. And not one person providing them with treatment would even bat an eye at someone offering relief."

One of the two objectors continued to protest, until she ultimately stormed out. However, everyone else stayed, some skeptical, but all listening. Jen turned bright red over the conversation, but even she stopped attempting to shut the brainstorming down. Rocky went on to explain how, by setting up a narrow chain of supply and demand, they could deliver a much-needed product to a small group of worthy recipients who would be highly motivated to both pay handsomely and keep their mouths shut. By the end of her sales pitch, everyone in the room at least considered the idea. And all, even Jen, admitted Rocky's insanity rose above any other idea offered.

By 5:00, Rocky took charge of a meeting for which she arrived thirty minutes late and of which she proceeded to sleep through the remainder of the first hour. Jen continued to shoot eye daggers toward her, but Rocky concluded the meeting by taking a vote. "So, by a show of hands, who here wants to explore our Half-Baked Bake Sale?"

Jen peered around the room to find every hand raised into the air. She kept her arms crossed and glowered up at Rocky, who motioned for her to raise her hand.

Which she did with reluctance and her middle finger extended.

Chapter 8

Driving away from the meeting, Rocky kept her sunglasses on and worked at clearing the last of her pot brownie cobwebs by rolling her jaw around. Jen stared hard at the road and either chewed on the side of her mouth or readied herself to spit on Rocky. After a full five minutes of painful silence, Rocky pushed her glasses up with a finger and snuck a glance at Jen before leaning forward and turning on the radio. Jen shot a hand out and turned the noise back off.

Rocky grinned and turned the radio on again.

Jen jabbed it off.

Their little dance repeated four times before Rocky mimed turning the radio on without doing so, which led Jen to yank it on, before realizing the trick and turning the music back off. "Goddammit, Rock. Could you take this seriously, please?"

Rocky scrunched her face up. "The radio?"

"No. Not the radio. The Junior League. Pot brownies? Are you kidding me?"

"I think we can go bigger than just pot brownies."

Jen pushed her eyebrows together. "What? Bigger how? Crack?"

Rocky shrugged. "I don't know. I was kind of wondering how many Junior Leaguers have their kids' Adderall in their purses."

Jen heaved a sigh and shook her head.

"Wondering." Rocky held her hands up.

"Rocky, you're going to get us arrested."

"Bullshit," Rocky scoffed. "We're the idea people. Did you ever buy an iPhone from Steve Jobs?"

"You're the idea person. I hate this."

Rocky nodded. "True. But did you ever buy an iPhone from Steve Jobs' cynical cousin?"

Jen threw her hands up in exasperation. "Why do you always do everything except the one thing someone wants you to do? I asked you for one thing. One thing! And that one thing was not starting a freaking drug ring in the Junior League."

"Well, I'm not sure I'd call one bake sale a—"

"Stop! Just stop, Rock. Please."

Rocky let silence fill the car again for a few minutes before squeaking out, "How—how many robberies again?"

Jen rolled her eyes. "I don't need you to throw me some sort of pity small talk."

"No. It's not that. I'm interested."

Jen shot her a look.

"I am. Jen, I promise. I want to hear about the robberies, or whatever." They shared skeptical glances, Rocky mimicking Jen's before throwing up a scout's honor hand sign and adding, "I'm ready to hear about them."

Jen bit at a lip and tried to hold a scrutinizing scowl of anger and resentment, but her countenance melted into pure giddiness as she reached around in the back seat.

Rocky held a hand out hovering near the steering wheel and grimaced as they swerved around so Jen could retrieve a folded section of newspaper. Jen flopped the folded paper into Rocky's lap and pointed. "There's a write up in there. From last week. After the Maplethorpe robbery. You have to search. The story's small and on page three. Little column on the right-hand side."

Rocky nodded. "Yeah, I see it. It's nothing."

"I know," Jen said, nodding. "But they started to link them. That's the important part."

After scanning the article, Rocky tossed the paper back into the back seat and pulled out her phone. "But they didn't give much at all. No names. No addresses. Just dates and a confirmation from the police of an apparent link." She scrolled through the calendar on her phone. "The 30th, the 6th, and the 13th. Those are consecutive Tuesdays."

Jen nodded with wide eyes. "I know. I noticed. And the 20th was Dot Dingledowd. And then the 27th?"

"Waverly St. Laurent," they said together.

Jen screwed up her mouth and cocked her head. "I know you think it's unrelated, but you gotta admit—"

Rocky took off her sunglasses and bit on an earpiece. "The date," she nodded. "Yeah, I get it." She frowned at Jen. "There were four. Who were the first two?"

"One was the woman from the Sip and Sign, who talked about her break-in to the group I pulled you into. Rhonda Thornhill. She was the first."

"I remember her. Hippy-ish?"

Jen nodded. "Yep. The second was Edie Gomez. I don't know her."

"At all? You don't know what she does, what she looks like, anything?"

Jen shrugged. "She hasn't been at any meetings. I think she may be a librarian. Seems like I remember hearing someone mention her being a school librarian, maybe."

Rocky nodded. "Makes sense. All four before Waverly were meek and mild. Not gun owners. The type to have cats instead of rottweilers."

"You think he picked them because they were easy targets?"

Rocky shrugged. "Could be. There has to be a connection. We're not just talking Junior Leaguers. There are lots of Junior Leaguers. It's *these* Junior Leaguers. What else do they share in common?"

Jen rolled her head around, thinking. "I'm not sure. I don't know them too well. I mean they all seem a little outside of the normal Junior League profile. The three I do know are very involved in the charity side of things. Not so much the social end. I assume the same for Edie, since she never even comes to events. I'm trying to think of what their husbands do."

"Jen! Jesus. Enough with the husband shit. Women are not defined by their husbands. I mean, they don't even all have husbands, for Sappho's sake. He didn't even see their husbands. He saw them."

Jen smiled wryly. "Oh, we're still on the feminist kick? I thought that was the pot brownies speaking earlier."

"No! Not the brownies. I am woman. Hear me snark." Rocky huffed and rubbed her hands together in a habit she'd practiced since childhood. Whenever she went into full-on contemplation mode, she rubbed her hands together as if she were applying lotion. "So what do you know about Rhonda Thornhill? She was first, right?"

"Yes, she was first. But I don't know much. I picked up her name, which you did not. Because, you know, I actually pay attention to things like names and other human things. You may know more than I do. Since you pick out other things to pay attention to. Like bird watching and piano hands."

Rocky shook her head. "She didn't have piano hands. More gardener hands. Had dirt under a couple of nails. And she made her own jewelry out of hemp or some shit. Somewhere with a window facing east."

Jen laughed. "Rocky. Seriously? What the fuck?"

"They were faded. Sun bleached, but only on one side. Like she had worked on them, dyed them, and hung them in a window to dry so the smell would waft out. She gardens, which means she's an early riser, toiling in the yard through the morning. Leaving her nights to work on the handcrafts, hanging them in the window to dry overnight."

Jen nodded. "And pick up the morning sunlight."

Rocky pointed to her. "But tells us nothing. There must be something more. She was first. Why? Did he know her? Maybe she lives in his neighborhood?"

Jen shrugged. "Maybe a relative?"

"Maybe. Try first with someone who may not turn you in if you're caught."

"Caught doing what?" Jen scoffed, "He didn't even take anything from the first one."

Rocky frowned and nodded. "You're right. So why break in? He looked around at things and left. But polite. On his first home invasion, he's not nervous, he's not barking orders, he's not panicky. He's polite. Calm. Collected."

"Maybe it's just his personality."

Rocky rubbed her hands and squinted. "Or maybe it's not his first one."

"What do you mean?"

Rocky buried herself in the tiny screen of her phone, tapping and scrolling, searching.

Jen tried to lean over to see. "What are you looking for?"

"The police beat."

"The police beat?"

Rocky nodded. "The police beat is a daily segment in the paper. They list any reported burglaries"

Jen nodded. "So you're checking—"

Rocky turned the screen around to face Jen. "Tuesdays." She pulled the phone back and read. "Tuesday, May 16th. Burglary in the 800 block of Elizabeth Street." She tapped and searched more. "May 9th, 700 block of Elizabeth. May 2nd, 900 block of Elizabeth."

"Elizabeth? That's a rough neighborhood."

Rocky nodded. "Yep. So, much more likely to be his own neighborhood."

Jen scrunched her face up. "You don't know he comes from—"

"Someplace close to his first break-ins? Of course he does, Jen. Think about it. If you start trying something like home invasions, you want to gauge your game clock. How much time do you have to work with before either the cops show up or the homeowner has had enough. And I know what you're thinking, response times would be shorter in rich neighborhoods. But I think you might be wrong. Police would patrol a rough neighborhood with regularity. So if a call went in, which it did, a patrol car would be nearby. Not to mention, homeowners on Elizabeth aren't going to be as patient as Dot Dingledowd. I think he practiced on some houses tougher than the real targets. And I think he had a house to run to nearby, where he could hide in a hurry. I would imagine there is even someone there—a wife or a girlfriend or a roommate—with a ready alibi if the police started knocking on doors."

"All I'm trying to say is you don't know that was him. I would imagine there are multiple burglaries there. Even on Tuesdays."

Rocky scrolled around through her phone. "There are a few. But only one on each of those three Tuesdays leading up to the Junior League break-ins."

Jen pointed and nodded. "Break-ins, Rocky. The Junior League homes were break-ins. Those are listed as burglaries. Why steal from lower income houses and then not take anything from these defenseless wealthy women?"

Rocky grinned patronizingly. "Jen. Sweetie. If you live on Elizabeth and someone breaks into your house, you're going to say something got taken. File an insurance claim and get a little cash out of the deal."

Jen recoiled. "Jesus, Rock. That's a little elitist of you. Just because—"

"Jen," Rocky eyed her. "I don't have the energy for this conversation."

"You don't even know what I was going to say."

"Yes, I do, Jen. You're like a rerun of *Law and Order*."

Jen curled her lip and mumbled, "Consistent and entertaining."

"Marry, fuck, kill: Lennie Briscoe, Rey Curtis, Jack McCoy."

"Easy." Jen raised her eyebrows. "Fuck the hell out of Rey Curtis."

"Given. Three times."

"Kill Jack McCoy."

"Also three times. Jesus."

They said together, "Marry Lennie Briscoe."

Rocky nodded. "The one liners alone. I would marry him for the one liners alone."

They drove and batted around a few more Marry, Fuck, Kill scenarios, laughing and arguing playfully. When they reached a lull in the conversation, Rocky retreated back to her phone, tapping and scrolling.

Jen glanced over. "Are you trying to find out who lives in the 800 block of Elizabeth?"

Rocky frowned at her. "What? No. Can you do that? Just pull it up on the Internet?"

Jen shook her head. "Yeah. Well, sort of, maybe. Wait, what are you doing?"

"Reading chat room comments about Waverly St. Laurent's dead kid."

Jen hung her head. "Shit, Rocky. Can you let it go?"

"I'm reading. There's no harm in reading." She flashed her screen. "Cowboymonster1982 thinks she's the killer, too. See? People agree with me."

"She didn't kill her son, Rocky. Or you know what? Maybe she did. Doesn't matter. This is a non-starter. We're already on a case."

Rocky made a sour face. "Since when do you talk like a 1960s advertising executive? There are no cases. I've told you a hundred times. And I'm only reading."

They stared each other down before returning to a moment of silence. Rocky broke the quiet without peeking up from her phone. "So what do you know about all this?"

Jen sighed.

Rocky answered the sigh with, "What? You said everyone knows about it. What do you know?"

"I know the basics. Somebody killed four or five kids in the 80s, and they called him the Rye Mother. No clue why. But they never caught him. He stopped after Jason."

"Do you remember it?"

Jen shook her head. "No, Rocky. We weren't born."

Rocky rolled her eyes. "I know. I mean talk about it. Do you remember rumors or anything?"

Jen shrugged. "I've heard my parents talking about it. They were in their twenties when the murders happened, so a little younger than the St. Laurents. I think everyone assumes the killer died or got arrested for something else or moved away after Jason."

"What about the St. Laurents?"

"You mean, were there suspicions? Of course. My mom said everyone assumed they killed him at first. The police leaned on them pretty hard. They had a lawyer, I think. Didn't talk at all to the public. Until his remains turned up. Then everybody shifted from suspicion to pity."

Rocky sniffed. "Well, I never saw the story on any of those true crime shows or anything."

Jen nodded. "Yeah, it was on one early. I saw the rerun. They did an *Unsolved Mysteries* about the murders, mostly focused on Jason. But Waverly thought the show made the family look bad, so she never allowed it again. Or at least, she never participated. I think it may have been on a local segment or two. She never commented again though. And the St. Laurents were the only family to be interviewed."

"Why?"

Jen shrugged. "I think the other families were lower income and less tied to the town. Seems like I remember Mom saying she thought most of them moved away."

"Like the killer?"

"I guess so. Moved or died. Mom and Dad talked about how fear stirred up every fall for a while. People kept their kids close around that time of year. But when nothing happened the next year, or the next, or the next, people sort of forgot. Assumed the guy must be dead or something."

Rocky grinned. "Or maybe she killed her one true target and stopped. Quenched her thirst for blood by eliminating the real source of her murderous—"

Jen laughed. "I've never heard the St. Laurents suspected of being the Rye Mother any of the times it has come up."

"How the hell often does it come up?"

Jen shook her head. "It's a major local mystery. People talk about that kind of shit."

"Why haven't I heard about it?"

"I don't know, Rocky. You don't pay attention to things not involving you. Like these robberies! Which could score us major points!"

Rocky snarled a lip. "Not robberies."

"Whatever!" Jen put a hand on Rocky's arm. "Just please drop the Rye Mother thing and think about these home invasions. If we—if you can figure this whole thing out, we will be Junior League Head Bitches."

"Is Head Bitch a real thing? Is there a sash somewhere with those exact words on it?"

"I will make one for you, Rocky. Just please. Solve this—"

Rocky put a finger to Jen's mouth. "Jen, if you say case, I will punch you in the twat."

Chapter 9

Rocky Champagnolle would make an exceptional elementary school principal. This fact would have come as a surprise to those who knew her at a younger age. Not to say Rocky ever failed to impress anyone with her intelligence throughout her entire life. She left quite an impression on most everyone. However, the same accusations Jen leveled against Rocky, such as not paying attention to things which did not apply to her, plagued her from day one. Rocky balanced out to a B student for the most part. Always smart enough to ace most tests, yet not interested enough to complete most homework. Her interests leaned toward literature and trivial matters, leaving such unessential topics…like math to pick up a low C (when lucky).

College came as a bit of a wake-up call. As her friends were planning to travel to the other end of the state to the University of Arkansas or at least up Interstate 30 to Central Arkansas in Conway or Henderson in Arkadelphia, at the very least Southern Arkansas a mere hour due east in Magnolia, Rocky weighed her options. They were few. Although her reading and English, even her science reasoning score on the ACT skyrocketed well into the thirties, math caught up with her. The math section lowered her overall score to better match a mediocre GPA, and the scholarship offers never materialized. Not to suggest they were necessary. Frank Champagnolle could have sent her to any of those in-state colleges.

Could have.

When a seventeen-year-old Rocky came bouncing into the living room with her prioritized college brochures, Frank said calmly, "Sweetheart, I've watched you yawn your way through four years of classes for free. Why do you think I want to pay for four more?"

Not that Frank didn't plan on his only child going to college. He did. He merely opted for the pathway of Texarkana Community College, followed by the local branch of Texas A&M. Opted at a fraction of the cost, when factoring in Rocky living at home under his watchful eye for the next four years. So Frank explained to a seething teenage Rocky how she would have to prove herself worthy of a college education before he planned on forking over thousands of dollars on one.

Rocky never took well to being underestimated. She never again made less than an A in any class. She spent the next four years earning an Associate's Degree, two Bachelor's Degrees, and three Master's Degrees. She also picked up her Special Education Certification, her Reading Diagnostician Certification, her English as a Second Language Certification, her Dyslexia Interventionist Certification, her Gifted and Talented Certification, and her Building Administration Certification.

And, however adept she would be at all of them, she would never use any of those.

Because Rocky Champagnolle cherished her summers.

After her long day of Junior League social events, multiple bottles of wine, and a few pot brownies, Rocky's aching head eased a touch upon finding her mother gone to Shreveport for the night with friends. Avoiding Darrelene allowed Rocky to also avoid a string of questions and stumble off to her room to resume full tilt summer activities.

Rocky started by soaking for almost an hour in a bathtub full of scorching water and Epsom salts. She followed the bath by pouring herself a tumbler of Diet 7-Up, chugging some Pepto Bismol, and downing a handful of Advil. On her way back to her room, she snagged three paperback mystery novels off her dad's bookshelf in the living room. Her normal summer routine consisted of finishing the first two and starting into the third before dozing off in the wee hours of the morning. Only to wake around noon and start back with a bowl of cereal next to her in bed. Rocky would knock out an entire series of mystery or slutmance novels in a week, and then switch genres and start again. And she loved every minute.

In her six years teaching, nothing interfered with the routine. Getting married disrupted her plans for a weekend. Illness and death of loved ones, maybe a day or two. Chet never bothered her. He would go off to work and to screw waitresses, so he loved her preoccupation with fiction and relaxation. Not one thing had thrown her off her summer game. Until Waverly St. Laurent.

When asked her greatest talent, Rocky, despite being adept at many things, named spite. And Waverly St. Laurent opened up every ounce of spite in Rocky's soul. She couldn't understand why the woman bothered her so, but her mind wouldn't leave the Junior League matriarch alone. Rocky didn't make it through one book before pulling up the chat rooms on her phone and exhausting the last bits of meaningless information about the St. Laurents. She fell asleep thinking about Waverly. Dreamed about Waverly. Woke up with Waverly still dominating her thoughts.

Rocky got up early enough for her mother to still be asleep. When she and her friends went to Shreveport, they would spend all night at the casinos and not get home until maybe four in the morning. So the next day she slept until at least lunch. Rocky also remembered her dad mentioning having to close the furniture store for a few days while he had the place repainted. So Rocky scurried to get dressed and rushed out to find her father sitting in the living room watching a morning news show with his giant boxer, Harper, draped across his lap like a throw rug.

"Dad!" Rocky burst into the room with a little more force than intended.

Frank shot up, wide-eyed, sending Harper bounding with a slight growl toward Rocky.

"Harper! It's just me. Jesus."

Frank stood up. "What's wrong, sweetheart?"

Rocky shook her head and grimaced. "Nothing. I'm sorry. I was bored. I didn't mean to make it seem like my room was on fire or something. Can you take me to the library?"

Frank frowned at her. "Honey, is your room on fire?"

"No. I just said it is, in fact, not on fire."

"The library?"

Rocky nodded.

"Is your car messed up, Rocky?"

She shook her head.

Frank closed his eyes and nodded. "You're scared to go by yourself because of the homeless people, aren't you?"

Rocky nodded.

"Damn your mother. Let me go throw on some clothes. Give me five minutes."

The Texarkana Public Library sat right across the street from the town's homeless shelter. This meant the front of the library always bustled with homeless men and women milling about, not panhandling, but always around. This posed quite a dilemma for Rocky. While she possessed a well-documented fervor for reading, she displayed an almost equally well-documented fear of homeless people. Her terror stemmed from childhood.

While it is true Rocky made B's in school, with a few C's in math, she did make one D. Once. Her distaste for math joined forces with her disdain for an algebra teacher named Ms. Snodgrass and the combination led to Rocky checking out altogether. When the D showed up on her report card, Rocky's mother decided to teach a valuable lesson. She loaded Rocky up in the car and drove her downtown. Rocky made countless trips to the library as a kid and recognized the path. The library, however, was not their destination that day. Rocky's mother pulled instead to the neighboring homeless shelter, where a line formed for lunch.

"There you go, Raquel. There's your future. These are your people."

Young Rocky eye-rolled her mother and laughed. "Mom, what are you doing?"

"Go join your people, Raquel."

After a momentary argument, Rocky was forced to stand in line and eat a community stew for lunch. Her mother picked her up an hour later, and Rocky came out a changed person. She would never make another D. But she also developed a near crippling fear of the homeless.

Therefore, an hour after their conversation, Frank Champagnolle wandered through the aisles ferreting out the latest Harry Bosch novel as Rocky checked out microfilmed copies of the *Texarkana Gazette*, circa 1985.

She didn't go back further, because she assumed the Rye Mother would be recounted in detail as soon as authorities discovered Jason's body. And, sure enough, eleven days after he went missing, the Saturday, October 12th edition featured a full-page article titled, "Rye Mother Killer Strikes Again." The photo contained a circle around a grainy zoom-in of a small boy being led by the hand into a wooded trail by a shadowy figure. The boy wore a dark green jacket with a hood, jeans, and sneakers. The alleged kidnapper appeared to be wearing a dress and a scarf—all black. The caption explained the picture to be one submitted by an anonymous bystander, who had been snapping family photos in a field. After discovering the image of the boy in the distance, the family turned the photograph over to the police, who enlarged the corner of the shot and matched the boy's clothing to the clothing worn by the third victim of the Rye Mother on the day of his disappearance. The outline of the dress, Rocky assumed, gave birth to the concept of the killer being a woman—thus the nickname, wherever it came from.

The article gave the names and timelines of each victim, dating back to October of 1981. The abductions and murders happened each October, beginning with six-year-old Ethan Sandberg and ending with Jason St. Laurent. Although the journalist referenced details being withheld to protect the integrity of the investigation, there were enough details to get a sense of how the killer worked. Each boy went missing from an area close to woods. Either they were last seen close to a wooded area, or, in the case of the photo, they were seen being led into a wooded area. All of these areas were on the outskirts of Texarkana. In some cases, they were in surrounding towns. Except Jason. He was last seen riding his bike toward a wooded area between a city park and a trailer park. Middle of town. But everything else fit. The boys were all between the ages of six and ten. They were all abducted on or around October 1st. And their remains were all found near where they went missing. In all cases, the remains were partial and left in a pile of burning ash believed to be the victims clothing. Next to the pile would always be a small bouquet of cornflowers. They even included a photo on page three of the flowers. Although cropped as to not show the remains, the top of the bouquet of blue flowers shone visible lying in the dirt.

While the salacious quality of the Rye Mother sparked morbid curiosity, Rocky flipped back through the first ten days of the search for Jason to find four articles which interested her much more. The first one came out on the Wednesday after Jason went missing. The article read like a missing poster, short and to the point. The next three came in the subsequent three days. Reading them in chronological order, she found the first article rather pedantic, ticking off facts she knew. The Friday article added the claim from Jason's friends that they last saw him riding his bicycle away from school, but not toward home. Jason attended Spring Lake Park Elementary and lived on nearby Washington Circle, a cul-de-sac of old money homes in a century-old neighborhood. He normally biked through the far end of the park, crossing through a field and coming out into a maze of residential streets which grew more affluent as he covered the four blocks to Washington Circle. According to the article, Jason's friends watched him enter the park and turn right, headed due north toward the Interstate. Spring Lake Park stretched along about seven or eight blocks parallel to a train track, ending at an overpass where the tracks and an access road curved off under the Interstate. The far south end of the park held the small lake and pressed up against the residential area where the St. Laurent's lived. The north end of the park, before hitting the Interstate came within spitting distance of a well-known area called The Trail of Pines. Locals shortened the name down to Trailer Pines, both out of a slurring of the words and as an appropriate nickname. Trailer Pines was the one trailer park in Texarkana. There were numerous similar locations on the outskirts of town. But Trailer Pines was a full-fledged trailer park smack in the middle of town. And the Friday *Texarkana Gazette* article stated Jason was headed there when he disappeared.

Which made zero sense.

Jason St. Laurent was the wealthiest kid in Texarkana at the time of his disappearance. His parents scheduled play dates for him with millionaire brats from Dallas. He had no business in Trailer Pines. And the article didn't shed any light on why he may have been going there. Saturday's article recapped the first two and added some mundane statements from both of the St. Laurents and one of Jason's teachers.

The St. Laurent disappearance received regular coverage the following week, with some mention every day. Every article seemed to be retreading the same worn ground, but the tone grew more suspicious of the St. Laurents, especially Bo.

One article even referenced an incident in Bo St. Laurent's youth where police arrested him following a drunken brawl with the husband of a woman ten years Bo's senior. The author laid out the suspicion trifecta: a penchant for alcohol, a temper, and a touch of womanizing.

On Thursday the 9th, the paper alluded to a "person of interest." No name. But the next day's headline read, "Primary St. Laurent Suspect Cleared." Not even twenty-four hours after naming a person of interest, police cleared some unidentified local man of suspicion following a thorough check of his alibi. The article did not offer much in the way of why the man came to be suspected, but the writer did confirm this person of interest as a male who lived near the area where Jason was last seen. The whole piece was only three paragraphs long, closing with a quote.

The quote read, "'We verified with multiple witnesses this suspect was accounted for during any possible window of Jason St. Laurent's disappearance,' stated lead detective Rondo Singer."

Rocky shot up. She started scuttling away from her table and stopped. She bit her lip, turning back to scoop up microfilm canisters and throw them back into the boxes. She struggled to balance the boxes against her chest as she scrambled out of the microfilm viewing room and into the main part of the library. Kicking over a chair, multiple people turned to stare as Rocky worked to pick up the chair and one of the boxes which fell and put her shoe back on at one point. Included among them, her father peered over his book with a sly smile. He reclined into the most comfortable chair available, his feet propped onto a table, and stuck a finger in the latter half of the latest Bosch novel as a bookmark. His reading glasses hung on the tip of his nose as he giggled to himself at the sight of his daughter fumbling her way to the counter to return her microfilm. She then practically skipped his way, bouncing to a stop at his feet and raising her eyebrows at him.

"Daddy?"

Frank blinked. "Yes, sweetheart?"

"Rondo Singer," Rocky almost shouted.

Frank frowned and shook his head. "What about him?"

"We know him, right?"

"Well, yeah," Frank laughed. "He's been to almost every one of your birthday parties, sweetheart. You've known the man all your life. You called him Uncle Rondo as a kid, Rocky."

Rocky waved a hand in the air. "Yeah, yeah, yeah. I thought so." She perched onto the table next to Frank's feet. "Can we meet him? For lunch? Dinner? Drinks?"

Chapter 10

Rocky had, indeed, known Rondo Singer for almost all of her twenty-eight years. Frank Champagnolle graduated with Rondo in the mid-seventies. As Rocky remembered, the story she heard as a child was that Rondo copied off a willing Frank's test papers, keeping state football championship hopes alive. Rondo Singer made All-State running back for three straight years. He bounced all over the field like a bowling ball, and opposing teams described him as being un-tackle-able. Rondo was the kind of player destined for a scholarship to a football powerhouse and a future in the NFL. Except for one problem. Rondo Singer stood about five foot one.

He still managed a scholarship. Rondo started all four years at nearby Southern Arkansas University, where he set and still holds enough records to get his jersey retired. After college, the diminutive star athlete tried out for every NFL team that didn't laugh him out the door, and even some who did. He spent a couple of years determined to make the league, convinced his size gave him an advantage, not a detriment. But after bouncing around some semi-professional leagues and failing to win the heart of any scouts, he returned to Texarkana with his head hung low.

Which is where Frank came back into his life. They happened upon each other as Frank took over run of the furniture store and Rondo made deliveries for UPS. After catching up over drinks, Frank pulled some strings and got Rondo putting his criminal justice degree to use fast-tracking through police training and onto the force. Since that day, Rondo Singer has credited Frank with renewing his spirits and sense of purpose. He poured himself into police work with every bit of the fervor he used to show on the football field, working his way to a detective rank in a little under four years. By '85, he earned enough stripes to snag a high-profile case like the Jason St. Laurent disappearance.

Frank owned a string of stories like Rondo's. If Rocky's greatest talent was spite, then Frank's was optimism. Frank Champagnolle thought the best of people. He encouraged their interests and curiosities. Without fail, Frank had fomented Rocky's curious nature since she wore diapers and toddled toward outlets with forks.

Even in the face of imminent danger, Frank always assumed her wonderment would lead her to positive outcomes. Which is why, without so much as an objection, Frank called up Rondo and invited him to grab a beer. Rocky listened intently as Frank ended the conversation with, "What time do you get off work?"

Without another word, Frank hung up and chuckled. Rocky held her hands up, "Well?"

Frank smirked. "He said he gets off work whenever I'm buying beer. He'll see us there in half an hour."

There was Pecan Point, a local gastropub and microbrewery Frank liked to frequent downtown. More than for what they served, Frank liked Pecan Point for where it sat, nestled in the shadow of Texarkana history. From the Public Library, they could reach Pecan Point by walking a few blocks due east. Travel about a block further and they could step from Texas back into Arkansas, while standing on a block home to both the local newspaper and the rundown Hotel Grim, an old eight-story brick building with a couple hundred rooms—abandoned now, but once the nicest hotel for miles around. Two blocks south of Pecan Point loomed the old Union Station, still functioning but nothing compared to its heyday. The railroad used to make Texarkana a hub of East meets West. "Little Chicago," they called the small town. Now, trains rattled along the edge of town like ghost chains. And next door to the little gastropub staggered the Perot Theatre, an ornate Italian Renaissance theater once known as the "Gateway to the Southwest." Now a venue for traveling stage productions, Frank used to tell Rocky about how his daddy watched *The Seven Year Itch* there and then walked a few blocks over to the Municipal Auditorium and watched Elvis and Johnny Cash.

"On your birthday, sweetheart. Everything good in pop culture converged right here at one time," Frank recounted the story for Rocky for the hundredth time. "It was one of those deals where they just drove themselves to the concert. Had a big pile up on the highway just outside of Memphis. So Elvis was late and Cheesie Nelson got up and did an impersonation. Supposed to be the first one ever. You remember Cheesie Nelson, honey?"

Rocky leaned against the open door of Pecan Point and tapped her foot. "Yes, Dad." She frowned. "Well, from this story, I do. I'm not sure I can picture him. I think he's always been a cartoon character in my head."

Frank stood staring wistfully off past the Perot toward a large mural painted on a brick wall facing the Perot parking lot. He pointed. "Did I ever tell you about that Scott Joplin mural? Texarkana's favorite son, Scott Joplin."

Rocky spun into the restaurant, calling out, "Let's hear it while I drink alcohol, what do you say, Frank?"

"Oh. Yeah. Yeah, yeah, sweetheart." Frank shuffled to hurry after Rocky.

Pecan Point stretched back from the road in two narrow rooms. On the side closest to the theater, there were long tables for family style dining. Rocky and Frank entered the bar side and set up at a pub table near the back. The dinner crowd hadn't started in yet, so the manager seated them himself and went ahead and took drink orders. Frank got his usual locally brewed pale ale and Rocky ordered a Cape Cod.

Frank marveled around at the old photos on the walls and shook his head at Rocky. "Rock, they make some damn fine beer." He jerked a thumb over his shoulder. "This is one of those deals where they brew it right back there. What's wrong? You watching your figure?"

Rocky rolled her eyes. "Dad, I butter Pop Tarts. No, I'm not watching my figure. I drink alcoholic beverages you would serve to a child. The ones that taste like sunshine and beachfront property. You know I don't drink beer." She said the last word like a piece of sour candy she tried to spit out.

When a waiter brought the drinks, Frank instructed him to go ahead and bring a couple more beers for the table. As the waiter walked away, Frank smiled at Rocky. "Well, Rondo does."

On cue, Rondo Singer strutted into Pecan Point like he owned the place. He stood about Rocky's height, a little less than the one inch over five feet programs always listed him at as a player. He still carried the bulk of a running back, with broad shoulders and ripped arms, but he added a small bulge of a gut with age. A fedora teetered to one side of a shaved bald head, and a touch of gray glittered in his black goatee. He and Frank were the same age, but Rondo's coffee-colored skin betrayed no wrinkles. He could have been sixty or thirty or anywhere in between. He wore a black sports coat over a rose-colored short sleeve Polo-style shirt. His shoes, pants, and belt were all black, with a gun and a badge visible peeking out from under his coat. Rondo walked with the confidence of the all-everything football player from forty years prior. There were four people in Pecan Point and three of them spoke to Rondo by name as he walked through the door. Each time, he smiled like they had told him a joke, pointed, and tossed out an "All right now" in a way that told Rocky he didn't know any of their names. His gravely and high octave voice somehow fit both a man of his stature and a man of his size.

Rocky greeted Rondo with a hug and then let the two friends catch up over three rounds of beers. She laughed along at stories and made a point to stay sober— at least more sober than Rondo. Rocky wanted him greased up enough to talk freely.

After an hour or so, Rondo rolled through one story after another of weird cases he had worked. He named them all, like episodes of some cop show he starred in. While finishing up one about a real estate agent who disappeared, leaving one shoe behind as the sole clue (titled, "Rondo and the Glass Slipper"), he put a hand on Frank and Rocky's shoulders and ducked his head in laughter. When Rondo came up for air, Rocky took a sip of her drink and asked, "Was the realtor your most high-profile case?"

Frank rolled his eyes. Rondo sucked at his teeth and tried to laugh, but the sound came out as more of a sighing cough. "Naw, girl," he shook his head. "Only high-profile case I ever worked on was those kids who got killed." Rondo had a way of stroking his goatee and staring off while thinking. He rasped, "Not even my case, technically." Rondo waved a hand for another round of beer, finishing the last of his current one, sucking at the foam at the bottom of the glass. "Frank, you remember when the St. Laurent kid got killed?"

Frank nodded and mumbled while cutting his eyes at Rocky, "Yeah. Yeah, it rings a bell."

Rondo shook his head. "Man. That was a big case. Biggest I ever caught."

Rocky shook her head and blinked innocently. "I guess it was before my time. What happened?"

Rondo snapped his fingers. "Oh yeah, Rock. Happened right around the time you was born. I wasn't on the child killer case. They'd been four kids killed before the St. Laurent kid went missing. In fact, I found the remains of one of them during my first year on the job. Freaked me the hell out." He laughed, "Awful to say, but I ran off to throw up so I wouldn't get shit all over the crime scene. But that's all I had to do with it until I got detective. Hadn't been in a suit and tie for more than a couple of weeks when I got put on the St. Laurent case. He was just missing at this point, now. Hadn't been for every homicide cop in the force working those kids, I'd never be given a case like that."

Rocky frowned. "Homicide? I thought you said he was just missing."

Rondo nodded. "Homicide cops got all the missing persons cases back then. Still do, most of the time." He shook his head. "When it gets to us? Ain't gonna end pretty."

Rocky nodded. "And this one? Didn't end pretty?"

"Naw. This one was never gonna end pretty. I knew from the jump." Rondo rubbed at his goatee some more and proceeded to walk through the basics of the case, nothing Rocky didn't know.

But at a passing mention of Trailer Pines, Rocky jumped at her chance. "Trailer Pines? The trailer park over by Spring Lake Park? What the hell is a rich kid doing there?"

Rondo cocked his head and pointed at her. "I'm saying. Craziest thing. Why you wanna go riding your bike to some trailer park when you got a mansion to go home to?"

"Are you sure he did?" Rocky asked. "Maybe he never made it."

Rondo shrugged. "I believe he did. He had a little group of friends. They said he was going there every day. Been acting all funny and hanging out with some friends they didn't know."

"Friends at Trailer Pines?" Rocky frowned. "Did it check out?"

Rondo cocked an eyebrow. "Those folks ain't gonna talk to no cop. Who knows? We found some kids there, yeah. Ain't a one of them in school. But they all swore they didn't know Jason. His friends said they were older. Seemed right. All those trailer trash kids were middle school age and up."

"Do you think one of them might be the killer?"

Rondo shook his head. "Naw. Ain't none of them kids started killing people in 1981. The oldest one of them would've been about ten years old back then." He pointed at nothing in particular. "Now, before we found Jason? Yeah. Those kids were on my list."

Rocky squinted at him. "Your list? Who else was on your list? Parents?"

Rondo shook his head. "Not in my book. I mean, yeah, we looked at them. Hard. Got to. But smelled clean to me." He rubbed his goatee. "Now, one of my partners on the case? He liked the dad for it early. We didn't see eye to eye though."

"Why? Why did he think the dad did it?"

Rondo laughed. "Because Bo St. Laurent is a fucking asshole. Mean son of a bitch. We both agreed he beat on the kid. But I didn't think he went past a hard ass whoopin every now and then." He slapped Frank on the arm. "Black folk got a different outlook on whoopins. Ain't that right, Frank?"

Frank grinned and nodded to Rocky. Rocky raised her eyebrows. "That's all? Your partner thought Bo St. Laurent killed his son because he was an asshole?"

"Well," Rondo cocked his head, "there was a life insurance policy."

Rocky grinned and nodded.

"I know, I know." Rondo held up both hands in surrender. "Sounds mad fishy. Two-million-dollar life insurance policy on your own kid." He closed one eye and pointed at Rocky. "But the man didn't claim it."

Rocky laughed. "Of course he didn't. Not immediately. His kid was missing, not dead. At least, in the public eye."

Rondo shook his head and sucked at his teeth. "Naw, Rock. He never claimed it. Not ever. Not even after we found Jason's remains a couple weeks later. I kept watching him. For years. Even after my partner passed. Never claimed it."

Rocky frowned. "So who did you like?"

Rondo leaned back in his chair. "Me? I liked this fella down in Trailer Pines." He rubbed his goatee and worked to remember. "Went by Spinny. Last name Spinelli. What was his first name? Something funny. Like Marcus, but longer. Marcellus, maybe."

Rocky shook her head. "Why him?"

"He was a perv. Kiddie porn and all kinds of shit. Got released after doing time for messing with a kid up in Memphis. Those sentences were such a joke back then. I tossed his place and found a whole closet of child porn. Mother fucker should've been put down."

Rocky nodded. "The person of interest they mentioned in the paper. It was him?"

Rondo laughed and trained one eye on Rocky. "You know a little more than you let on, girl."

Rocky smirked. "Maybe."

"Yeah," he laughed. "Yeah, that was Spinny. We found him drunk out front of his trailer and went through his shit. No warrant. So it got tossed. We fucked up. But his alibi also checked, I guess. I never liked his story, but it checked. His job gave us a time card showing he was at work the day Jason went missing."

"So what didn't you like?"

Rondo clucked his tongue. "The shit was handwritten. Could've been faked easy. But a co-worker put him there. And then, of course, Jason got tied to those other kids. Spinny was in a Tennessee jail during two or three of those killings, so I had to accept it. I still wonder what all the fucker did while he's living in Trailer Pines, though. Spinny's dead by now, but I still wonder."

"But you're certain Jason St. Laurent was killed by the Rye Mother?"

Rondo threw his head back and let out an exasperated groan. "Fucking Rye Mother. Get out of here with that shit, Rock. Ain't no cop ever going to acknowledge some bullshit name like Rye Mother."

Rocky smiled. "Okay, okay. So what do I call her?"

Rondo curled a lip. "I don't know. Crazy?"

"But you do believe it was a woman?"

Rondo rolled his head around and shrugged. "I don't know, man. I mean, I didn't work those cases, so ain't my place to say. I got involved a little after Jason, because he was my case and it connected. But you had a lot of veteran cops working those killings. I was still green. They didn't want me too close. And after I fucked up the search of Spinny's trailer like I did? I got froze out of several things for a while after."

Rocky shook her head, frowning. "So you didn't think it was a woman?"

"Maybe. I don't know. They brought in some dude. Like a criminal profiler. He said woman. After the profile got created, the photo showed up and seemed to confirm woman. I guess I never wanted to believe a woman could do that. But what do I know?"

Rocky shook the ice in her empty glass and Frank scooped the tumbler up and headed to the bar to get her another. "Did you ever think it was a local woman?"

"Like who? You got a local woman in mind, Rock?"

Rocky gave him a series of little curt shakes of her head. "Oh, no, no. Nobody in particular."

Rondo ducked down to catch her eyes. "Why you care about Jason St. Laurent?"

Rocky shrugged and kept shaking her head. "No reason. Just an interesting case."

Rondo laughed big and shook Rocky by the shoulder. "Naw, Rock. I been knowing you all your life. Who set you off?"

Rocky pursed her lips and shook her head around in something between a denial and a shrug. "Nobody."

Frank stepped up to the table with another drink. He leaned in between them and whispered, "Waverly was mean to her."

Rondo roared with laughter as Rocky blushed and sighed. "This is not about Waverly. I'm just interested."

Rondo struggled to catch his breath. "Oh, she's a right bitch, no doubt. No doubt. You ain't gonna find anything she did wrong, though. She was wrecked. Barely could talk. I could see maybe the dad acted a little funny, but she was spot on. I seen plenty of moms lost they babies since then, and she was no different. Seen a couple who killed babies, too. Ain't her, Rock. It just ain't."

Rocky frowned. "The dad acted funny?"

"Yeah, I guess. It's why my partner suspected him in those first days. Bo was a cold man, though. Ice cold. He ain't got any emotions other than greed and asshole. So I never thought much of it. And he paid a fortune hiring private eyes and shit, trying to track Jason's killer down all over the country. Way I see it, ain't no mother fucker greedy as Bo St. Laurent gonna spend money searching for a mystery killer he know ain't out there."

Rocky started in on her second drink, lost in thought and pulling pink liquid through the straw way too fast. She faded out as the two men returned to talk of high school and college and catching up on life. Rocky drank until her dad had to help her to the car, and she passed out on the drive home while attempting to suppress both looping spins of a dizzy head and creeping feelings of sympathy for Waverly St. Laurent.

Chapter 11

Rocky slept through dinner and straight into mid-morning of the next day. She woke to an empty house with a hangover, struggling to separate what she learned the night before from the weird, rambling Rondo Singer movies she dreamed. In the last one, Rondo dressed like Sherlock Holmes and Rocky stood by as his Watson. They were constructing a trap for Waverly St. Laurent straight out of an episode of *Scooby-Doo*.

The desire to sleep lost out to the need for water and some aspirin. Rocky clambered into the kitchen and swigged a bottle of water, tossing back a few pills one at a time. She then made herself some chocolate milk and a bowl of cereal. While she ate, Rocky scrolled through Pinterest, bookmarking teacher ideas to keep her mind from wandering to Waverly St. Laurent. The inspiration drove her straight into a shower and a pair of yoga pants. Rocky scavenged her father's storage room for a can of black paint and headed toward town to do some work in her classroom.

Under normal circumstances, Rocky would turn to the best classroom decorator in town. Darrelene Champagnolle could teach a class in elementary classroom decor. Rocky received near constant praise for her interior design by principals and peers alike. But the designs all came from her mother. Rocky would find a Pinterest board, show the idea to Darrelene, and, by the following morning, Darrelene would present Rocky with everything needed to make magic happen on the school house walls. Unfortunately, Darrelene slipped out to work before Rocky could wake up and leverage her mother's unfaltering dedication to all things Rocky. Jennifer was her backup. But Frank called Jennifer in to help decorate the newly remodeled front room of his store, so Rocky was on her own. She found a revolutionary idea for organizing cubbies. All of Rocky's classroom ideas were revolutionary, but this one had her extra excited. The Pinterest board vision drove all thoughts of robberies and murdered kids out of her mind as she cleaned out her back shelves to repurpose them into a stylized system of student storage. S.S.S.S., she coined the idea in her mind.

Frank had drop cloths and tape and everything she needed in his storage room. Everything except the skill with which to paint. Rocky had many talents. But she was horrible at painting. Horrible. Those shelves were her Everest.

Rocky excelled at the pre-game warm ups. She dressed next-level adorable in her tennis shoes, yoga pants, and tank top, with her hair tied up in a neat ponytail. She positioned a tumbler of Diet 7-Up at the ready along with a variety of snacks laid out on her desk: an assortment of dark chocolate covered fruits and nuts and some Cheetos Puffs (sweet, salty, savory). She pulled the image of the cubbies online up on her large smart board at the front of the room and set her phone to cycle through a Pandora station of stand-up comedy. Everything fell into place to tackle the job. Everything except the skill with which to paint. Because Rocky was just horrible at painting. Edging, rolling, taping off, even the drop cloth lay crumpled at her side because she couldn't get the damn thing unfolded.

With her sunglasses pulled down to cover her eyes in case she started to cry, Rocky sat in the middle of her classroom floor staring at the image of what grew into an impossible goal. Behind her, she heard a timid tapping. She turned to find three blondes standing in her doorway wearing various degrees of apologetic smiles. Rocky recognized them from her Junior League new member class. The one in the back with the dirtier shade of blonde hair was the cynic from the last meeting who ended up agreeing about the pot brownie idea.

Rocky swiveled on her ass to face them. She curled a lip, pointing at the one closest to her, "Bridgette? Britney? Brandy? It's a *Br-* name, I know it."

The girl cocked her head and smiled in a touched expression of gratitude. "Yes. Hey, girl. It's Brene."

Rocky shook her head. "Nope. That's not real. That's a made-up name. I'm calling you Britney."

The girl next to her raised a hand sheepishly. "But my name's Britney."

Rocky glanced at her chest and cocked her head. "More of a Christina. I'm calling you Christina." She stood up and brushed off the seat of her pants. Peering through to the girl in the back she grinned. "And you're a Kesha."

The girl in the back laughed. "I can live with Kesha."

Rocky pushed her sunglasses back up into her hair and frowned. "So, Britney? Christina? What are you doing here?"

Brene threw out a nervous laugh at being re-christened Britney and said, "I'm sorry to show up like this. We didn't have your number."

Kesha smirked and spoke toward the floor. "Because the number you put in the Junior League member's book is to a guy who is very tired of getting calls for you."

Rocky shrugged. "He gave me his number in a bar a couple of years ago and told me to not let those digits go to waste. I don't understand what he's so upset about. I've gotten a lot of use out of them."

Britney grimaced. "Yeah. So, we called your cousin, Jennifer. She said she thought you'd be here."

Rocky nodded. "And look how right she was. Is this one of those scavenger hunts for your church youth group? Do I need to sign something or take a selfie with you? You don't have to take back my panties, do you?"

Christina chimed in with, "Could we sit and talk for a minute?"

Rocky's classroom was filled with first grade furniture pushed to the sides of the room. The sole piece pulled out was Rocky's desk chair. Her chair sat in the center of the room, with a curved table rounding one side so she could pull kids in for small groups. The table curved away from the bulk of the class, situated at small tables with six-year-old-sized plastic chairs. Her teacher's desk and computer were pushed off to one side, near the smart board controlled by her desktop. The set-up allowed Rocky to work with her small groups, but still swivel to the rest of the class or roll over to her desk. She pilfered the chair—an extravagant leather desk chair on a swiveling base with casters—from her dad's shop. The chair sat up a bit, mahogany-colored Italian leather hoisting Rocky to tower over the small plastic chairs of her students.

Pointing to a stack of muted green and gold chairs in one corner, Rocky directed the three Junior Leaguers to gather round her, seated in her Italian leather throne at their center. The three of them sat with their knees jutting out into their necks, trying to find someplace to put their hands, staring up at Rocky who rocked in her chair with legs crossed and prim hands folded on her lap. Rocky kicked herself for not being able to find the "Scepter of Silence" she used in class to rule over her children.

Rocky fought the urge to cry out, "What say you, peasants?" Instead opting for a much more sensible, "What did you want to talk about, ladies?"

Britney-Brene started out. "We met with the people at CASA. They are super excited about our project. They said they send an average of four kids a week into a living arrangement with their belongings in a black garbage bag. It's terrible. Just awful. They think our project could make a significant difference in the lives of these kids."

"But," Rocky squinted.

Christina nodded. "Yes. But. They said to pull off what we are wanting to do—backpacks with toiletries and some essential items—we would need somewhere around ten thousand dollars."

Rocky nodded. "We figured it would be high. Which is why we needed a fundraiser and a donor."

Britney grimaced and nodded. "Yes. Well, our donor has," she stared at the ceiling, thinking of how to choose her words, "experienced a life crisis, which has caused—"

"The cops froze her bank accounts," Kesha interrupted.

Rocky smiled before catching herself and frowning. "How sad."

Britney continued, "Yes, so we are back to square one. We have no donors and one fundraiser to make ten thousand dollars."

Christina added, "And no Junior League fundraiser in Texarkana has made more than five thousand. Ever."

"So," Britney picked up, "that means we either need to secure another donor or—"

Kesha broke in again, "Or we need to put on one bad ass fundraiser."

Rocky propped her elbows on the arms of her chair and put her hands in a praying position, placing her thumbs under her chin and her index fingers against her mouth. She drummed her fingers together as she talked. "Well, this puts us in a very interesting predicament, indeed." She flopped her hands into her lap and cocked her head, frowning. "Whatever shall we do?"

Britney sighed. "Well, we gave your idea a lot of thought."

Rocky shook her head. "What idea would that be? I toss out a lot of them."

Christina swallowed. "The proposal you made the other night. At the meeting."

Rocky scrunched her mouth up and squinted hard.

Kesha laughed. "They want to make pot brownies."

Britney and Christina jumped all over each other adding, "We don't think we have a choice. I mean, it won't be bad if we do everything like you said. We could find old people and sick people. We'd be doing a public service."

Rocky nodded solemnly and said, "Oh. Oh yeah. Yeah. Public service. Definitely."

"And we still might not make enough," Kesha tossed out while picking at a fingernail.

Britney shot her a scowl. "Think positive."

"But she's right," Christina admitted to Rocky. "If we play things safe like you suggested," she held her hands up, "which I am one hundred percent in favor of. But if we do, what are we talking about? Connecting with a few places and making quiet regular deliveries? Pulling in several hundred dollars a week for a month or two? We're talking about what? Seven or eight thousand dollars max?"

Rocky shrugged and nodded. "I'll be honest. I don't even know how much weed costs, so I'm not sure what we even need to charge."

Everyone eyed Kesha. She rolled her eyes. "Jesus. Screw you, bitches."

Rocky grinned. "Yeah, but ..."

Kesha sighed. "You could charge about ten bucks a brownie and make money. If you're the only supplier, which is possible if you find the right market, then you could double that easy. I think we could clear maybe fifteen a brownie."

Britney furrowed her brow. "We would need to move about five hundred brownies in ten weeks' time."

"Doable," Christina shrugged.

"Yeah," Britney said, "but that's for seven thousand. We need ten. Something else needs to happen."

Rocky rubbed her hands together like she was applying lotion and stared off into the distance. She spoke to no one in particular. "Do you have friends with kids?"

All three of the ladies looked around at each other, frowning. Kesha said, "How do you know we don't have kids?"

Rocky shook her head. "Please. Your nails are manicured and you carry designer purses. Two of you are wearing heels in the middle of the summer, and all three of you are uncomfortable in an elementary classroom. You don't have kids. But do your friends?"

The nodded in slow unison.

Rocky nodded along with them. "Adderall."

Britney frowned. "Adderall? Like, ADD medicine?"

"Yeah. I heard someone mention it the other day. Every kid is on that shit now, right?" Rocky waved a hand around absently.

Christina shrugged. "I guess. I know of a couple of kids on it, yeah."

Rocky nodded again. "How many do you think we could get our hands on?"

Kesha frowned. "Why?"

"Isn't it like, speed? If you don't have ADD?" Rocky asked.

Kesha shrugged, "Yeah. I took some in college to study. Gets you going pretty good."

Rocky cocked her head. "And we have access to a metric fuck ton of bored housewives and stay-at-home moms who would love a little pick-me-up."

Britney's eyes grew wide. "Like, a care package?"

Rocky shrugged. "Sure. At thirty or forty dollars a pop? Call them caffeine pills. Or oxygen pills. Is that a thing? Organic Oxygen Pills. Throw in some fun little items. Maybe a bottle of wine or something. We could move a couple hundred of those in two months, I'll bet. Talk some men into sending one to their wives. Get the wives coming back for more. There's your other three thousand dollars."

Britney and Christina eyed each other, both sheepishly wanting to admit Rocky's Adderall care package was a good idea, but neither willing to say it out loud. Kesha rolled her eyes. "They love the idea. We all do. It's brilliant. Two months, ten thousand. We minimize risk and cut and run when we clear what we need. But there's one problem."

The other two turned to Kesha, but Rocky spoke. "We need product."

Christina raised a hand. "I can get Adderall, I think. I'm not sure how much, but some. And I'll ask a couple other girls if they can gather some up, too. I know girls who are married to doctors. Maybe we could even get our own prescriptions. For two months, we'd get sixty per person."

Britney nodded. "Good. Keep everything within the Junior League. No extra people involved. But what about the pot?"

Everyone studied Kesha again. She laughed, "Don't look at me. I haven't smoked in a couple of years. I wouldn't even know where to begin."

Rocky sniffed. "Let me take care of that."

Britney whipped around. "Really? You can buy pot?"

Rocky rubbed at an eye. "I think I can figure it out. You'll all just owe me."

Christina nodded. "Of course. For real, girl. I'm not even joking. If there is anything we can do, you just say the word."

Rocky swiveled around toward her cubbies. "How are you girls at painting?"

Chapter 12

The three Junior Leaguers finished painting Rocky's shelves in about an hour. Rocky, of course, provided direction and guidance, managing after a few redirects to match the project to what she found online. Rocky did, as a thank you, offer to buy the girls some chips and salsa and a round of midafternoon margaritas at the nearby Taco Shack. The gesture seemed kind, but Rocky just needed to kill time in order to get home at the right moment.

Rocky's mom worked at a school on the opposite side of Texarkana from Rocky's own, but unlike Rocky, Darrelene Champagnolle decided early on that teaching children was a surefire way to land herself a second-degree murder charge and an insanity defense. So she found peripheral jobs in the school district—working in the library or the technology department or, even more secluded, the print shop. Darrelene loved the lack of human interaction, but a school district's print shop ran most of the year, which meant no summers off.

All of this, coupled with Frank Champagnolle running his own business, meant Frank found a glorious hour most days he could spend at home—somewhere between around three and just after four—utterly alone, sitting out on his back porch and staring up at the pine trees of rural Palermo, a little bedroom community outside Texarkana. Palermo was quiet and country, more backwoods than quaint, but still more charming than redneck or trashy. Frank always said he would trade a little bit of culture for a whole lot of peace.

Rocky aimed to interrupt his peace at precisely 3:15. Since living with her parents again, she grew mindful of allowing them both their privacy, attempting to stifle her powers of deduction to keep from unearthing some guilty pleasure of Frank or Darrelene. But even with her keen eye turned down a few notches, she wasn't blind. She came home around 3:30 one day and found Frank acting odd. He walked in from out back just as Rocky bounded in the front door. He looked frazzled and hid something. Darrelene had spent the past year or so winning a battle with cancer. But the battle did involve some chemotherapy once a month. Frank and Darrelene weren't the most loving couple in the world, but Frank Champagnolle would do whatever he could to help any of his people be a little more comfortable.

These factors were enough clues to convince Rocky to park out by the road where no one up at the house (or on the back porch) could hear her coming. And she walked on the grass instead of the gravel driveway, padding her way up around the side of the house and around back, sliding up the side of the raised porch and coming around the corner unannounced.

Frank reclined in a hammock stretched across the far end of the porch. He crossed his legs at the ankles and laid with his eyes closed and the sun on his face. One arm propped his head up like a pillow. His free hand held a joint pinched to his lips as he puffed.

Rocky clopped three quick steps up the noisy porch stairs and called out, "Hey, Daddy!"

Frank tried to shoot up, fumbling in the hammock and dropping the joint. As he bobbled the roach trying to catch the unlit end, he let out a "Shit" and reeled back a burned hand. The hammock did one hard spin and emptied him out onto the deck on his hands and knees. He scooped up the joint and jumped to his feet, hiding it behind his back. When he got upright, he shut his eyes tight and held his forehead with his free hand. "Goddammit, Rocky. You scared me half to death."

Rocky struggled to keep from laughing. "I didn't mean to scare you."

Frank rolled his eyes and held the joint out in front of his face. He looked back at Rocky with a sigh. "Bullshit. How long?"

Rocky batted her eyes. "How long what, Daddy?"

"Cut the act, Rock. I know you. How long have you known?"

Rocky shrugged. "How long has it been going on?"

Frank shook his head. "Not long." He held his hands up toward her pleadingly. "I swear, honey. Your mother had so much nausea with the chemo, and I read where this stuff was supposed to help. Well, a buddy of mine, he's offered before. It's one of those deals where he and I ran around together back in the day." He nodded. A conciliation. "And yes. Yes. I enjoyed a little marijuana in my running days. Nothing crazy. And never anything more than some grass. But I always turned him down." Frank cocked his head. "But you know, I got to thinking. If a little bit could help your mother, then what's the harm?"

Rocky nodded along, solemnly. "I'm sorry, Dad. I wish you told me sooner. I wasn't aware you were also having to go through chemotherapy."

Frank held his hands up, palms toward Rocky. "All right. Okay. I knew you were going to say something along those lines. Rock, you know your mother. She's stubborn. She wouldn't touch the stuff. Made me swear to throw it out." He held the joint up and stared at it. "Seemed like such a waste." He raised his eyebrows. "I take a hit or two at a time. This one joint has lasted me quite a while, you know."

Rocky frowned and nodded. "Oh, I'm sure it has. He gave you one, did he?"

Frank sighed. "How much?"

"I'm sorry?"

"How much? How much is this going to cost me?"

Rocky shrugged. "Nothing much. I just want the name of your supplier."

Frank frowned and shook his head. "Now, wait a second—"

"No, no, no. Not for me. It's for a," Rocky paused and tapped a finger on her lips, "a project, let's call it."

Frank laughed. "Rocky, you know I've never been one to withhold my support, but you cannot honestly expect me to tell you—"

"Where you got five joints?"

Frank eyed her.

Rocky curled a lip. "I'm assuming five. I mean, you're smoking the one there. Which I'm betting is your second from your current batch." She pulled a folded napkin out of her purse. "And then, of course, there are these three."

Frank reached for them.

Rocky shook a finger at him. "Mm, mm, mmm. Supplier. Then joints."

"How did you—"

"Find them? You hid them in an empty can of old paint. You should put a weight in there. Otherwise, if someone lifts it, like I did, and finds it far too light, said person gets curious."

Frank shook his head. "Do you have any idea how difficult it is to be your parent?"

Rocky nodded. "I can imagine." She held the joints toward him. "Name, please."

Frank mumbled some curse words and snatched the joints from Rocky's hand. He sighed into his chest and mumbled, "Hamilton Hallmark."

Rocky shook her head and laughed. "Give me the joints back. That's not a real person."

"Hamilton Hallmark? The reporter? H.I. Hallmark? People call him Hi?"

Rocky gave him her meerkat look and said, "You're just saying names from old movies right now."

Frank pulled out an overstuffed wallet and fished until he came away with a business card. He handed the card over to Rocky and raised his eyebrows. "Hi Hallmark. We go way back. Graduated with me and Rondo. We were all buddies. Hi wrote papers for us all through high school. Damn near made me fail freshman English in college. I didn't have the first clue how to write an essay on my own."

Rocky studied the card and frowned at him. "This better be a real person or I'll find them wherever you hide them next."

Frank laughed. "Sweetheart, I quit thinking I could hide things from you around Christmas Eve of 1995."

"Well, to be fair," Rocky shrugged, "you were using a combination lock with my birthday as the code. Come on, Daddy. I got it in two tries."

Rocky bounced off down the steps and Frank called after her, "Wait. What was the first try?"

Rocky called back over her shoulder, "The dog's birthday."

Chapter 13

Hamilton "Hi" Hallmark agreed to meet Rocky at his office anytime. He talked about coming to visit Frank and Darrelene soon after Rocky was born and how she pooped while he held her for the first time. Hi laughed retelling the story. Rocky did not. But the nostalgia landed her an open invitation, which she cashed in the same day.

The *Texarkana Gazette* offices were downtown very near where Rocky and Frank met Rondo Singer for drinks. The building was nondescript, save the large black letters spelling out *Texarkana Gazette* in an old newspaper script font sprawled across the beige brick. The entryway and front lobby was a cross between a DMV and a cheap hotel check-in desk. A couple of teenage girls manned the newspaper's front desk and directed Rocky to an elevator between stereotypical smacks of their gum.

Rocky sauntered off with a, "You two should share a piece so one of you can talk."

Hi Hallmark's office hid away in the basement. Along with nothing else. Rocky stepped off the elevator into a horror movie. The lighting crackled and buzzed overhead, and the pathway wound like a maze around dusty boxes stacked all the way to the six-foot ceiling. Rocky couldn't remember ever coming as close to a ceiling as she did in the claustrophobic basement of the *Gazette*. The girls at the desk claimed "ya' can't miss him," but Rocky began to wonder if they had been jacking with her sending her down here. But before she could muster the courage to move forward or the sense to turn around, a voice bellowed out, "Who goes there?"

Rocky jumped and called out, "Mr. Hallmark? It's Rocky Champagnolle."

A tiny man ran out from behind a stack of boxes and beamed a smile and open arms. "Rocky Champagnolle! As I live and breathe!"

Hamilton Hallmark stood at least two or three inches shorter than Rocky. He may even almost qualify as a little person. She smiled for a moment at the fact that her dad, at a shorter than average five and a half feet or so, was, by far, the tallest of this group of high school friends. Hi was shorter and stockier than Rondo Singer. He had short arms and legs, with a round body and large head, making him seem to wobble when he walked. His hair was chocolaty brown and wavy, not betraying any of the gray of Frank's short-cropped hair or Rondo's beard. Hi boasted quite a head of hair—the kind anyone would be drawn to run his or her fingers through, which Hi himself did almost obsessively. Making him seem even younger was his big baby face and devilish goatee, and a twinkle of mischief in his eye marking him as the troublemaker of Frank's group of friends. Rocky wondered, if Hi had been the rebel and Rondo the jock, what about Frank? Something in Rocky made her think he might be the lady's man, which made her shudder a touch.

Rocky smiled. "Mr. Hallmark? It's nice to meet you. Thank you for seeing me."

Hi waved off her greeting. "Nonsense. Frank's daughter is family in my book." He started back around the corner he sprung from, waving her to follow. "Come on, come on. Come take a seat. You'll have to excuse the mess. Just throw everything on the floor."

Rocky rounded the corner to find a single chair sitting in front of a desk, shoved back into a corner of the basement and surrounded on both sides with metal filing cabinets. The desk overflowed with papers and file folders and notepads. The chair held a stack of four hardcover books and a stack of handwritten notes. Rocky set the pile gingerly on the floor and sat on the edge of the chair leaning onto the edge of the desk, sort of teetering between both. Hi collapsed into a squeaky desk chair and rocked back and forth. Rocky could see the top of his face over the pile of paperwork on the desk when he rocked forward.

Rocky tapped her fingers on the desk. "I'm going to assume my father has contacted you."

Hi held a hand up. "I'm going to stop you right there, Rocky. Your father contacted—" He frowned at her. "Wait. What?"

Rocky nodded. "He told you not to sell me anything, I'm sure."

Hi raised an eyebrow.

"And I would try to persuade you? Tune me out? Don't let her charm you, Hi? Is that about right?"

"Yeah. Pretty much word for word."

Rocky nodded. She leaned back in her chair and glanced around the room as Hi poured them both a cup of coffee in a pair of Grateful Dead mugs. He placed Rocky's on a stack of spiral notebooks near the corner of the desk. She thanked him, but she wouldn't touch the mug, as she never drank hot liquids.

"But you," Rocky shook a finger at a poster on the wall displaying a series of blue jean and leather vests with motorcycle club emblems on their backs, "you, Mr. Hallmark, are a non-conformist."

Hi chuckled. "I won a Pacific Northwest Excellence in Journalism Award for that piece. Wrote it when I lived up around Portland." He closed one eye and pointed. "See the two in the top left corner and the one at the very bottom in the middle? I rode with those three clubs for almost a year, all told. Which is quite an accomplishment, let me tell you. Because they did not get along at all. Didn't like what I wrote either. I thought it was honest, but they didn't like being compared to one another. That's one of the reasons I moved back down here, to be honest. They were scary dudes."

Rocky stood up as he reminisced and stepped over to a bookshelf. She examined a row of framed certificates for volunteer work. The Texarkana Chamber of Commerce recognized Hi for his charitable contributions seven out the past eight years. "And," she glanced back at him with a warm smile, "you have a big heart."

Hi squinted. "I feel like this is you doing what Frank said you would be doing."

Rocky raised an eyebrow and moved back to her chair. "Is it?"

"You did inherit your father's charm," Hi laughed. "Here's the deal, little Champagnolle. I am a big proponent of legalized marijuana use. I think it's ridiculous we're still even having the conversation as a society. And I am more than comfortable in the ethics and legalities of my involvement in the exchange of marijuana. I don't deal pot by any means, but I do serve as a middleman to a few select friends every now and then. I have plenty of friends in positions of authority in this town, and they all accept me as a non-threatening, productive member of the community. So, under normal circumstances, if Frank Champagnolle's adult daughter wanted a little grass, I would offer it up as a repayment on any one of a million favors your father did for me over the past fifty years. But, even if you are a grown-ass woman, if my friend says to not give his daughter any illicit drugs, I think I need to respect his wishes."

Rocky nodded. "And what if they aren't normal circumstances?"

Hi cocked his head. "I'm listening."

Rocky proceeded to make an impassioned pitch on behalf of the many suffering citizens of Texarkana—those with cancer and Alzheimer's and arthritis and multiple sclerosis. She painted a portrait of the Junior League helping these long-suffering locals get the relief they deserve. At certain points, Rocky worked herself up to the point of (very fake) tears, closing with, "We know we can ease the pain of hundreds of people in this town. And if we know that's possible, isn't it our responsibility to do something?"

Hi smirked throughout the entire speech. When she finished, he shook his head and sighed. "Jesus. Your father didn't warn me what I was up against." He hung his head back and stared at the ceiling. "How much would you need?"

Rocky shrugged. "I'm not sure, to be honest. Did you ever make brownies?"

Hi laughed into the air. "Brownies? Jesus. You're going to do a goddamn bake sale." He rocked forward. "All right. Give me a few days and I'll get you enough for several batches of brownies. I trust you know someone who can teach you how to make them?"

"I'm working that part out. We'll be ready."

Hi shook his head and laughed as he studied his phone. "This number?" He held the screen up to her. "Is this how I reach you?"

Rocky leaned forward and studied the screen, nodding. "Yep. That's me." She sat back and crossed her legs, feeling like she would be rude to just leave after working out the details. "So where does this stuff come from?"

Hi flailed a hand off toward some invisible place in the distance. "Ah, some guy I know from my time on the west coast. He's a northern California hippy with a bunch of cross-country trucker friends. He sends a batch to me and a handful of other folks out this way. Doesn't overcharge because he grows the stuff himself. He's a simple farmer, if you strip away the cultural stigma. Grows gorgeous plums, too."

Rocky smiled at the thought. "How long did you live out west?"

Hi thought back. "Oh, about fifteen years or so. I started out in the newspaper business here. Did everything from running a paper route to writing obits to doing real stories. Covered one in the mid-Eighties got picked up for syndication. Allowed me to apply different places, so I moved around a little to see the country. Kansas City, Minneapolis, Denver, and then on to Sacramento, Seattle, and Portland. I was in Portland for the last nine of those fifteen. Moved from there back to my old stomping ground. Doesn't pay as well, but this is home."

Rocky frowned. "Mid-Eighties? What was the story? The syndicated one?"

"The Rye Mother." Hi smiled with wide eyes. "Serial killer. Missing kids. Perfect storm, baby."

Rocky could have kicked herself. She hadn't even paid any attention to by-lines. She tried to play it cool. "Oh, wow. I've been reading all about that case. So fascinating."

"No shit it's fascinating. They never caught her. No significant leads. Nothing." Hi jumped up, excited to talk about the old case. He hoisted a box down from one of the stacks after studying labels for several minutes. "I kept all my notes. You never know when a story may come to life again. That's why I asked to be put down here. Nobody else could stand the dimensions of the space." He pointed to the ceiling. "There are a few advantages to being short, you know." He pushed a stack of papers on his desk aside, knocking a pile on the far side to the floor, and flipped the cardboard lid off the box. "Check this out."

Hi pulled a sprawling sheet of butcher paper out of the box. Rocky could tell Hi had folded the aging, thick sheet over several times, but he managed to flatten it out across the piles of mess on his desk. He disappeared onto the floor for a minute, crawling around and throwing things until he came up with a box of thumb tacks. Motioning for Rocky to help him, they managed to hold the butcher paper up to a stack of boxes and pin the corners so Hi's "murder board" formed a wall in front of them. When visible, Rocky could see Hi had created a map of people involved in the case, with notes under each person and lines drawn from one to the next and from everyone to a picture in the center: the grainy zoomed in shot of the Rye Mother leading a kid into the woods.

Rocky took a step back and put a hand to her mouth. "Holy shit."

Hi ran a hand through his hair. "You think I'm crazy, don't you?"

Rocky backhand slapped him across the arm. "Crazy brilliant. This is a thing of beauty." She stepped up to the map and ran a finger along a couple of the lines. "Are these all suspects?"

Hi stepped around her and pointed as he talked. "Some are, some aren't. I mean, you've got parents and other relatives here who were never considered suspects."

Rocky nodded. "Okay. So who was?"

Hi tapped on a wrinkled photo of an old woman. A candid shot taken when the woman slouched on a row of concrete steps and appeared to sleep. She dressed in a series of rags with a nervous hand perched on the handle of a shopping cart loaded with various items. "Well, there was a flurry of suspicion on a local homeless woman. She drifted around and people knew her as Crazy Mary. Her real name was Juniper Greenleaf, if you can believe that. Not as old as she looks, but she never had the mental capacity to pull off a string of crimes like these."

Rocky nodded, squinting at the picture and the captions around it. "So why so much suspicion?"

"She was crazy. And homeless. And hell, she looked like a damn witch. She was also seen kind of close to a couple of possible abduction sites around the time the kids were taken. But it was a stretch. She disappeared several years back. Nothing weird. Just sort of drifted away. She'd be pretty old now."

Rocky poked at a photo. "Who's this?"

"Jason St. Laurent's little league coach. He wasn't suspected back then, but I added him not so long ago because news came out he messed with some kids he coached back in the day."

Rocky's eyes grew wide. "Jason?"

Hi shook his head. "Nobody thinks he did anything to Jason, necessarily. It's just a possibility. Two of the other kids also played little league. Not for this guy, but they played. He was around them at tournaments and what not. Of course, damn near everybody played little league back then. Asshole offed himself before he could go to prison, so we may never know any more about him." Hi flayed his fingers across a series of headshots of women. They were all professional photos. "These are women who fit the profile. Not much reason to suspect any of them, but they fit the profile. So I added them."

Rocky shook her head. "The profile?"

Hi nodded and smiled. "Yeah. If you ever ask Rondo Singer, he will cuss me up and down for coming up with the name Rye Mother. Damn near ruined our friendship. But the cops got nobody to blame but themselves. They were the ones who allowed Waverly St. Laurent to bring the circus to town."

As Hi laughed at some inside joke, Rocky frowned at him. Her ears perked. "Waverly? What circus?"

Hi nodded. "The profiler. Waverly paid for the guy. Some private consultant from Little Rock. He's the one who built the profile and gave me all the information I needed to come up with the name."

Rocky shook her head. "I don't understand. I thought the name existed before Jason got abducted."

Hi nodded and traced a series of notes on the butcher paper with a stubby finger. "Yeah. The horrible irony of the story. Waverly wanted to reach out and help the parents who lost children. She was big into the Junior League at the time, and I think she tried to turn her efforts into a League project. But she ended up funding the search herself. It's the reason most of us amateur sleuths believe the killer targeted Jason. We think she put her own kid in the crosshairs."

"By hiring this—this profiler?"

"Yep. The guy was good. Still is, from what I hear. His name's Linus Rolando. And he is weird as shit. But brilliant. He swept into town and fluttered all over the place for a few weeks. Came up with a profile under the blessing of the local police force. He believed the killings were being committed by a woman. His theory connected the string of murders to the loss of a child, when her mental stability suffered a catastrophic break. He compared what she did to the efforts of a changeling from the old folk tales. She took children and made offerings to the harvest. Her addled brain hoped her actions would bring back her own child somehow. Her sacrifices would yield a new crop, so to speak. I did a little research into the folk tales he talked about and found a story about something called a Rye Mother, who left cornflowers in place of kids. Fit so perfect I couldn't help but run with it."

"Why would Waverly St. Laurent bring in some consultant for some missing poor kids?"

Hi shrugged. "Valid question. But she claimed to just want to help. And, to be fair, everyone tried to pitch in however they could."

"Did anyone ever suspect her?"

Hi laughed. "No. She was too wrecked. Now, Bo, the dad? He was a rough guy. They considered maybe he went too far one day, and he and Waverly covered up an accidental murder. But that was early. Even before the pedophile who lived in Trailer Pines." Hi tapped on a mug shot. "Pretty good alibi, though." He tapped other pictures. "Other Trailer Pines residents. Older kids, single nurse who moved shortly after Jason died, abusive boyfriend to a mother of a couple of kids Jason may have known. The place was pretty ripe with possibilities."

Rocky pointed to the pedophile. "Yeah, I asked Rondo about the case a little the other day. He said he liked this Spinelli guy for it."

Hi shrugged. "I don't blame him. The guy was a creep. And abuse of some sort checked out with people close to Jason." He pointed to a photo of a school. "This was his school. Spring Lake Park. A teacher there described the way he acted right before he went missing. Sure sounds like a kid getting messed with."

Rocky glanced over at the picture of the school and did a double take. Off to one side of her photo hung a yearbook-style photo of Rocky's own uncle. "Hey! That's my Uncle Jim!"

Hi laughed. "Yep. He was principal of Spring Lake Park Elementary when Jason went missing. I talked to him a few times, but he didn't know Jason too well. Didn't offer much to note."

Rocky had to fight to keep her mouth closed, managing to ask to take a picture of Hi's board of suspects before exchanging pleasantries and rushing out to plan the cussing she would give her parents for failing to inform her Uncle Jim had been Jason St. Laurent's principal.

Chapter 14

Before Rocky even got the chance to dole out a cussing to either of her parents, she sat slumped in the passenger seat of Jennifer's car receiving one of her own. After a late night spent poring over the photo of Hamilton Hallmark's suspect board, combing the Internet for information on any and all names, Rocky woke up to a midday call from Jen. Although half-sleep made it difficult to decipher what Jen said over the phone, proximity and blistering sunlight brought the topic into focus.

"You're going to get us all arrested, Rocky! You have been in the Junior League for all of a month and you're about to bring the whole organization crashing down around you in a front-page scandal." Jen drove with one hand while the other waved around in frantic punctuation of her lecture.

Rocky made a face. "No one's going to get arrested."

"Adderall? Adderall? Seriously?"

Rocky shrugged. "I just suggested the *idea* of Adderall."

"Brittany Bumpers has talked three girls into going in to see about getting a prescription."

Brittany Bumpers?" Rocky laughed. "These names aren't even real anymore, are they? You gotta be fucking with me at this point."

Jen continued, undeterred. "Rocky, this is our last chance to salvage the train wreck you've created. You realize that, right? Please tell me you realize that."

Rocky frowned and nodded. "Of course I realize it."

Jen eyed her. "If she hadn't asked for you specifically, I would be going alone. I know this is hard for you."

"Nah." Rocky shrugged off the apology.

Jen continued glaring at Rocky out of the corner of her eye. "Shit. You don't know where we're going, do you?"

Rocky winced. "I was still asleep a little bit when we were on the phone. You said so many words."

"Goddammit, Rocky. Waverly St. Laurent's. We are going to talk to Waverly St. Laurent about donating the money for our project."

"We're going to a prison?"

Jen sighed. "No. She is home awaiting trial. Seriously, Rock. Read the paper once in a while. She agreed to talk to us about our options, but only if you came with me."

"We're going to her house?" Rocky's face went sour. "Stop the car. Or slow down and I can roll out."

Jen locked the doors, leading Rocky to unlock them, and they flipped them back and forth several times until Jen hit the child safety button. "We need this money, Rocky. We can't sell drugs to fund a Junior League new members' project. You don't even have to talk. I can do all the groveling and begging. You just look solemn and nod a lot."

Rocky pouted as they drove, mumbling, "She called me fat."

"I know she did. She's a horrible woman. But she's a horrible woman who may still be able to access some part of a fortune. Which we need to keep from resorting to a plan that could land us all in prison along with her."

Rocky continued mumbling and moping on the drive to the St. Laurent mansion. Or, at least, what Rocky and Jen expected to be a mansion. The St. Laurent home looked impressive, no doubt about it. But unlike some of the newer five thousand square feet sprawling homes in the north part of town, Waverly St. Laurent still lived in a relatively modest hundred-year-old house half that size. Near the center of town, the houses in the St. Laurent neighborhood were all old and brick, most stood two stories and larger than the surrounding area, but nothing crazy. Washington Circle was one of several cul-de-sacs named after presidents: Adams, Jefferson, and Roosevelt were closest. There were others, but those four stood out based on the preservation of the homes. The street signs all boasted the neighborhood as a Historic Area, with the seal of the Texarkana Preservation Society stamped to one side. The roads were red brick and the streetlights replicas of a bygone era. The area even earned its own local nickname: Rushmore. North Texarkana may offer the largest homes, but true status came with a Rushmore address. And in Rushmore, Washington Circle held the greatest esteem.

At the crest of Washington Circle perched a red brick two story house with navy shutters and a crisp white front door. A colonial house, built like a big box with five windows arranged around a framed entrance. Two shorter structures jutted off to either side, one an obvious garage and the other what appeared to be some sort of mother-in-law's suite. A circle drive with hundred-foot-tall oak trees at each of the elbows bisected the front yard. Colorful flowers dotted beds around each tree and rows of deep green bushes lined the front of the house from the tip of the garage to the far end of the mother-in-law's suite, where the corner of a small porch and one end of a rear carport were visible from the street.

Jen pulled into the circle drive and stopped next to a Mercedes parked in front of a short walkway to the door. Rocky walked around the back of the Benz and waited for Jen to catch up. She jerked a thumb at the license plate—a personalized plate, reading "FREDDY"—and made a masturbation motion with her other hand. Jen shook her head and dragged Rocky toward the door.

Rocky waited like a scolded child behind Jen at the door. After one ring of the doorbell, a woman in stained jeans and a ratty t-shirt opened the door holding a rag and a bottle of Windex.

Rocky mumbled. "Can't even afford a uniform like civilized rich assholes."

Jen talked over her to keep the woman from hearing the comment. "Hi! We're here to see Ms. St. Laurent. She's expecting us."

The woman smiled and nodded. "Ms. Waverly's in the parlor." She pointed through a set of double doors to their right. "Right through there."

Rocky mumbled, "Fucking parlor," as Jen thanked the woman and they made their way toward the doors.

Everything in the St. Laurent home held true to the turn of the 20th Century when it was built. Even the paintings were all oversized portraits of St. Laurent ancestors from, according to little brass plates at the bottom, the 1800s up to no later than the 1940s.

The double doors were glass, with dark wood framing out fifteen small windows. But a billowy curtain blocked the view, so Jen had to ease open a door before she and Rocky could see who waited on the other side. Only the natural light from the one window at the front of the house offered any reprieve from the cavernous feel of the dark parlor. The room felt more like an office or a library than a parlor. The far wall did have a wood-framed fireplace with a pair of couches jutting out from the corners of the hearth. But sticking out from the mahogany trim and yellowed wallpaper were several floor-to-ceiling bookshelves lining the back of the room, with a huge mahogany desk planted in the middle of them. The desk held two lamps on either end, and there were three floor lamps positioned around arm chairs in the room, but none were turned on.

Waverly St. Laurent reclined on a white high-backed sofa and stared out the window. She wore her sunglasses and smoked a cigarette in an actual cigarette holder. She wore a white pantsuit this time, and gold jewelry glittering over an emerald green, silky blouse. Matching gold buttons adorned the jacket to her suit, but she had it draped over an arm of the couch next to her. She didn't look up when they walked in, but she waved her cigarette in their direction, sending a narrow flume of smoke spiraling in the light. "Come in, ladies. Sit." She motioned toward the matching couch opposite her.

Jen offered pleasantries as she and Rocky shuffled over to sit facing her. A man sat next to Waverly on the couch. He wore a gray suit with a red bowtie. The bald surface of his pink head reflected the narrow rays of light from the window. He sat leaned back with his hands cupping the bottom of his belly, which hung down over his lap and pressed at the buttons of his white shirt. Rocky made eye contact with him, trying to decide if his expression revealed smugness, boredom, or annoyance. He could have been any of the three. Back in the shadows, a man in a darker suit sat in one of the reading chairs. He was just as bald, but in much better shape and, at least in the absence of much light, his complexion didn't seem as ruddy.

Jen leaned forward and held her hands out in almost a praying motion. "Ms. St. Laurent, I am so sorry about everything you've been through. You didn't need to do this."

Waverly brushed the comments aside. "Jibber jabber. Bunch of rattling bullshit. I don't need all that." She noticed Jen's shocked reaction, glancing their way for the first time. "Don't be offended. I appreciate the gesture, sweetie. But I don't take to patronizing small talk. We're not peers. Hell, we aren't even equals. You're here for a reason, so let's get on with it."

Rocky sat with her legs crossed in a manner as to not show too much leg under her linen summer dress. "You called us. I was going to get my nails done."

Jen leaned back and mumbled, "I didn't think you were listening."

Rocky shrugged. "I might have picked up a bit."

Waverly's sunglasses met Rocky's eyes and the two stared for a moment until Waverly grinned. "True. I did. And I don't want to hold you up from," she glanced down at Rocky's hands, folded on her knees, "a much-needed appointment."

Rocky glowered and folded her fingers under her palms.

"As I'm sure you've heard by now, my recent troubles caused a minor hiccup in my finances." Waverly took a quick puff of her cigarette and smoke seeped out of her nose. "However, I do possess a few rainy-day options still floating around here and there." She motioned to the man to her right. "I've been talking to my lawyer and he assures me I will still be able to donate the ten thousand dollars to fund your project."

Jen shook her head. "Such amazing news, Ms. St. Laurent. You have no idea how much this means to us. I know how much of a strain this must be on you with everything going on."

Waverly nodded. "It hasn't been easy, no. But your project touched my heart."

Rocky snorted and Jen elbowed her.

Waverly nodded toward the lawyer again. "Mr. Van Vleck here will set everything up for you."

Jen gushed, "Thank you so much, Ms. St. Laurent. Thank you."

"Ms. St. Laurent has one stipulation." The lawyer's voice boomed from his nostrils, cutting and echoing through the room.

Rocky laughed. "Oh, is that so, Freddy?"

Freddy Van Vleck chuckled and sucked at his teeth. "Only people who can afford me call me Freddy, honey."

Rocky raised one side of her mouth and nodded. "Well, only people who can afford me call me honey, Freddy. Bet my list is shorter."

Jen put a hand on Rocky's arm and leaned forward, almost in front of her. "Anything, Ms. St. Laurent. Whatever you need. You name it."

Waverly St. Laurent stared off toward the fireplace and smoked as if she were no longer a part of the conversation. Freddy Van Vleck breathed in through his nose in what bordered on a snort, preparing himself to speak. "It has come to my client's attention you are," he eyed Rocky hard, "at least one of you is looking into the series of robberies leading up to the unfortunate incident at my client's home."

Rocky steeled her gaze in silence, but Jen nodded vigorously. "Yeah. Yes. Yes, we are. She is. Rocky is good at this sort of thing. She can figure out—"

Freddy Van Vleck held up a chubby pink hand. "I'm going to stop you right there, honey. I'm sure your little sister is real good at playing Nancy Drew. But my client would prefer to leave these matters to the actual authorities."

Rocky frowned. Jen blinked at him. "Wait, what? So you're saying the stipulation is," she shook her head, "Rocky *doesn't* look into the burglaries."

Freddy glanced at Waverly, who gave an ever-so-slight nod. He turned back to Jen. "My client would prefer to leave these matters to the authorities."

Jen hung her head and sighed. "Shit. Here we go."

Rocky rubbed her hands together in front of her face. "So let me make sure I'm clear, Freddy. Your client, who is sitting in silence right next to you, is willing to pay us ten thousand dollars to not look into some home invasions? Is that the sum of it?"

Freddy glanced at Waverly, who made some imperceptible sign with one of her hands. Freddy turned back to Rocky and swallowed some unspoken annoyance. "Twenty thousand."

Jen's head shot up. "What?"

Freddy nodded. "Twenty thousand. Ten for your project. Five straight to each of you."

"If we agree to not investigate the home invasions?" Rocky frowned.

Freddy held his hands out and cocked his head, nodding once.

Rocky moved her eyes from Freddy to Waverly and held the glare until the old woman turned her head back toward her. Rocky couldn't see her eyes behind the sunglasses, but they faced off for a painful thirty seconds. Rocky let a smirk creep onto her face.

"Nah," Rocky tossed out, standing up.

Freddy laughed. "Nah?"

Rocky nodded. "Yep. Nah. We'll find the money ourselves."

Rocky started out, with Jen shuffling behind her. Freddy bumbled and struggled to stand. He managed to blurt out, "What the hell is wrong with you?"

Jen brushed past him, muttering, "I've been asking the same question for about twenty-eight years."

Waverly put a hand out to stop Freddy from following Rocky and Jen. Once out the door, Rocky slipped her own oversized sunglasses back on as she made her way to the car. She called back, "Well, it wasn't a total bust."

Jen jingled her keys out and laughed, "Oh yeah? How do you figure?"

Rocky shrugged. "You got what you've been asking for. Because I am sure as fuck going to look into this now."

Chapter 15

"Can you believe that bullshit?" Rocky asked for the fourth time since Jen pulled out of the St. Laurent driveway.

Jen let her vent without comment for the first block or two before she replied, "I'll admit, it is weird."

"It's more than weird! Why would she want me to back off? Why?" Rocky tapped a finger on her lips. "Unless she's behind all the break-ins."

Jen laughed. "She isn't behind anything, Rocky. It's weird. I told you, I agree it's weird. But a ridiculously wealthy old woman is not behind a string of robberies by some petty thief. There is no logical reason for her to—"

"Not robberies, remember? Which means he is no petty thief." Rocky rubbed her hands together. "Can you take me to Elaine Maplethorpe's house again?"

Jen eyed Rocky. "Why?"

Rocky held her hands out and shook her head in little jerks. "What do you mean, why? You've been wanting me to figure this out. I'm doing it, aren't I?"

"You aren't about to attempt to buy marijuana from Elaine Maplethorpe, are you?"

"What? No. Of course not."

Jen frowned. "I feel like I'm being tricked. You know, just because we aren't taking Waverly St. Laurent's money, doesn't mean I am going to be okay with your criminal enterprise."

Rocky scoffed, "Criminal enterprise."

"By definition, that is exactly what this is. And I do not condone criminal enterprises."

"Well, to be fair, since when do you *condone* anything? I mean, you don't hold press conferences or something where—"

"Rocky, I need you to tell me in a way I know I'm not being tricked."

"Tell you what, Jen?"

"Are you or are you not about to attempt to procure marijuana from Elaine Maplethorpe?"

Rocky twisted in her seat to face Jen. She held her hand up in a Scout's Honor position. "Jennifer, I, Raquel Champagnolle, hereby referred to as Party of the First Part, do solemnly swear I am not, in any way, attempting to buy or otherwise obtain any type of marijuana from Elaine Maplethorpe of the first order of the Maplethorpe coven of Texarkana, Texas, hereby referred to as Party of the Second Part. If said Party of the Second Part is to offer any illegal substance to Party of the First Part, aforementioned Party of the First Part will categorically and emphatically decline said offer from aforementioned Party of the Second Part."

Jen rolled her eyes. "Jesus. Okay, Rocky." She shook her head. "I still feel like you're tricking me."

Rocky flipped back around and leaned back in her seat, returning to rubbing her hands and staring off at nothing. "I'm very sorry you feel that way."

Although Jen couldn't get Elaine Maplethorpe on the phone, she agreed to still stop by, conceding Rocky's point: "the Bohemian lifestyle begs for surprise visits." When they arrived, Rocky hung back and let Jen ring the doorbell. As predicted, Elaine lit up as she opened the door. "Ladies! What a wonderful surprise! What brings you to my doorstep again so soon?"

Jen opened her mouth to speak, but Rocky leaned around her and said, "Hi, Ms. Maplethorpe. I was wondering if you could teach me how to bake brownies."

As Jen turned and gave Rocky an icy stare, Elaine flailed her arms up and smiled broadly. "Of course, dear! I would love nothing more! Come in, come in. Head on to the kitchen, honey, and let me run grab an apron."

Jen's lips drew tight and lost their color as her face pulsed scarlet. Rocky edged around her, offering, "Excuse me," as she did, and bounced off into the house.

Once in the kitchen, Elaine busied herself gathering baking paraphernalia, while Jen brooded in the corner and Rocky perched on a counter recounting the plan for an innovative Junior League fundraiser. "We think we can fly under the radar. No one suspects a bunch of Junior Leaguers. So we should be able to raise some much-needed funds while providing a service to those in need."

Jen harrumphed something about Adderall, but Elaine's gasp overshadowed the sound. "I couldn't agree more, dear. We, as a society, are letting our elderly and our sickest citizens suffer needlessly. People misuse all kinds of medicinal products. Why is marijuana treated any differently?"

Rocky nodded. "I know. Just the other day I heard about how people use ADD medicine as some sort of speed." She tsked and shook her head.

Elaine dropped a spatula into a bowl with a clang. "Yes! And I'm sure no one is starting a campaign to make those drugs illegal."

Rocky curled a lip. "Nope. In fact, I'll bet there's someone out there getting a prescription for Adderall right now."

As Jen fumed, Elaine pointed to Rocky in agreement. "Oh, I'm sure there are multiple people!"

Rocky mumbled, "A girl can dream."

Elaine pulled a small bag of pot out of a cookie jar and plopped it next to the baking equipment. "I'm guessing you want me to teach you, so you can, in turn, teach some other first years?"

Rocky squinted. "If you don't mind. I have to warn you, I'm terrible at baking."

Elaine laughed, "But that's why you're here, right?" She motioned toward Jen. "Jennifer is wonderful at baking. I remember those cookies you brought to last year's Christmas fundraiser. They were delightful!"

"Of course," Rocky nodded at Jen. "Jen is such a good baker. She can't wait to pitch in."

Jen glowered at Rocky but managed a smile to Elaine. "Of course."

Moving over to the refrigerator, Elaine started pulling out milk and eggs and butter, chattering as she did. "I love to see projects where everyone can apply their skills. We are all blessed with such unique and wonderful strengths. And so often, we are forced to set them aside and struggle to do other, even opposite things. I think this is going to be a beautiful project, girls. Let's see, we just need a few more ingredients." She spun around with wide eyes. "Ingredients! Oh! Do you ladies need a supplier? I could talk to my guy for you."

Rocky nodded at Jen and then turned back to Elaine with a resolute expression. "Categorically and emphatically, no."

Eliane recoiled from Rocky's serious tone until Rocky smiled and added, "I have a guy, but thank you."

Elaine chuckled. "Well, okay. Good." She clapped her hands at Jen. "Shall we begin?"

Despite herself, Jen got into baking. She enjoyed the process far more than she anticipated. And although she still threw hard stares at Rocky, who sat in the same spot on the counter the entire time flipping through a magazine, Jen found herself laughing and enjoying realizing how necessary she would be to the whole project. Rocky, for all her brilliance, couldn't heat up cosmic brownies in the microwave, much less bake pot brownies from scratch. And she would never have a prayer of teaching anyone else how to do it.

As they put the brownies in the oven, Elaine pulled off her apron and shook her head sadly. "Well, girls, I am excited about the potential of this project, but I sure do hate the circumstances forcing your hand." She sighed, "Poor Waverly."

Rocky put away her magazine and zeroed in on Eliane. "How well do you know Waverly St. Laurent, Ms. Maplethorpe?"

Elaine stared off in thought. "Oh, years. Years and years. We go back to even before our first year on the Junior League together." She giggled. "We co-wrote a skit for the end of the year celebration. You should have seen us. We sold candy as our fundraiser, so Waverly and I did a little bit like the *I Love Lucy* scene. You know the one. With the candies on the conveyor belt."

Rocky and Jen smiled and nodded.

"Oh, we had such a grand old time." Elaine grew solemn. "Before Jason, you know. Such a tragic story. Waverly has endured so much."

Rocky cocked her head. "And Baudouin."

Elaine blinked and looked up. "What?"

"And Dr. St. Laurent? *They* endured so much."

Elaine nodded. "Yes. Yes, of course. They both did. I didn't—I wasn't as familiar with Bo. I met him multiple times of course—at parties and events. He never seemed like the friendly sort. This may surprise you, but I read auras."

Rocky and Jen shared a look.

"Bo St. Laurent had the most rage-filled aura I ever saw." Elaine held her hands up. "I am not suggesting anything. I know the rumors, and I am not about to add any fuel to those fires. I'm simply saying he wasn't very approachable, in my opinion."

Rocky shook her head and frowned. "Rumors?"

Elaine sighed in frustration with herself. "I forget how young you girls are. There were many people in town who believed Bo St. Laurent was abusive. They thought he may have even hurt Jason himself. And I detest repeating gossip. There is no basis in fact for any of this. I never saw any signs of abuse myself."

Rocky nodded. "I'm sure they're nothing but vicious rumors. After all, it was so long ago. The police would have done something had there been any truth to the claims. How long had you both been in the Junior League when everything happened?"

Elaine grinned. "I think three or four years. We always worked the Mistletoe Fair together. I can remember doing the Fair at least three times, maybe four before Waverly stopped. She stopped after Jason…"

Rocky let her trail off before continuing. "And you joined together? Who else was in your class?"

Elaine stared off and smiled, counting on her fingers. "Oh, let's see. Edie. I doubt you've even met her. She seems to never come around much anymore. I think Mary Margaret Moneyham was in our class. I loved Mary Margaret. Sweet, sweet lady. I haven't seen her in a few years, though. Of course, Waverly. And Dottie Dowdy, she's still around. And Rhonda Martindale." She tapped her head. "Oh, but they both remarried since then. What are their last names now?"

Rocky and Jen both said, "Dot Dingledowd and Rhonda Thornhill?"

Elaine nodded and laughed. "Yes! We kidded Dottie because she wouldn't have to change her monograms. That's right."

Rocky hopped down off the counter. "Does it strike you as odd all of the home invasions happened to ladies from the same new member class?"

Elaine shrugged. "It hasn't even occurred to me until now. I suppose that is a little odd, but you must understand, we had a very strong class. If someone is targeting active Junior League members for some reason, then it would make sense to see an abnormally large number from our class. We've remained so engaged. And as much as I hate to admit, we've all done well for ourselves in one way or another."

Rocky strolled around the kitchen and scrutinized the wall hangings. "You mean financially?"

Elaine nodded. "Yes. I can't stand talking about physical wealth, but I can acknowledge, if someone were trying to, I think they call it 'score,' I could see why he might target those of us he did."

"The thing is though, Ms. Maplethorpe," Rocky leaned against a wall and rubbed her hands together in her characteristic way, "he didn't score. He didn't take a single thing. He snooped around and left." She pointed at Elaine. "And something about you stands out to me. I can't quite put my finger on it, but something is different about this one."

Elaine frowned. "I don't know. I think I'd say Dottie's stands out."

Rocky matched her expression and shook her head, almost laughing. "Dot Dingledowd? Why?"

"Well, you said yourself, he didn't take anything." Elaine raised her eyebrows. "Except at Dottie's. He took—"

"Her son's pills. From her purse." Rocky nodded and went back to rubbing her hands together.

"Yes. Dottie and David had little Davey Junior so late in life." She whispered, "I think that's why he has as many problems as he does."

"You are right." Rocky chuckled. "The one thing he took was bottle of Adderall from Dot Dingledowd's purse." She craned her neck toward Jen. "So why does this one stand out to me?"

Jen laughed. "No clue, Rocky."

Elaine grew excited. "Are you trying to solve the home invasions?"

Rocky rolled her eyes. "Well—"

"Jen mentioned how smart you are with all of this type of thing. How exciting. Oh, I do hope you can figure this out. I mean, as much as I hate to be judgmental and presumptuous, if this is a drug addict we're talking about, it's just a matter of time before—"

Rocky frowned and interrupted Elaine's rambling thought. "A drug addict. If he's stealing prescription pills from a lady's purse, then he's a drug addict, right? Does this seem like the behavior of a drug addict to you? Taking nothing and letting himself out after exchanging polite banter? You have bags of marijuana in a cookie jar, for Christ's sake, and he pokes around, apologizes, and leaves. It doesn't make any sense."

Elaine shook her head mournfully. "Well, dear. It never does, you know," she winced, "with drugs."

Before Rocky could reply, a bell dinged and Elaine proclaimed, "Oh! Our brownies are ready."

Chapter 16

Although Jen rebuffed Rocky's efforts to sample the brownies and proceeded to low-key scold her the entire ride home, Rocky could tell her plan worked. She played into Jen's strengths. Gave her a sense of purpose. Between comments on how dangerous the pot brownie bake sale would be, Jen caught herself starting to brainstorm which Junior League members would be best in the makeshift bakery she planned on setting up in the large kitchen of Frank's furniture shop. Whatever the building had once been used for needed a large kitchen, and Frank left the space intact through a couple of remodels. Jen even slipped and mentioned her idea in passing, to Rocky's oversized grin, before catching herself and returning to fuming. Jen tried to dismantle Rocky's gloat by tossing out, "Yeah, so where do you plan on keeping all this illegal shit, smarty pants?"

Rocky shrugged. "I don't know. We can just keep it at home until we need to bake another batch."

Jen raised her eyebrows. "We?" She laughed. "Rocky, no one is going to want drugs in their house. And you—well, must I remind you? You live with your parents, Rock."

Rocky frowned and nodded. "Yeah. There is that, huh?" She flopped her hands into her lap. "I guess I'll just go get my own place."

Jen roared with laughter. "Like picking out a new dress, huh?"

Rocky ducked her chin into her chest and snarled a lip.

Jen continued, "You honestly think you can just waltz out into the world and 'get your own place?'"

Rocky tutted. "People buy houses all the time."

"Yes, Rocky. People with their shit together. You've never done anything like this in your life. You need to apply for a loan. You have to secure a down payment. Can you even find all your tax information from the past few years?"

"I don't know. Maybe. What does it look like?"

Jen guffawed. "Oh, Rocky."

She pulled into Rocky's parents' driveway, and Rocky got out before the car even stopped. Jen tried to offer half-hearted apologies, but Rocky had never taken to being laughed at. She knew Jen leaned into the ridicule because Rocky tricked her, which, admittedly, was a dick move. But still, Rocky didn't like being laughed at. Hearing someone discredit her with laughter filled her with determination. Which meant getting serious about finding her own place. Which meant retrieving her financial information from the past few years. Which meant talking to Chet.

On the surface, talking to her ex-husband would seem like no big deal. However, even during marriage, Rocky and Chet could go weeks without speaking more than a few passing words in the morning and the evening. Chet worked as an insurance adjuster, which meant he never had to arrive at work until around nine. Rocky would be out of the house before he even woke up. In the evenings, Chet almost always "got a drink with the boys" after work, which involved watching some game and could wind into the early morning hours. He would stumble home drunk and curse about the fact Rocky fell asleep by nine. Monday nights were their date nights, and *date* is used rather liberally. Chet would send a text asking if Rocky wanted to "grab dinner and touch base tonight," as if they were business partners instead of spouses. And weekends? Well, they were reserved for golf and fish fries and barbecues and mud racing and a litany of other activities Rocky found repugnant. She often recounted one Saturday afternoon when their one physical interaction of the week came as they high-fived passing to and from their respective cars and headed to separate events.

Since the divorce, Rocky and Chet had not spoken one time. No contact at all. So texting him to ask if she could come to the house and pick up some documents felt like peeling one of her own fingernails off. And his response made her sick at her stomach: "Sure, babe. I'll get them ready for you." With a little winking, kissy face emoji. Gag.

They agreed to meet the following day during Chet's lunch hour, which Rocky knew would be a long two hours at worst. She always envied public sector lunch "hours" as she wolfed down a bowl of cereal in the twenty minutes she got to hide from school children.

The day of their meeting Rocky spent two solid hours getting ready. Ironically, she hadn't spent much of any time getting ready on Chet's behalf during the majority of their marriage. But as happy as she was to be rid of him, Rocky couldn't help feeling the desire to make him regret losing her. She put a subtle curl in her hair, wore a shade redder lip gloss, and slipped into a flowy little dress which hugged all the right curves.

Chet and Rocky, to Rocky's knowledge, owned two pieces of land while married. As it turned out, Chet's father owned them both, a fact which Rocky found out the hard way. But, in all honesty, she didn't even care. Houses always proved to be a sore subject in their marriage. Rocky and Chet both hailed from Palermo. And Palermo is where they settled after they got married. They built a house an equal distance between their parents. And Rocky loved their house. Although Chet and his father, who built the house with his construction company, played the man card multiple times during construction, Rocky managed to set up the interior the way she wanted. She picked out all the colors and the floors and the decorations throughout. All by herself. Having married at twenty-two, setting up her house was the first time Rocky ever felt in control of her own adulthood. So when Chet sold their home out from under her without so much as an advanced notice, it stung.

Chet swore they were getting a once-in-a-lifetime deal—one they couldn't refuse. They owned two pieces of land they could use to build an even bigger and better house and, as he put it, "Rocky, you can play with all your flowers and wall hangings and shit over there, too."

The two pieces of land were within a block each of their respective parents. Again, without consulting her, Chet started construction on houses near both their parents. He and his dad's company had spent two years working on a labor-of-love French Provincial two-story out by his parents. And a quick construction of a half-finished two-bedroom starter home near her parents. So Rocky, the new Queen of the Junior League of Texarkana, spent her last two years living in a twelve-hundred-square-foot doll house with an unfinished bathroom. And sure, Rocky and Chet walked away from the sale of their house with about a hundred grand. But over the two years of false starts and delays, Chet spent most of the money on race cars and golf clubs and a motorcycle and two new trucks and a four-wheeler and any other grown man toy he could find. They were left with little money and no house to show for it. So when Chet took her for everything, Rocky shook off her initial indignation with a shrug of the shoulders.

The drive from Rocky's parents' house to Chet's took less than two minutes. Chet stood outside waiting on her when she pulled up. He wore a pair of khakis and a bright green polo shirt. He had put on a few pounds and grown his beard out to distract from the fact he had lost a few more hairs on top over the past month. A pair of Ray Bans, with a tacky neck strap strung from earpiece to earpiece, hid his eyes. But he flashed a wistful smile as Rocky stepped out of the car.

"Hey, Rock." Chet shook his head. "Mm, mm, mm. I always did love to watch you crawl out of a car in a dress."

Rocky froze. She cycled through this meeting in her head a hundred times. She rolled through any number of quips to any number of statements. But she never, in any of her imaginings, pictured a greeting which could make the bile rise up her throat quite as far as it just did. All of her comebacks and snarky insults left her in a moment of absolute disgust. She pushed her sunglasses up into her hair to buy herself some time. And then she said the first thing that popped into her head. "I fucked your brother."

Chet's mouth dropped open. He pried his sunglasses off and let them hang at his chest by their gaudy lanyard. Rocky breezed past him in a flutter of hair and perfume as he stammered and stuttered, trying to get any words to leave his mouth. Rocky bounced up the steps and into the house like she still lived there. She scrambled to think of a next move. Chet's younger brother, Chance, was at least seven years younger than Rocky. The Arnolds had him a little late in the game, a pleasant surprise. He became the babied golden boy of the family, and Chet grew a little envious. The thought of Rocky sleeping with Chance would drive him insane.

Of course, she had not slept with Chance.

The technicality gave Rocky some slight twinges of guilt. Chance would deny her claim. Chet wouldn't believe him. The scandal would drive a wedge in the family. And Chance wasn't a bad kid. Rocky kind of liked him. But, she reasoned, Chet's mother always hated Rocky. And Chance was her baby boy. So she would side with Chance, leaving Chet out in the cold. And that guilt she could live with.

Chet came storming into the house. "Rocky, what the fuck are you telling me here?"

Rocky whirled around. "I didn't feel like I minced words. Do you want me to say it again?"

Chet's eyes watered. "While we were married?"

Rocky frowned. "Oh, no. I never slept with your brother while you and I were married, Chet." It felt good to be back to the truth.

Chet heaved breaths and stomped around the house.

Rocky tapped her fingers on the table. "So, were you able to find those papers?"

Chet laughed. "Rock, can you give me a second? I'm a little discombobulated here."

Rocky's eyes grew wide.

Chet nodded. "Yeah. Didn't see that one coming, did you? I'm improving myself, Raquel. Word of the day. They got a calendar and everything."

"Wow, Chet. I'm impressed. In a Leap Year? Going straight for the deep end, buddy."

"Don't think we ain't talking about this, Rocky."

"Aw, sweetie. Next year maybe Santa can bring you an English usage calendar."

"My own brother, Rocky?"

Rocky scowled. "Come off it, Chet. How many girls did you sleep with while we were married? Huh? How many? I know you counted. You're a notches in the bedpost kind of asshole. So how many? Five? More?"

"This ain't about me, Rocky. How many guys did you sleep with? Huh?"

Rocky shook her head. "None!"

"Bullshit. I know you were fucking somebody, Rocky."

Rocky laughed. "Chet, I barely slept with *you* when we were married."

Chet pointed at her words. "I know. Believe me. So you had to be getting it somewhere. Was it Chance?"

"No. I told you. Never while we were married. I never slept with anyone, Chet."

Chet curled his lip in a skeptical expression. "Yeah. I'll bet. So why does some guy keep cruising by here to see if you're home, huh?"

Rocky turned to scan the counter for her papers, but Chet's statement got her to spin back around. "What?"

Chet nodded. "Yeah, you know him. I'll bet you've been giving it up to him for months, haven't you?"

"Chet, what are you talking about? What guy? What does he drive?"

Chet flung a hand out toward the road. "Old brown pickup. Older guy. You always said you liked older guys." His voice cracked. "So why Chance, Rock? Why?"

Rocky shook off the question with annoyance, brushing a hand around to sweep the irrelevant topic away. "I don't know. He's better than you in bed. Whatever. Tell me about this guy. What does he look like?"

Chet started to cry. "How much better?"

"Jesus, God."

"Is he," Chet struggled to get the words out, "is he bigger?"

Rocky put her head in her hands and swallowed. "I can see this is not going to be very productive." She raised up. "Do you still have my nine millimeter? The one you bought me?"

Chet shook his head. "Well, yeah. It's got a goddamn pink handle, Rocky. You don't think I'd be using it, do you?"

Chet had gotten the pistol for her for a birthday. He made sure to get one with a pink handle, so she would never forget she was the woman in the relationship. Of course, when they took their concealed firearm course together, and Rocky outshot everyone, including Chet, she turned to him and asked, sweetly, "Want to switch guns?"

After several more awkward attempts to ask questions about Rocky's fictional escapade with Chance, Chet shuffled to the back of the house to retrieve Rocky's gun and a file folder of tax papers. As he handed them to her, he stared into her eyes with such sadness, regret. He tried to say several things, but only managed to whisper, "What do you say, Rocky? One more time for the road?" He continued to lean closer, closer, licking his lips and inching toward her face.

Rocky leaned back, putting a hand to his chest to stop him. "Actually, Chet," she said as he continued to lean in, Rocky having to press hard against him to stop his momentum, "he is bigger."

Chapter 17

Rocky left her ex-husband dealing with his discombobulation on the porch steps and drove across the highway to park behind a cluster of trees on her uncle's property. The cover allowed her to watch her old house to see any brown trucks cruising by. She rolled down her windows and got comfortable, pulling up a book on her phone to read. With the windows down, she would hear any approaching vehicles or other movement in plenty of time to look up from her slutmance novel.

After about an hour and a half with no brown trucks, Rocky heard a car pulling up behind her. A long gravel driveway to the home of her aunt and uncle stretched off into her rearview mirror, which meant anyone coming would be a relative. She checked the mirror and found Jen climbing out of her car with a perplexed expression. Jen climbed into the passenger seat of Rocky's car and gestured across the highway, "Rocky, are you spying on Chet?"

Rocky shook her head. "Not primarily, no. I mean, he did leave on a four-wheeler to ride off into the woods about thirty minutes ago, which I found strange. I took the opportunity to drive over and rifle through his truck for something of mine I left there. But I would not say I am spying on him."

Jen closed her eyes. "Rocky, please tell me you got your paperwork from him."

Rocky nodded. "Oh. Oh, yeah. A good while back. He tried to make out with me."

"Gross."

"Yep."

They both watched back and forth through the trees up and down the highway for a moment. Jen winced. "Rock, what are we doing?"

Rocky rubbed her hands together. "We are watching for a brown truck."

Jen nodded. "Okay. Why?"

"Chet said one has driven by several times. He assumed the truck belonged to someone I'm fucking. I'd kind of like to know who it does belong to."

Jen sighed and shook her head. "That's it. Drive."

"What?"

"Drive, Rocky. We are going to get a drink."

Rocky frowned. "I am busy, Jen."

"No, Rocky. You aren't. You are sitting here staring at your asshole ex-husband's house watching for some imaginary brown truck he made up in his asshole head. You need to drink and laugh and get hit on and forget about Chet for a while. Just leave my car here. It'll be fine. Now, go. Go. Drive."

Rocky groaned but rolled up her windows and fastened her seatbelt with a begrudged pout, pulling out from behind the cluster of trees as she did. They made the fifteen-minute drive back to Texarkana and let themselves slip into Palermo gossip as Jen scrolled through an app on her phone dedicated to publicizing local mug shots. Rocky drove them to a steakhouse chain restaurant in Texarkana because she happened to like the piña coladas they made there. Jen made every effort to get them seated at the bar, but Rocky insisted on a booth by a window about as far away from any semblance of a crowd as they could get.

Jen made a face as they sat down, "You're never going to get hit on all the way over here."

Rocky's eyes grew wide. "Exactly."

A passing waiter threw a little side eye toward them both and mumbled, "I wouldn't be so sure," as he passed by with a tray of drinks.

Jen howled laughing at the pained expression on Rocky's face. But after a couple of drinks, the waiter's prediction came true. He showed back up with a piña colada and a cape cod on a tray. He smirked and rolled his eyes. "Hate to say I told you so, but …"

Rocky sighed. "I figured. He's been staring at us pretty hard for the past half hour."

The waiter started to set the drinks on their table, adding, "Not to tell you how to live your life, but they're both pretty huge tools."

Rocky shook her head. "Wait. Both? Who sent these? The guy at the bar, right?" She nodded toward a nondescript guy in jeans and a t-shirt—shaggy, dark brown hair and a touch of face stubble. He sat alone at the bar and nursed a beer.

The waiter peeked back over his shoulder at the man. "That guy? No." He pointed at two college-age men at a table. They were grinning from diamond studded ear to ear with smiles as greasy as their hair.

Jen let out a noise of disgust. Rocky couldn't stop looking back and forth between the greasy pair and the solitary man, who called for his check and fished in a pocket for his wallet. Rocky snapped back to the moment and started waving off the drinks. "Wait, wait, wait. No. We are not taking these."

The waiter chuckled. "Oh, don't worry. They never touched them."

"I don't care. I'm not taking them."

He frowned at Rocky and glanced over to Jen, who shrugged. "Yeah, she's not going to back down. You might as well take them back."

Rocky twisted in her chair and face the interior of the restaurant. "Or ..."

Jen groaned. "Rocky. Just let it go."

Rocky motioned slyly to a table of three large men in motorcycle leathers. At a table next to them sat two teenage girls—maybe fourteen—who entered with them. The girls carried all the awkward mannerisms of the daughter and friend of one of the men or even daughters of more than one. "I want you to take them over there."

The waiter frowned. "To those guys?"

Rocky nodded. "Yes. Well, kind of." She pulled out a twenty. "I'll pay you twenty bucks to take these to those bikers and tell them Guido and The Situation over there asked you to take them to the girls. But you don't feel right about it. You just wanted to make sure they are of age before you serve them alcohol."

As Jen buried her face in her hands, the waiter's grin grew. "Save your money. I'll do this one on the house."

Rocky turned away from the bikers and begged Jen to give color commentary on what happened. As Jen ducked her tittering chin into her chest and tried to watch through her fingers, Rocky overheard the man at the bar still trying to get his check by calling out to the bartender, "Pardon me? Could I get my check?"

Rocky shook her head. "Did you hear that?"

Jen cringed. "Yes. They are getting so pissed off. I think they're getting up. Rocky, you're going to start a fight."

"No, no, no. Not that. The guy. The one at the bar. He said 'pardon me.'"

Jen glanced back over her shoulder at the man before turning back to the awkward scene in front of her. "Okay. So?"

Rocky held her hands out to Jen pleadingly. "Pardon me? Jen, come on. Pardon me. Just like the guy."

Jen shook her head. "What guy?"

Rocky scrambled to get up and gather her purse. She dropped the twenty in front of Jen and whispered, "The Neighborly Knave. The Courteous Crook. Whatever we're calling him."

Jen tried to grab Rocky. "Where are you going?"

Rocky slipped her grasp and darted for the door while cursing and commotion distracted everyone around her as a rowdy group of bikers made their way toward the greasers. Rocky tossed back, "Meet me at the car in five minutes."

Jen tried to whisper-shout, "What?" But Rocky was gone.

Once outside, Rocky broke into a trot over to her Lexus. She fell into the driver's seat, ass up, and fished through the middle console until she came out with a cell phone. She had pulled the burner phone from Chet's truck just a couple of hours earlier and left the cell charging in the console of her car ever since. She punched the power button to make sure the screen came to life, and then closed her door and straightened her dress.

Fiddling with the phone, Rocky started to make her way through the parking lot, rounding the front of the restaurant and coming up the single row of cars on the far end. Past the carry-out spots, she came to a back parking lot dotted with cars in about half of its spots. She zig-zagged in between cars and trucks until she rounded the corner from a minivan and found what she had been searching for.

An old brown pickup truck.

She reveled in being right for half a second before dropping the burner phone into the bed of the truck and hurrying back up to the restaurant. She hugged a corner of the building over by the carry-out door, waiting and watching. Anyone walking to the brown truck would come out the other end of the building and walk right through Rocky's line of sight without ever being able to see her.

Sure enough, within seconds, the solitary man from the bar, having finally gotten his check amidst all the ruckus, jogged out into the parking lot and made his way to the brown truck. The engine roared to life with the sound of an old muffler and pulled out of the back of the lot, speeding away.

Once clear, Rocky ran along the back of the building toward the other side where she parked her Lexus. As she rounded the corner, Jen walked out and flailed her hands at Rocky in confusion. "Rocky! What the hell are you doing?"

Rocky waved Jen on. "Come on! Hurry! It's him! The guy! It's the guy!"

Jen shook her head. "What? Rocky, how do you know?"

Rocky kept ushering her toward the car. "An old brown pickup, Jen! It is the guy!"

Jen made it to the Lexus and started around to the passenger side. Rocky shook her off. "Oh, no. You need to drive. I'm going to track him."

Jen frowned at her. "What? Rocky, are you drunk?"

Rocky cocked her head and shrugged. "Yeah. I guess there's also that. You should really drive."

Chapter 18

As Rocky stared at her phone and barked out directions, Jen drove and fretted, "Rocky, what the hell are we doing?"

Rocky pointed. "Take a left. This is how I caught Chet at the hairdresser's."

"Waitress."

Rocky shrugged. "I've heard it both ways." She pointed frantically. "Right, right, right. Yeah, I got one of these burner phones and turned on the Find My Phone feature. You can track it on this website."

Jen nodded. "That's what you got out of Chet's truck today?"

Rocky nodded. "Take another right up here. Yep. Charged it all afternoon. You never know when you'll need something like this."

Jen laughed. "Something like this? A tracking device, you mean? You never know when you'll need a tracking device?"

"Yes, Jen. We are tracking a murderer, here."

"Burglar."

Rocky spoke out of the side of her mouth. "Never stole anything. Now, slow down. I think he stopped."

Jen pulled to a stop on the side of the road in front of a vacant house with a For Sale sign in front. She gasped. "Um, Rocky? Look where we are."

Rocky peered up from her phone to find Jen pointing at a street sign. "Holy shit. We're on Elizabeth. And he's parked one street over. This is his neighborhood. Where the first break-ins happened. I was—" she raised her hands up in an awkward robotic dance, "I was right. Right, right, right, r-right-right-right."

Jen rolled her eyes. "Okay. Yes. Maybe you were. So now what?"

Rocky kept dancing for a moment, signing, "Rocky was right. The rightest of the right. Righter than the right and the righter and the more right—"

Jen sighed. "You shouldn't show this much surprise. It's like a touchdown dance. Act like you've been here before."

Rocky stopped and stared at Jen. "Oh, I have been here before, Jen." She put fingers to her temples. "In my mind."

Jen nodded. "Okay. Great. Can we leave now?"

Rocky frowned. "What? No. We need evidence, Jen. Evidence."

"Evidence? What the hell kind of—" Rocky jumped out of the passenger seat in the middle of Jen's sentence. "Rocky! Rocky?" Jen got out and gave chase, swiveling her head around to take stock of the rough neighborhood.

Rocky called back, "Did you lock my car?"

"Rocky! Rocky, stop! Shit." Jen turned back and fumbled with the key fob until she heard a beep, then ran to catch back up. "Rocky, what the hell are we doing? We need to leave."

Rocky pulled her phone out, twisting the screen around trying to orient herself on the map. She cut through a side yard over to the next street, Victoria. She stopped in the middle of the street with Jen at her elbow. Rocky pointed. "He should be right about," she closed one eye and cocked her head, "is that a brown truck in the carport of the little yellow house?"

Jen looked up and squinted. "Yep. Now, let's go." She tried to tug Rocky by the arm, but Rocky squirmed out of her hold and started walking toward the house. Jen flailed her arms in exasperation. "Rocky, come on." She hurried to catch up. "At least get out of the middle of the damn road."

Rocky let Jen guide her over into the empty front yards of the four or five houses leading up to the yellow house with the brown truck. Once off the street, Rocky took the lead back, stumbling her way over some scattered toys and a sprinkler. Coming up on the side of the house, Rocky crouched down and peered back over her shoulder to give Jen a shushing motion.

Jen crouched behind her and scrunched her face up in an annoyed "no shit" expression.

Rocky duck walked up to the edge of a window and strained her neck to peek in. The cheap vinyl blinds were closed, but they didn't quite reach the window sill. So Rocky and Jen both were able to rest their almost identical noses on the outside window ledge and stare inside at what appeared to be a living room. A woman lounged on the couch in a tank top and a pair of panties. She barked indecipherable orders at someone as she flipped at channels with a remote. Within a few seconds, the man from the bar passed by, barking back at her. And then again, walking past—he mouthing at her with disgust, she swearing back at him. The words were hard to make out, but the couple displayed all the mannerisms of an argument.

Rocky eyed Jen and motioned for her to follow as she started toward the back of the house. She paused to scout in another window to a kitchen and another to a bathroom. As she rounded the back of the house, she raised up and walked more leisurely. Jen jerked her head around, which led Rocky to wave her off. "Don't worry. They're fighting about her not having a job, I think. I picked up on a few tired phrases. The type they each say a lot. This is a conversation they've had plenty of times. And one that could go on for a while. I want to have a look around while it does."

"A look around? For what, Rocky?"

Rocky shook her head. "I'm not sure yet." She glanced at random trash in the backyard and paused at each window: the backdoor window into a mudroom or laundry room, a bedroom, another bathroom, and, on the other side of the house, just before coming up on the brown truck parked in the carport, the living room from a different angle. She stopped Jen and shushed her again.

Jen narrowed her eyes and whispered, "I know to be quiet, Rocky." She pointed at the continued shouting coming from inside the house. "They aren't going to hear me over all that."

Rocky nodded. "This is the angle I wanted." She crouched down and eased over in front of the window. The blinds had a similar gap, allowing for a view of the back of the couch and, beyond the small living room, the front door. Rocky rolled back away from the window with her back leaned against the house. She went back into her "Rocky was right" dance, whispering the accompanying song.

Jen frowned at her. "What are you talking about? Right about what?"

Rocky jerked a thumb at the window.

Jen crouched and peered in. She glanced up at Rocky and shook her head.

"By the door," Rocky whispered.

Jen nodded. "Yeah, what? The coat rack?"

Rocky nodded. "And what's on the coat rack?"

Jen flopped back around and slumped down out of sight with eyes wide. "Holy shit."

Rocky danced some more.

Jen giggled a little. "An army green jacket and a—"

Rocky said it with her, "Plain black baseball cap." She mimed a sexual thrust with both hands to punctuate her words, "And I'll bet you there's a ski mask in the pocket of the jacket."

"Holy shit." Jen shook her head. "This is the guy."

"This is the guy."

"God, Rocky. We need to get out of here before—" Jen stopped mid-sentence and cocked her head, listening. "Hey. Do you hear them arguing anymore?"

They both strained to hear anything coming from inside, each placing an ear against the side of the house. Their faces were turned toward Victoria Street.

Toward the brown truck parked in the carport. And toward the man from the bar who stood with a key in his driver's side door lock, frozen in confusion and staring back at them.

"Shit," they all three said in unison.

Jen spun on Rocky and shouted, "Run!" She pushed her in the direction of the back of the house, with Rocky stumbling over her feet, needing to be dragged by the time they reached the backyard.

"Jen, this is the wrong way!"

Jen kept dragging. The man's pounding footsteps grew louder. "Rocky, he is the wrong way. Just trust me here. Please!"

Neither the yellow house nor the one backed up to it had a fence, which meant Jen could lead Rocky by the hand all the way into the next street over from Victoria. Rocky fake cried, "Our car is way over there, Jen."

Jen jerked Rocky into a sharp right, barreling through front yards. The man ran behind them, panting, cursing. Jen passed one house and another and another, waiting for any without fences to use as a cutback. When they came upon a setup like the one they used before Jen forced them to take a hard right, cutting back across to Victoria street. They were about four houses away from their car—two down and two more over, but Jen jerked a protesting Rocky down into a clump of bushes at the side of a house on Victoria. The man's footsteps came near—near enough to hear his frantic breathing. He lingered there above them as Jen clamped a hand over Rocky's mouth. In a burst of noise, he darted away from them, back the way they came.

Rocky pulled Jen's hand away. "Whew. That was so close."

Jen rolled her eyes and drug Rocky up from out of the bushes. "Rocky, come on. It's not over!"

As they ran toward the car, Rocky whimpered, "What do you mean it's not over?"

"I mean you basically announced where we parked the damn car!" Jen held the key fob out to Rocky as they approached the car.

Rocky shook her head. "Oh, no. You better still drive."

"Rocky, we don't have time for this!"

"Jen, I'm still a little tipsy, if we're being honest."

Jen's face wrinkled in agony. "What? You had two drinks!"

Rocky winced. "I ordered one while you were in the bathroom." She grinned and held up two fingers with each hand. "Both times."

Jen started some retort, but the sound of a truck rumbling to life interrupted her. They both glanced back toward the house and then to each other. "I'll drive."

"You should drive. Good call."

Jen started the car and spun out into a turn up and over a curb before Rocky could even get her door shut. In the rearview mirror, they could see the man from the bar spinning out into the road at the same time. Jen hopped off the curb and took the first turn off Elizabeth at thirty miles per hour and climbing.

Rocky's eyes grew wide and she smiled even wider. "Did you know you could do that? Look at you go."

Jen squealed through two more turns, catching a yellow light and rolling through a stop sign before opening up on a larger straightaway. "Rocky, stop grinning like an idiot and pull the app up on your phone!"

Rocky shook her head. "What app?"

Jen sighed. "Rocky, for a brilliant person, you are a fucking moron sometimes. The app! The app or whatever the hell it is where you can tell me where this guy is!"

Rocky nodded and pointed at her, pulling out her phone. "Ohhh. See, it's not an app. Just a website I go to and enter this code. I mean the app is just Safari. Which, you know, what's funny is I Google websites on Safari. What I should do is get the Google app. Do you have the Google app?"

"Rocky!"

Rocky held a hand up. "I'm typing while I talk. Calm down." Jen caught sight of the brown truck in the rearview and took two more sharp turns until she doubled back onto another straight road. Rocky tossed around in her seat. "Well, I can't type when you're swerving all over the place, can I?"

Jen craned her neck to see if he was anywhere behind them while stretching the Lexus out, pushing it up over a hundred miles per hour. "Rocky, please."

Rocky nodded at her phone. "Okay, okay. He is," she pointed as they passed a spot, "riiiiight there." She pointed back. "There. Now there. There. Turning, turning, turning. There he is. Here he comes." Rocky leaned over to observe the dash. "Are we going over a hundred miles per hour?!? I've never gone over a hundred miles per hour! I didn't know this car could go over a hundred miles per hour. Can your car go over a—"

"Rocky! The phone!"

"Oh yeah, he's still back there."

Jen slowed as she came into some slight traffic. She took a side road, zigzagging to miss a traffic light. "Watch him and tell me if he stops at the light." She continued winding around to make her way back to the main road.

Rocky frowned at her. "It doesn't tell me what he's doing, Jen. It's not a crystal ball. I can't tell you what radio station he's listening to. I mean, unless we got close. I'm pretty good at the thing where you watch someone dancing along and you flip through the stations—"

"Rocky!"

Rocky scanned the phone and flopped her hands. "I don't know, Jen. He slowed down or something."

Jen worked her way past the traffic light, coming out onto the same main road on the other side.

Rocky returned to the phone and raised a finger up, orienting herself by looking around at street signs. "Hold on. I think he's, maybe …" She glanced back at the brown truck stopped at the light just a couple of blocks behind them. "Oh! There he is. See him?"

Jen cut her eyes at Rocky. "Yes. Thank you, Rock. I see him." She wheeled out into the road just as the light changed and the truck lurched forward. "I need to get on Interstate."

Rocky bounced in her seat. "Ooh, yeah. You could go hella fast on Interstate. Have you always been able to drive like this?" She cocked her head and twisted her mouth. "We should go go-karting. I'll bet you're so good at go-karting." She pulled her phone up. "Shit. Sorry." she studied the screen. "Yeah, he's right behind us pretty much."

Jen nodded. "I know, Rocky." She made her way to Interstate, catching a light and zipping through slower cars. The Lexus overtook a delivery truck and got onto the Interstate highway doing eighty. The brown truck roared behind them trying to keep up.

Rocky sighed. "You know, I hate to even say this out loud, but—"

"Rocky, I swear to Christ. If you say you need to pee, I will drive us into oncoming traffic."

Rocky nodded and paused, sucking at her lips. "Don't even need to say it now though, huh?" She kept nodding and sniffed. "Kind of implied, you know?"

Jen swerved into the left lane to pass a semi-truck. The brown truck chugged up road behind her, coming up onto their bumper fast. Pushing toward them. Almost touching. Jen eyed approaching signs for an off ramp, gauging the distance. She kicked at the accelerator, revving up past one hundred again. The brown truck struggled to keep pace. She drew even with the cab of the semi and threw everything into one last surge—up and around the semi. She broke hard right, cutting off the semi, but crossing all the way into the exit lane. The Lexus glided off the Interstate to the sound of a blaring truck horn. A pissed off trucker pinned the brown truck into the far-left lane, forcing him to miss the exit and continue sailing down the Interstate. Jen let out a cry of "Yes!"

Rocky edged her eyes open and unfolded herself from the defensive position she had sunk into. "Holy fuck balls. That was so intense." She looked at her phone. "Yeah, he's still on Interstate."

Jen nodded. "And the next exit isn't for seven miles."

Rocky mouthed "Wow" and nodded her approval. They sat in silence for a moment until Rocky leaned toward Jen. "So now? Is now okay to say I need to pee?"

Chapter 19

As Rocky came prancing out of the service station bathroom looking relieved but grossed out, Jen leaned against the side of the Lexus with her phone pressed to her ear. She waved her hands around, animating the story for someone who couldn't see any of her motions. Her voice squeaked, shouting, "Yes, ma'am. Yes. We don't know his name, but we can describe him and give his address."

Rocky's eyes grew wide. "Jen, what are you doing?"

Jen reared up with scrunched together eyebrows and mouthed, "The police," pointing to the phone.

Rocky tittered and shook her head in rapid jerks. "No, no, no, no." She grabbed the phone away from Jen. "I'm sorry, ma'am. My daughter was playing on my phone again. The rascal. I apologize for wasting your time, but everything is fine. Thank you." She ended the call and handed the phone back to Jen.

"Rocky, what the hell?"

"We aren't calling the police, Jen. Not yet."

"Not yet? What do you mean not yet? We just got chased by a killer."

Rocky cocked her head. "Not a killer."

"Okay…burglar…whatever."

Rocky winced, "Well…."

"Rocky! It doesn't matter! He wanted to hurt us! We have to call the police."

"Jen, we can spend all our time stomping out flying monkeys. Or we can go straight for the wicked witch."

Jen shook her head. "You are so bad at analogies." She turned and got back in the car.

Rocky scurried around to the passenger side and jumped in as Jen started up the car. "Hear me out. Please. Please?"

Jen sighed, but nodded.

"Thank you." Rocky straightened up and sobered up. "So this guy, Mr. Victoria Street. He breaks into a string of Junior Leaguer houses and takes nothing, hurts no one. He raises the level of panic to socialite gossip level red. Right?"

Jen shrugged and nodded. "Yeah."

"And this all leads up to Waverly St. Laurent, in a moment of fear for her own safety, shooting and killing her husband."

Jen nodded. "Yes. All true."

Rocky pointed. "A husband who knew of her true identity as," she placed a finger to Jen's mouth to stop an interruption, "wait for it, no…wait for it…" Rocky leaned in dramatically. "The Rye Mother."

Jen laughed. "Rocky, Waverly St. Laurent is not the Rye Mother."

"Okay, so maybe she isn't. I don't know why she wanted her husband dead yet. Maybe money or she couldn't stand being with him anymore or something else. But," she flapped her hands at Jen to get her to stop laughing, "but! Hear me out! What was yesterday, Jen?"

Jen frowned. "I don't know. The…"

"No. Not the date."

"Oh. Tuesday." Jen looked up at her. "Tuesday. It was Tuesday. And there wasn't—"

Rocky finished the sentence with her, "Another break in." They both nodded, and Rocky continued, "Right. They've happened every Tuesday until last night. After Waverly, nothing. And for that matter, including Waverly. Because the accepted theory is not he broke into Waverly's house. It's Waverly thought he broke into her house and shot her husband."

Jen twisted her mouth and nodded. "I guess you're right."

"Jen, of course I'm right. And then Waverly herself warns us to back off the break-ins. Why?"

Jen shook her head.

"Because she's behind them. That's why." Rocky waited for a protest, but, hearing none, continued, "Waverly St. Laurent wanted to kill her husband—and no, I don't know why…yet, but she wanted him dead—so she hired Mr. Victoria Street to break into houses of meek and mild Junior League sustainers to create a panic. Then, when it came her turn to become victim of a break-in, she shoots her husband in an act of mistaken identity and self-defense."

Jen swallowed any doubt for a moment. "Okay. So let's pretend you're right for a second. Why does any of this mean we shouldn't call the police?"

Rocky grinned and nodded. "Oh, Jen. We just shook the apple tree. Now it's time to line up with a basket and—"

Jen held a hand up. "Rocky."

Rocky nodded and lost the grin. "Bad at analogies, yeah, I heard it. Couldn't stop it, but I heard it. We tracked the guy to his house. His next logical step is to go running back to Waverly and let her know what happened. And here's the thing, I can't prove any of this. Waverly is clean. For now. But whatever she does next? There's the proof."

Jen nodded. "And what if whatever she does next is to have us killed?"

Rocky stared off and nodded thoughtfully. "Huh. Okay, I can see a flaw in the plan. Maybe not a flaw, but a crack. Hairline crack, at worst. I will admit, there is a fraction of a chance Waverly St. Laurent has us killed."

Jen laughed maniacally.

Rocky waved her hands in Jen's face. "But, Jen! Jen, Jen, hear me out. The fraction of a chance is because there is a fraction of a chance Waverly St. Laurent is—"

"Don't say it."

"The Rye Mother."

"I said don't say it, Rocky. You sound crazy."

"Crazy like a fox."

Jen shook her head. "So if we don't call the police, what do we do? Assuming we live long enough to do whatever nonsense you're about to suggest."

"Well, I need more information. And I may need some help to get it. Like the kind of help your sister can provide."

"Lexi? What the hell kind of help can Lexi provide?"

"She still comes in town every Wednesday and Thursday, right?"

Jen nodded. "Yeah, she's got her practicum at a clinic in town. She spends the night at Mom and Dad's. Drives back Thursday night or early Friday morning."

"Perfect. I may need her help. But in the meantime, I need you to take us home. I need to pay a visit to my Uncle Jim."

Rocky and Jen continued to walk back over the same theory on the drive back to Jen's car. After separating, Rocky made a quick call to her Uncle Jim. Rocky's Uncle Jim and Aunt Jeanie lived sort of between Palermo and Texarkana. Their house sat within Texarkana city limits, but in an older neighborhood off Highway 82 headed out of town. A series of quiet roads and cul-de-sacs snaked and stretched out into the woods between 82 and Highway 196, which sliced right through Palermo. So Jim and Jeanie moved out of Palermo, but, as the crow flies (as Palermans would say), they had only gone about a couple hundred yards. However, without a cut through from 196, Rocky's fifteen-minute drive there gave her time to think of a reason to be showing up on her uncle's doorstep asking about Jason St. Laurent.

Jeanie greeted her at the door. "Rocky! Come here and let me hug your neck."

"Hey, Aunt Jeanie. How are y'all?"

Jeanie squeezed Rocky's head. "Oh, we're just old, retired, and worthless, sweetie. Can I pour you some iced tea?"

"Yes, ma'am. Thank you." Rocky followed her into the kitchen and watched as she poured tea from the pitcher always perched and ready on her aunt's kitchen table. As always, she adorned the glass with a pink bendy straw dropped down through the ice. When Rocky was a kid, her Aunt Jeanie used to assign a color to all of the cousins so everyone could identify their drink. Rocky always held a firm grip on the color pink, no matter how much any female cousins protested. Rocky sat with her Aunt Jeanie at the kitchen table, sipping sweet tea and listening to updates on various relatives. She then had to give Jeanie a recap of her recent divorce. Each and every detail elicited a gasp from Jeanie, who seemed to be struggling to believe anything so scandalous could happen to her own kin.

After managing to collect herself, Jeanie asked, "Well, I'm sorry, Rocky. Here I am jabbering and forcing you to relive the whole nightmare of troubles you've been through. I didn't even ask what brings you by. I mean, I do love to get to put my eyes on you, but I'm sure there's some reason for your visit."

"Yes, ma'am, there is. As much as I love to visit, I'll admit, there is something specific I came to ask about." Rocky glanced around. "Is Uncle Jim around? I'm working on a little research project, and I ran across something I think he'll be able to help me with."

Jeanie slapped at Rocky's knee. "Sweetheart, are you ever going to stop getting these degrees? How many will this make? Four? Five?"

Rocky nodded and danced around a lie, "Six."

Jeanie whistled to herself as she stood up to go rouse Jim from elsewhere in the house.

Jim soon came into the kitchen alone and went through a very similar song and dance greeting with Rocky—hugs and small talk and a much shorter recap of the divorce, more focused on "how you're holding up" than on "what did that so-and-so do to you." After the requisite formalities, Jim poured himself some tea and sat down across the table from Rocky. He took one long sip and let out an "Ahhh" with a smack of his lips. "So, Jeanie says you're working on a paper of some sort."

Rocky moved her head from side to side. "You could say it's something like a paper, sure." She winced in hesitation. "I'm afraid the topic is a little morbid, to be honest."

Jim's eyebrows raised. "Oh yeah? So not an education class?"

Rocky shook her head. "No, sir. This is not for an education class." She grinned to herself, happy for the brief respite from her lie of omission. "I'm working on a little research project dealing with the Rye Mother."

Jim shook his head. "Mm, mm, mm. Dark stuff." He looked up, his face lighter. "You picking up a history degree? You know how I love history."

Rocky smiled and nodded. "Oh, I do. I know you're quite the history buff. Especially local lore, right?"

Jim held out his hands in a motion of humble brag. "I've done my fair share of poking around. Now, I'm usually drawn to lighter topics, but I can appreciate the importance of a story like the Rye Mother in our local history."

Rocky held out a hand in agreement. "I completely agree. Unfortunate, but important. Which is exactly why I knew you'd be more than willing to help when I found out you have a tiny little role in this story."

He frowned at her for a beat, and then nodded once and chuckled. "You're talking about Jason? Well, I had a tiny role, that's for sure. But I did know Jason. And Bo and Waverly. They helped out quite a bit. Always more than willing to donate when I needed something up at the school. I paid for quite a few coats with St. Laurent money every winter."

Rocky nodded. "So I read correctly? You were the principal at Jason's school when he went missing."

Jim's face grew somber. "And when they found his remains. Tough times. We had counselors cycling through daily. Those kids were pretty torn up over the ordeal."

"I would imagine. And before they found his remains?"

Jim shrugged. "Before? Oh, well, that was a different time, keep in mind. People weren't jumping to the worst possible conclusion right away. Everyone got concerned and scared, but I don't think any of us expected the worst. And, as horrible as this is to say, we'd had kids go missing before. They'd slip away for a couple of days one way or another, and then always turn up at some friend's house or something. I hate to sound flippant, but, like I said, that was a far different time. This type of culture led us to need Amber Alerts and the like. We needed more of a sense of urgency, Rocky. We did. So don't misunderstand me. I'm simply telling you how it was, right or wrong."

Rocky waved her hands. "Don't worry, Uncle Jim. No judgement. Times were different. But, from the sound of things, the police were taking the disappearance pretty serious."

Jim nodded and shrugged. "Oh, yeah. I think they were. The St. Laurents were very wealthy and well-to-do. Still are. When a family like them has a problem, the police won't be dragging their feet."

"Which means they talked to you?"

He nodded. "Yes. They talked to me a couple of times. Your dad's friend Rondo worked the case. And he's a good cop. Leaves no stone unturned. I remember how much I admired his tenacity. I've investigated many issues as a principal in my day. Smaller issues, mind you, but still requiring investigation. And you can't let emotion or any preconceived notions," he cocked his head, "or even tact get in the way of finding the truth."

Rocky frowned. "Why do you say tact? Did Rondo—"

Jim shook his head. "Oh, no, no. Nothing serious. All water under the bridge now, as they say."

Rocky's eyes widened. "Are you telling me Rondo looked at you?"

"Me? Heavens no. Rondo investigated Bo and Waverly, I believe. His questions to the school seemed to be designed to rule out the parents."

"How so?"

"Well, like I said, it didn't matter in the long run. All was forgotten when they found Jason." Jim shook his head and tsked. "Those poor, poor people."

"But what were the questions?"

Jim frowned, remembering. "Well, Jason had some issues right before he went missing." He held his palms up, dismissing them. "Coincidental, mind you. Turned out the poor boy just had a rough fate and bad luck, I suppose. But, yes, in the days, maybe a week or two, leading up to his disappearance, we experienced some problems. Nothing major. Nothing the boy did wrong."

Rocky shook her head. "Then what kind of problems?"

Jim hesitated. "Well, I hate to even say, since it turned out to be unrelated to his death, but a teacher reported some odd behavior in Jason."

"What kind of odd behavior?"

"Jason grew very withdrawn and almost depressed. He exhibited behavior we would associate with abuse, to be honest."

Rocky recoiled. "You thought the St. Laurents were abusing Jason?"

Jim frowned and shook his head. "Now, I'm not saying abuse. His teacher was concerned. Just concerned. The first step would be to schedule a meeting with the parents and learn if anything happened to cause strange behavior."

"But you didn't get to?"

"No. His teacher reported his behavior to me the day before he went missing. I planned on watching him myself for a day before contacting his parents. I wanted to hear from more than one witness to the behavior before the meeting."

"And did you?"

Jim nodded. "I did. And she was right. He acted very strange. In fact, I called Waverly the afternoon of his disappearance and scheduled a meeting for the next day. Of course, as you know, we never got to hold that meeting."

"And this all interested Rondo?"

"At first, sure. It interested his partner even more. I'm afraid his poker face wasn't too great. He suspected Bo early on."

"Suspected Bo of what?"

Jim shrugged. "I think they viewed Bo as the disciplinarian in the St. Laurent household. And back then, being a disciplinarian meant you maybe got a little rough from time to time. There weren't many rods spared in those days."

Rocky frowned. "Yeah, but why would being strict cast suspicion on you? Spanking to killing is a big leap."

Jim laughed. "Oh, I couldn't agree more. I thought they were being rash and borderline irresponsible. But, as I said before, I respect an effort to explore every angle. No stone and all." He shook his head. "But after what those poor parents went through, I thank the Lord those suspicions went no further than they did. As far as I know the investigation ended with a few questions to people like me. They found Jason before too long and those depressing theories were laid to rest with that sweet little boy."

Rocky nodded respectfully. "What about his teacher? Is she still around?"

Jim nodded and pointed over his shoulder. "Oh yeah. She's back there folding sheets, I think."

Rocky frowned and shook her head. "What?"

Jim turned back and yelled, "Jeanie? You still around?"

Jeanie's voice called out from the other room, "Yep. Folding sheets."

Jim turned back to Rocky and pointed again. "Yep. Folding sheets."

Rocky blinked in flutters. "Are you telling me Aunt Jeanie taught Jason St. Laurent the year he died?"

Jim nodded. "Oh yeah. Year before, too. She looped up with his group. Taught them both years, and taught the rest of them the next year, too."

After several painstaking minutes of getting Jeanie and Jim at the same table, rehashing the same set of basic details, and wading through all of the near-tears and wistful memories, Rocky sat in front of her aunt and leaned across the table. "Aunt Jeanie, can you tell me what about Jason's behavior made you feel the need to report suspicions of abuse?"

Jeanie clutched at a ragged tissue she turned to multiple times throughout the conversation. "Well, the rapid change more than anything. Jason was always such a happy boy. He had friends and most everyone liked him. Of course, no one wanted to miss out on an invitation to a St. Laurent birthday party or swim party or whatever the season may hold. That helped his popularity, I'm sure." She laughed at the memory. "But those kids loved Jason. He was the center of the playground. King of the mountain and all. Until right before…it happened."

"What changed?"

Jeanie shook her head. "I have no idea. I first noticed a change right after we did health screenings. You know, vision and hearing? With the nurse? We did them every year. And honestly, I thought maybe they told him he needed glasses. I've seen kids get upset over less. But pretty soon, when his odd behavior kept up, I knew there was more going on."

Jim slurped at the last of his tea. "Never got glasses."

Jeanie shook her head. "Nope. Never did. Like I said, more going on. He started keeping to himself at recess. His friends made comments about how he would take off right after school. They liked to hang around for a little—maybe play at the park or something. But Jason quit hanging around. His grades slipped. He seemed despondent. I couldn't help but wonder."

Rocky nodded along. "But why abuse? Why did you suspect abuse, specifically?"

Jeanie cocked her head. "Well, I'll admit, abuse was maybe a bit of a leap. Around the same time, Jason grew very angry with his father."

"How did you know?"

"He wrote a few things—and I'm sorry, I can't remember specifics—but they displayed a lot of anger. And in the front of our journals, we pasted a questionnaire. One of the questions was, 'Who is your hero?' Jason had put his father, but during the week before he died, he scribbled that out. Maybe it wasn't enough, but I had to say something. I reported my concerns to Jim at first because I didn't see any evidence of actual abuse. Just concerns."

Rocky addressed both of them, "What about the nurse?"

Jim and Jeanie shook their heads, confused.

"The nurse? The one who did the screenings? Did she notice any signs of abuse?"

Jeanie looked at Jim, who shook his head. "No. She didn't report anything. And I feel certain she would. Good woman."

Jeanie patted at the table in front of him. "Oh, but Jimmy, remember? Nurse Hill was out the year Jason died. She had a baby."

Jim nodded. "That's right. We had to call in some local nurses from the clinic." He snapped his fingers. "In fact, Bo helped me find someone. He sent some of his staff over to help us out. Sent an older African-American lady to check vision and a young blonde girl to check hearing." He stared off. "Yeah, I remember. Real looker."

Jeanie slapped his arm.

Jim shrugged. "I can't notice when a woman is attractive to the eyes?"

Jeanie frowned. "You can't talk about her twenty years later, no." Jeanie turned to Rocky and shook her head. "I suppose you heard plenty of comments like that with Chet, didn't you, dear?"

Rocky shrugged. "Well, to be fair, Chet would be off boning the pregnant nurse."

Chapter 20

A Wednesday shouldn't even register to a summertime Rocky Champagnolle. But, waking up the next day, Rocky remembered that on some Wednesdays, Frank Champagnolle met what he referred to as some "old buddies" at Ye Old Burger Shoppe for lunch. Rocky passed on the burger, but she grabbed a table, ordered a grilled cheese, and waited in the hopes one of those buddies would be Rondo Singer.

Rocky had long finished her sandwich and sipped on her third glass of tea when Rondo walked in. She put down a paperback and eyed Rondo as he made the rounds, glad-handing almost every person in the diner. A waiter hurried by, pointing at Rondo and checking with a point if he wanted his usual Coke. Rondo pointed back with a nod, and then noticed Rocky.

Rocky pushed a chair out with her foot and smiled up at Rondo. "Mr. Singer. How are you today?"

Rondo squinted at her. "I'm good. I'm good. Now, usually when I catch lunch with a Champagnolle in this burger shop, he picks up the check."

Rocky smiled and whipped a credit card out of her purse. "Well, seeing as how that particular Champagnolle has made the mistake of giving this one his credit card, I suppose he still can."

Rondo settled in across from Rocky, motioning to the waiter where to bring his Coke. Rondo settled in, removing his pageboy cap and placing it in the seat next to him. "Now, what makes me think you came here to talk about Waverly St. Laurent?"

Rocky smiled and gave Rondo time to order a bacon cheeseburger and spicy fries. "You are a detective. Nothing gets past you, huh?"

Rondo grunted. "What did this woman do to you, girl?"

"It's not about her. I promise. Not directly, at least." Rocky bowed her head. "I will admit, at first, yes. I hoped to find dirt on Waverly St. Laurent. Now? I'm curious. Call this a summer project. The more rocks I turn over the more buggy this whole thing gets."

Rondo snorted. "You telling me. Shit was always buggy. Everything about the Jason St. Laurent case."

Rocky raised her eyebrows. "So we can talk about the case? Not Waverly…directly. Just…the case."

Rondo spread a napkin on his lap and cleared room for his plate of a teetering, greasy burger and fries spilling off the side onto the table. "You paying. I suppose you get to pick the topic of conversation."

"Well, I talked to Uncle Jim and Aunt Jeanie. They told me about the report on Jason right before he died."

Rondo nodded while chewing. "Yeah. Never got to follow through, though."

Rocky nodded. "Because of the Rye—"

Rondo raised an eyebrow.

Rocky raised her hands. "Sorry, sorry. Because of the way you found Jason, I mean."

He eyed her and swallowed, but answered, "Yeah, I guess so. I mean, I don't know who killed them kids, but I know who didn't. So yeah, all suspicion on either of the parents went out the window when we found the body. Or what was left of the body."

"And there is no way either of the St. Laurents could be involved in Jason's murder?"

Rondo laughed. "Man, you don't let up, do you?"

"I'm just making certain."

"No. Ain't no way. When Jason disappeared, both the mom and the dad were accounted for. As in, different city accounted for. The St. Laurents had some house help supposed to meet Jason at home and stay with him until they got back from a trip to," Rondo tapped at his bald head, "New Orleans, I think."

"Alibis checked out?"

Rondo laughed again. "Yes, Rocky. Whoever took Jason, it ain't his father and it damn sure ain't his mother. Sorry to disappoint you."

Rocky frowned. "So why all the attention early on? And you even said your partner liked the dad for the murder. Why did any of that make sense if they both had alibis?"

"I paid attention because I thought the kid had run away. I figured Daddy got a little too rough and Jason split. I had a couple of guys you'd call my partners on this case, I guess. And yeah, one got tunnel vision for Bo St. Laurent. Shit like that happens. You zero in on somebody and nothing shakes you off. Not an alibi, not nothing. He didn't know what he thought. He just didn't feel right about the

dad. But even he backed down when Jason tied back to the serial case. Somewhat."
Rondo grinned. "He kept checking the life insurance right up until he died. Just in case."

"What about the other one?"

Rondo frowned. "Other what?"

"You said you had two partners on the case. What did the other one think?"

Rondo laughed. "Oh. Face?" He shook his head at the memory and wiped at his mouth with a napkin. "Patterson Lord Fillmore, the third. Looked like the guy on *The A-Team* they called Face. So we started calling him Face. I don't even remember what we called him before Face. Would've been sometime after this case we started up with the nickname. But Face was always the same. Good cop, but he chased skirts a little more than leads, if you get my meaning." He waved a hand between them. "No offense or nothing. But that's Face for you. He would follow up any lead taking him back to talk to the cute nurse or the receptionist or neighbor. Seems to me he was working one at Bo St. Laurent's clinic, one at the school, hell, even one at the trailer park."

"Did he have any theories?"

"Face didn't collect theories. He collected phone numbers." Rondo laughed at his own joke.

"Is Face still alive?"

Rondo nodded. "Oh yeah. Ain't changed one bit."

"Do you think he'd talk to me about his memories of the case?"

Rondo raised an eyebrow at her. "As much as I hate to say this, cause you like a daughter to me…looking the way you do? Yeah," he rolled his eyes and shook his head, picking at one last fry, "Face'll love to talk to you."

Rondo wasn't wrong. An hour later, when Rocky tracked down Patterson "Face" Fillmore in a coffee shop across from the courthouse, he welcomed her into the booth across from him and even offered to buy her a drink. When Rocky told him she didn't drink coffee, he informed her he wasn't talking about coffee. To which she used a polite smile to stifle a gag.

Face Fillmore looked just as Rondo described him. He was late fifties, a few years younger than Rondo and Frank Champagnolle. He had a full head of dark brown hair flipped over into a silky wave across one ear. The other side ruffled, like he ran his hand through his locks over and over again all morning. His face held onto sharp angles, though time wrinkled and sagged them a touch. He wore a tan sport coat with a light blue shirt unbuttoned a few down and tieless and dark gray pants. A knit navy tie lay tied and ready to slip on beside him.

His smile may have faded to an off-white over the years, but even Rocky would admit she could see how the grin won him a couple of phone numbers. "So you're Frank Champagnolle's daughter, huh?"

Rocky flashed a winning smile right back at him and framed her face with her hands. "Yes, sir, I sure am."

He winked at her. "I suppose I should behave myself then?"

Rocky winked right back. "Oh, I'll bet you're always on your best behavior."

Face laughed. "So what can I do for you, Little Champagnolle?"

"I'm doing some research into an old case you worked with my Uncle Rondo." Rocky made sure to use the familiar term with Rondo to give the old hornball one more deterrent.

He sucked a breath in through his teeth. "Whew. Me and Rondo. A lot of cases, sweetheart. Which one? I'll see if I can remember."

"Jason St. Laurent."

The grin left Face's face. He nodded once. "I remember."

"Any theories?"

Face laughed and gave a condescending shrug. "Theories? The way I recall, we didn't get much time to develop many theories. As soon as they tied Jason to the serial case, they chased us right off."

"What about before then?"

He shook his head. "There wasn't much before then. Everything happened pretty fast. And I was young. So young. They had me doing interviews. Canvassing, we call it."

Rocky nodded. "Rondo said you had a way of," she paused, rolling her head around, "seeking out female interview subjects?"

Face laughed loudly. "He would. The asshole. You tell Detective Singer I picked up some good leads on the St. Laurent case before it went serial."

Rocky frowned. "Like what? Do you remember?"

He frowned, thinking back. "Well, the one I remember most was one I tried to track down right before they found the body. There was a connection. Between Trailer Pines and Bo St. Laurent's office."

Rocky leaned forward. "What connection?"

Face nodded. "A nurse who worked for Dr. St. Laurent lived in Trailer Pines. She moved right around the time of the disappearance."

"Right before or right after?"

He cocked his head. "Well, I never found out. Place like Trailer Pines kept shoddy records, so she could've left anywhere in a five or six day span. And that sounds fishy, I know. But people moved in and out of those places all the time. Still, the connection piqued my interest."

Rocky shook her head. "But you didn't get to follow up?"

"Kind of. We passed all our stuff on to the serial squad. I flagged her, of course. And I checked back. But the woman's alibi checked out for all the previous murders. And they could pinpoint about the time Jason's body got dumped. She checked out then, too."

"Do you remember her name?"

Face strained to remember but shook his head. "No. Sorry. Real cute. But I'm sure Rondo told you she was just my type, didn't he?"

Rocky grinned sheepishly. "Something like that."

The talk slid into trash talk about Rondo and stories of run-ins Face had with Frank Champagnolle over the years. In short, Rondo was an ass and Frank was salt of the earth. They chatted until Face finished his cup of coffee. As he drained the last sip, he reached for his tie and adjusted the slipshod knot as he told Rocky, "Well, I hate to run out on you, but I'm due in court. Tell your dad I said hi, will you?" He paused and glanced back over his shoulder. "And kick Rondo in the shin." He smiled and left.

Once outside the coffee shop with a bag of donut holes for her troubles, Rocky started for her car, keys in hand. The little black Lexus angled toward her in a parking spot on Broad Street about three buildings down. Before she took three steps, Rocky noticed a man loitering across Broad watching the area around her car. He filled out his suit in a frightening series of bulging muscle right up to his bald head. She recognized him from his shadowy perch behind her at Waverly St. Laurent's. Freddy Van Vleet's tough waited on Rocky in the street, watching her, following her.

They made eye contact as Rocky started to walk toward the car. Mr. Clean flicked a toothpick from his mouth and started ambling across the street to block her path to the Lexus. Rocky kept walking, calm bounces and confident strides, but panicked in her head. She scanned the street for any escape or help. The tough grinned at her not-so-subtle surveying of surroundings and leaned against the trunk of her car.

Rocky slowed down and looked to her left. She stood next to The Lonely Indian, Texarkana's oldest bar. Even in the middle of the afternoon, The Lonely Indian would have a few patrons. And more than likely, those patrons would be about as scary as Freddy Van Vleet's henchman.

She undid a button on her neckline and tucked a little skirt into the tie at her waist to raise her hemline. And she swiveled on one flat, sashaying into the bar.

Sure enough, three bikers sat at the bar. They were bearded and tattooed and burly enough to do the trick. Rocky held up the bag of donut holes and jutted out one hip. "I would be more than happy to share some of these donut holes with any gentleman willing to do me one eensy weensy little favor." Three rough, grease stained hands shot into the air.

Chapter 21

Wednesday night brought the first baking class at Elaine Maplethorpe's house. Jen led a group of five Junior Leaguers with kitchen experience through a first lesson in folding a fourth of an ounce of marijuana into a batch of brownies. Rocky added a sixth member to their student group. But, as she pointed out real quick, she was merely auditing the class. Which meant sitting on a counter and licking spoons.

As it turns out, making pot brownies isn't as simple as dumping marijuana leaves into some batter and mixing everything up. The proper way to prep for edibles is to make what's called cannabutter, which is nothing more than a stick of butter whipped together with a fourth of an ounce of finely ground cannabis buds. Elaine guided the group through the process of baking the buds for an hour or so at low heat to "decarboxylate them."

Rocky watched on as they placed the buds on a baking pan. "Decarboxylate? Is that a spell?"

Elaine laughed, "Oh, no, sweetie. Science. This is how they let off their potency. Without this step, I'm afraid you'll make nothing more than brownies with green butter."

Rocky nodded. "Yeah. My Granny used to help me decarboxylate Shrinky Dinks."

The lesson went on through the afternoon, three brownie batches, and about four bottles of wine between them. Elaine relished the opportunity to share stories of her New Member Class with the next generation. She gazed off as she spoke. "Oh, I suppose I was always the free spirit of the group. Always suggesting we go camping or," she giggled into her hand, "skinny dipping. I remember how I would drive poor Dottie crazy. Always so reserved."

One of the bakers glanced back over her shoulder while mixing a bowl of batter. "So who was the Rocky of your group?"

Another burst out laughing and shrieked, "I doubt there's ever been another Rocky."

Rocky scrunched up her face in annoyance, but Elaine shook her head, "No, no. We had our Rocky, all right."

Rocky shot a look at her, and Elaine smiled. "Irreverent and witty. Brilliant and brash. Always there with a retort or a takedown of some pompous ass who thought he could pick one of us up."

Everyone stopped and turned, asking in unison, "Who?"

Elaine smiled at Rocky. "Waverly St. Laurent."

Jen howled with laughter. Rocky went into full meerkat face and shook her head. Elaine just nodded. "It's true, I'm afraid. I know she can be a pill as a grumpy old woman, but as a young lady, I can see a lot of similarities between the two of you."

Jen clapped. "This is the best thing I ever heard. Please. Please. Tell us exactly how they were alike."

Elaine twirled a wooden spoon in the air and thought back to a young Waverly with a smile enveloping her whole face. "Many, many ways. Waverly, like our Rocky here, was a beautiful woman. Striking and always so classy. Waverly didn't boast your figure, I'm afraid."

Rocky grumbled, "So like a skinny me. Great. Thanks."

Elaine grinned off the comment. "No, no, now. She was a stick. Waverly St. Laurent would kill for an ass like yours, hon. But the charisma." She shook her head and closed her eyes. "Wow. You both radiate brilliant auras. Magnetic charisma. Everyone wants to be near you. Waverly was the same. We gravitated toward her. Like planets to a sun. She always glowed a little brighter than the rest of us. Had more," she cocked her head, "gravity to her, I suppose."

Jen leaned in next to Rocky, elbowing Rocky's knee and enjoying the hell out of the conversation. "So Waverly was funny?"

Elaine recoiled. "Funny? She was hilarious. I know she just comes across bitter and mean now, but in our day, she kept us rolling." She pointed at Rocky to pull her from her pout. "But I'll say this for you, dear. Waverly never had the balls to leave her husband."

Rocky shot back alert and squinted at Elaine. "Why would she leave her husband?"

Elaine waved off the question. "Same old reason, honey. Same old reason."

"What reason?"

"Same as yours, I think," Elaine shrugged. "Bo always ran around on her."

Rocky leaned forward. "Bo cheated on Waverly?"

"Lord, yes. Many times." Elaine took a swig of wine. "I'll bet he screwed every nurse who ever worked for him."

"Well," Rocky nodded along and held out her glass for a toast, "I definitely know how that feels."

Elaine met her glass. "Damn right. And you kicked him to the curb. Good for you, girl! I can't tell you how many times we tried to get Waverly to do the same. They weren't married a year before she caught him the first time. Nurses, secretaries, maids, nannies—"

"Nannies?" Rocky held her glass to her mouth and paused.

Elaine nodded. "Yep. Two of them. Waverly fired one and then he still screwed the new one. Hell, I remember one time when Waverly had to stay in the hospital after her surgery for endometriosis, for God's sake, she hired a maid to look after the house while she was gone. And guess what happened?"

Rocky cocked an eyebrow. "He screwed her?"

Elaine shook her head. "Nope. He screwed her." She waved her glass around, sloshing wine. "All over the place."

"This was all before Jason?"

Elaine swallowed and lost her smile. "Yes. All before Jason." She drained the rest of her wine. "Oh, I'm sure Bo continued to screw anything with tits who would smile at him. But Waverly changed after Jason died. She lost all her fire. Whatever hope she had of kicking Bo out died with Jason. She was never the same after Jason."

Rocky nodded. "So after Jason died, she became the miserable old cunt we know today?"

Jen elbowed Rocky, but Elaine shook her off. "No, she's right. That's pretty accurate. Waverly was always cynical and sarcastic and borderline mean. Just in a funny way. Like Rocky. After Jason, all she had left was the cynicism and the bite. Which stopped being funny." She nodded and stared into space. "She became a raging cunt."

Rocky smiled at Jen, who rolled her eyes. A burning aroma and a fog settled in around them, slicing the smell of baked brownies which filled the kitchen. Jen spun away from Rocky. "Shit!"

Everyone scrambled around to clear a path for a burning pan of brownies. Rocky snarked, "What you get for laughing about me being like Waverly St. Laurent."

"Shut up, Rocky!" Jen squawked back over her shoulder as she fumbled with potholders.

Elaine flipped on a fan and waved at the smoke with a magazine. "Don't you worry, Jennifer. We distracted you with our jabbering. You're ready to bake to your heart's content."

One of the other girls said, "So all we need now is a supply."

They all eyed Rocky, who raised her eyebrows and shrugged. "I said I'd take care of it, didn't I? I'm meeting my guy as soon as I leave here."

Jen rolled her eyes. "Your guy?"

Rocky nodded and studied a fingernail. "Yes. I have a guy."

On the way to the car, after a lengthy set of goodbyes with Elaine, Rocky asked one of the girls (Brittney from the visit to Rocky's classroom), "What about our other endeavor?"

Brittney sighed. "Well, we are making progress, but this isn't as easy as we expected."

"Why not?"

"Well," Brittney explained, "apparently no doctor is going around writing scripts for his own kid. They get a colleague to do it. So we need to find a doctor's wife to pair up with another doctor's wife."

Rocky shrugged. "Shouldn't be too hard."

Brittney nodded. "No, you're right. We've matched two sets. Plus we found three moms who think their kids get twice as much as they need. Just takes time."

"So what does all that mean?"

"About three hundred Adderall are coming our way. Eventually."

Rocky slapped her on the shoulder. "Three hundred ain't too shabby, Brittney. Keep up the good work."

As Rocky and Jen climbed into Jen's car, Jen glanced over and said, "Her name's not Brittney, you know?"

"Jen, you overestimate my ability to give a fuck. They're all Brittney."

"And since when do you have a guy?"

Rocky bobbed her head around and shrugged, but Jen glowered at her until she caved. "Since I caught my dad smoking a joint and forced him to fork over his supplier."

Jen gasped. "Frank Champagnolle smokes pot?" She blinked and looked around. "What is happening? Fred would blow a gasket."

Fred Champagnolle was Jen's father and Frank's twin brother. They were not identical in any way. Frank was short and built pretty solid, like a fullback. Fred was tall and lean, wiry and country strong. Frank picked up every sociable gene in the Champagnolle line—the gift of gab and the discernment of a politician as to when to use it. Fred was stoic and much preferred the company of a few cows and a cattle dog. But Fred picked up all the morality left in the Champagnolle genetic gas tank. And those respective qualities were passed on accordingly to Rocky and Jen.

Rocky laughed and shook her head. "Well, Fred isn't going to find out about this. Frank isn't even going to find out why I wanted it. As far as he's concerned, I got a couple of joints to dull the pain of my divorce."

"And what did you actually get?"

Rocky shrugged. "Enough for about twenty batches of brownies."

"You got," Jen started in a scream, but finished with a whisper. "You got five ounces of marijuana?"

Rocky held up a finger. "I got five ounces of premium marijuana." She waggled the finger. "At a discount."

Jen closed her eyes and shook her head. "How? Who is this guy? You aren't going alone, are you?"

"No, of course not. You're taking me."

"What? Since when?"

Rocky glanced at her ornate gold watch. "Since I realized I'm almost late." She pointed toward the road. "If you could just drive me downtown to the alley behind the newspaper offices, that would be great."

Jen grumbled, but started driving. "This is unbelievable, Rocky. You are taking me to a drug deal. In an alley. What happened to Steve Jobs' cynical cousin?"

Rocky frowned at her. "Steve Jobs didn't drive, Jen. Everyone knows that."

"I don't think that's true. Who is this guy, anyway?"

"He's a reporter my dad knows. You won't believe this, but his name is—"

"Hi Hallmark?"

Rocky reeled back in shock. "How did you know his name?"

Jen laughed. "Hi Hallmark sells pot? Oh my god."

"How do you know this man?"

Jen looked at her incredulously. "Rocky, Hi Hallmark is one of your dad's oldest friends. He and Hi and Rondo go back to grade school, I think."

Rocky's mouth dropped open. "You know Rondo?"

"Of course I know Rondo, Rocky. He came to every one of your birthday parties. He came to Thanksgiving one year after his mom died. He picked us up from school when our parents took their trip to Germany."

Rocky nodded along, squinting at memories.

Jen shook her head. "How do you live so oblivious to everyone and everything around you?"

Rocky took a deep breath through her nose. "It is a struggle. Takes constant dedication."

Jen agreed to drop Rocky around the corner from the alley so Hi wouldn't get nervous about including extra people in this part of the plan. Rocky left her purse in the car after extracting an envelope full of cash. She paused and pulled something else out of her purse. "Oh, I almost forgot." She handed Jen a folded document.

Jen took the paper with a perplexed scowl. "What is this?" She unfolded and studied a series of numbers. "Rocky, is this an invoice?"

"No rush."

"This is an invoice? A bill. You created an actual bill to give to the Junior League New Member Class treasurer—"

Rocky nodded along, pointing at the end. "Which is you."

"Yes, me. But you made a bill for," Jen studied the category labels, "overhead expenses and baking supplies."

"Both accurate."

"We're going to jail."

Without further comment, Rocky strutted off in the direction of the alley, her dress swishing behind her with every step. When she rounded the corner, Hi waited by a door into the newspaper offices. He leaned up against a brick wall with a paper bag folded into a roll and tucked under one arm. When he saw her, he smiled. "I thought maybe you wised up."

"Not yet, but I'm twenty-eight. There's always time."

"Probably what Hank Williams thought, too."

"I've never bought drugs in an alley, but I expected less talk about country music."

Hi laughed and shrugged. "Everyone always says that." He tapped his bag in the palm of a hand. "And for future reference, don't telegraph it so much. People will think you're wearing a wire."

Rocky glanced down at herself and held her hands out to draw attention to a clingy summer dress. "Not in this dress, they won't."

Hi snorted and handed her the bag, taking the envelope of money at the same time. "Or they won't care? Is that your whole plan?"

Rocky winked. "My plan is to look good enough to not need a plan."

"Yeah, and if I were twenty years younger and not like an uncle to you, I'm sure that would work."

Rocky shook her head. "Nah. I'm awkward as fuck when it counts." She pointed to the envelope. "Are we all good here?"

Hi glanced at the bills bulging out and frowned. "Yeah. I'm not going to count it in front of you. If you're short, I'll just call your father."

"No different from how I got my prom dress." Rocky started away and stopped. "You know, I talked to my aunt and uncle about Jason St. Laurent."

Hi raised his eyebrows. "Oh yeah? Turn up anything interesting?"

Rocky tapped a finger on her chin. "They said the year Jason went missing the school nurse went out on maternity leave. And they did screenings just a couple weeks before everything happened, so they filled in with local nurses."

"Oh yeah?"

"Yeah. From Bo St. Laurent's clinic."

Hi frowned. "Oh yeah? Did they describe any—"

Rocky nodded and cut him off. "Cute blonde?"

Hi's faced betrayed something very interesting to him. He thought back. "If I'm remembering correctly, Detective Fillmore found a nurse from Bo St. Laurent's clinic who—"

"Lived at Trailer Pines?" Rocky nodded. "Yeah. I talked to him, too."

Hi smiled. "You've been busy."

Rocky shrugged. "Interesting case."

"And one that'll suck you in, girl. Be careful."

Rocky flashed her winning smile. "Always."

As they started to walk away from one another, Hi stopped in the doorway to his offices. "I wouldn't get too swayed by anything Fillmore says. He's a good detective, but—"

"Has a thing for the ladies?"

Hi laughed. "I see you talked to Rondo, too."

Rocky nodded. "Twice."

"Yep." Hi started through the door. "I don't know what the girl from the trailer park looked like, but if the nurse from the school was a cute blonde? Well, then she's just Fillmore's type."

Chapter 22

Rocky met Jen at Jen's parents' house, which meant going back there to pick up the Lexus. Which meant going in to say hello to her aunt and uncle. With a bag full of pot in her tiny purse. This, of course, made Jen an absolute wreck. All throughout Rocky's lengthy retelling of her divorce hearing and the events leading up to the separation and how she'd been doing since then, Jen alternated between sweating in a corner of her parents' kitchen and trying to usher Rocky out the door.

Jen's mother and Rocky's aunt, Diane, shushed Jen, "Jennifer, will you stop! What's the hurry?"

Rocky swatted Jen's hand away from her hold on Rocky's elbow. "No hurry at all, Aunt Diane. I love catching up with y'all. Feels like forever since I got to just sit and chat with somebody."

Jen mumbled, "That is literally all you do. All day long. Every day."

Rocky laughed. "You know Jen. Just like when we were kids. She gets tired of me and wants me to go home. You remember my sixth or seventh birthday party? The one we had here when Uncle Fred took us on the hayride? Jen started asking if 'Rocky could go home, please,' because she didn't want me to get any of your chocolate chip cookies." She looked at Jen, "Remember, Jen?"

Jen pursed her lips. "The feeling is coming back to me now, yes."

Rocky turned back to Diane. "I did love those cookies. Oh, it's been ages since I've gotten to taste those. Best chocolate chip cookies in the world. I've claimed that all my life."

Jen mumbled, "This is the first time I ever heard you say any of these things."

Diane beamed. "Well," she jumped up, "I can make some right now."

Jen mumbled, "Of course you can."

Rocky put a hand to her heart. "Oh, I don't want to put you out."

Diane waved off her objection. "Nonsense. No trouble at all. Do you have time?"

Rocky nodded. "There's nowhere I'd rather be." She plopped her purse down in the middle of the kitchen table, causing Jen to choke trying to swallow whatever she had been about to say next.

For the next thirty minutes, Jen wiped sweat from her brow as she kept her eyes locked on Rocky's purse, but all three Champagnolle women sat and swapped memories and laughed. And then, as if she planned it, just as the timer went off for the cookies, Alexandria Champagnolle burst into the kitchen like a Broadway diva doing a curtain call. She carried two matching Louis Vuitton overnight bags from a much larger luggage set and she hoisted them onto the kitchen table, pushing Rocky's purse onto the floor. Diane Champagnolle almost dropped her pan of cookies trying to place them aside. She squealed, "Lexi!" in glee and ran to grab Alexandria around the neck. Rocky grinned. Jen fumed.

The life of Rocky's cousins included countless scenes like this. The three girls—Rocky, Jennifer, and Alexandria—grew up as close as sisters, which meant they hated one another for about twenty years. Sometime during college, things started to turn around, and, as adults, they would all name each other as their best friends. But also like sisters, they couldn't be more different. Jen was the oldest by a couple of years over Rocky, who was a year older than Lexi. In the Champagnolle line, all of the compassion, all of the charity and heart and philanthropic spirit passed right down to Jen. With zero leftover for Rocky or Lexi. Jen resembled Frank Champagnolle's daughter more than Rocky did. While they were both black-haired, short, and curvy, Jen had the dark complexion and dark eyes the Champagnolles were once known for. Jen and Rocky had similar family smiles and the inherited beauty of the Champagnolle line. Going back as long as there were records, Champagnolle women were known as town hotties—whichever town they may inhabit: Palermo, Texarkana, or all the way back to the little French village of Le Chambon-sur-Lignon where one of their great-grandmothers came from. The big difference between the physical appearance of Jen as compared to Rocky or Lexi was Jen's level of give a fuck. While Rocky grew annoyed by the amount of attention paid to her due to appearance, Jen took things a step further. She spent a large portion of her life rejecting physical attention hard—preferring to carve out paths for herself with other things, whether kindness or creativity or sheer work ethic. Rocky leaned on wit and intellect, but, at the same time, never looked a gift flirt in the mouth.

Lexi? Well, Lexi bathed in any type of approval and appreciation. Lexi reached a level of driven the other two never quite reached. She leaned into the bit and made for first in any race she entered. And to Lexi, everything was a race. Lexi Champagnolle would be the prettiest girl in the room no matter what it took. If that meant waking up at four in the morning to exercise, done. If someone possessed more natural beauty, then Lexi would be sure to wear the best makeup or dress or jewelry. Something always set her apart. She made the best grades in school, earned the best rating as an employee, snagged the cutest boyfriend, bought the nicest car, claimed the best of anything and everything she came into contact with. This drive made her come home from Conway to Texarkana once a week—a three-hour drive—just to finish her residency a semester early. Lexi worked as a nurse for less than a year before starting the process of becoming a nurse practitioner. Being a nurse was fine. She just set out to make sure she became the best nurse at the top of the possibilities of the profession.

So, like everything else in her life, Lexi approached being a daughter as a competition, too. Jen accused her of even willing herself to look more like their mother—slender, with red hair and dark, puppy dog eyes. Lexi seemed to form herself into the epitome of what Diane Champagnolle envisioned in a daughter, while Jen spent a lifetime trailblazing a unique path for herself. Rocky lived the life of the introvert pretending to be an extrovert. Jen: the extrovert living like an introvert. Lexi was two hundred percent extrovert all the time. She lived with both hands in the air and her tits out.

And every time she came home, her visits turned into The Lexi Show. On a normal Wednesday night, Jen would make herself scarce, opting to catch up with her sister later, when not around their mother. But Rocky orchestrated this. She needed to ensure some facetime with Lexi.

After an hour of family talk around cookies and milk, Rocky got what she was after. Diane left for bed with a grumpy frown at a bottle of Cupcake Moscato Lexi brought as a present for Jen. The wine had been chilling in the fridge the whole time and Lexi broke out the bottle along with three glasses for the younger generation. They all knew alcohol would drive Diane to bed, as she was a staunch teetotaler.

Jen pushed the glass away from her. "Lexi, you know I don't even like this shit. You bring it as a present to me so Mom gives me the evil eye for drinking instead of you."

Lexi laughed to Rocky. "What? I thought you loved this stuff." She winked and poured a glass for herself and one for Rocky. "So Jen says you're playing Nancy Drew again?"

Rocky made a face. "Playing Nancy Drew? I don't play Nancy Drew."

Jen and Lexi both scoffed. "Yes, you do," they said in unison.

Lexi wagged a finger at Jen. "Remember in middle school, when Ms. Mitchburn thought something was wrong with her water?"

Jen nodded and laughed. "And Rocky figured out Julia was going in during lunch, swiping her water bottle, and filling it with toilet water. Yes!"

They all laughed. Lexi added, "Rocky noticed Julia watching the teacher parking lot from the playground or something."

Rocky nodded. "She watched for Ms. Mitchburn to go to her car to sneak a cigarette. She did it every day at the same time."

Jen tried to control her laughter. "I let you talk me into spending my birthday money on a nanny camera to hide in the bathroom."

Rocky cocked her head. "Not only did we catch Julia, but we found out—"

They all finished the sentence, "Rachel Barden peed standing up," and howled with laughter.

"And in high school," Lexi continued. "You figured out who wrote on the bathroom mirror with a bloody tampon."

Rocky shook her head. "Nasty ass bitch."

"You've always done this shit, Rocky." Lexi refilled their glasses. "So what is this one about?"

When Rocky sat quiet, Jen leaned forward. "There were some break-ins. Several Junior League ladies had their houses broken into while they were home."

Lexi recoiled. "Oh my god. Were they hurt?"

Rocky shook her head. "No. The weirdest thing. No one got hurt and nothing got stolen." She took a drink. "But this all culminated with a Junior League matriarch shooting her husband. She mistook him for the guy breaking into houses and shot him in fear."

"However," Jen held a finger up, "Rocky thinks she set everything up to murder her husband and get away with it."

Lexi raised an eyebrow and opened her mouth wide. "Scandalous."

"Isn't it though?" Jen and Lexi shared a smile.

Rocky rubbed her hands together over the table between the three of them. "I could actually use your help, Lex."

Lexi choked on her wine a little, spitting out, "Me? How?"

Rocky squinted at her. "Didn't you date a cop in town for a little bit?"

Lexi twisted her mouth up. "I wouldn't say date."

One of the more intriguing aspects of Lexi's life was her lack of romantic entanglements. Not due to a lack of men, but rather due to her drive to be the best at everything. In most any relationship Lexi entered, the guy brought with him a set of male dominated opinions of societal norms. Most men dated like they were planting flags. They wore the pants and ruled the roost and brought home the bacon, or whatever other macho cliché made sense. Lexi didn't allow for any of that bullshit. She didn't need anyone to bring her bacon; she ruled her own roost; and, she found little use for men with pants on. In her efforts to take life by the balls, Lexi took quite a few men by the balls in the process. She lived a very sexually liberated lifestyle—one typically reserved for men. But she claimed sexuality in the same way she had taken a spot on an all-boys little league team as a kid or forced her way into a college sorority claiming to not accept new members during her freshman year. Lexi took most men and turned their lust for her into an obsession for her, and then she turned the obsession on its head, used their fawning to her advantage, and moved on with her life. Lexi Champagnolle was not the type to keep a scrapbook.

Lexi took a swig of wine. "But I messed around with a cop for a bit. I think he turned out to be married, if we get honest. Which is why I cut him loose."

Rocky nodded. "I thought I remembered something about a cop. What's his name?"

Lexi frowned. "Brandon Greenleaf. Awful name."

"Do you still have his number?"

Lexi pulled a phone out of her pocket and scrolled through her contacts. "No. Sorry." She held a hand up. "Oh, but wait. He's on my Facebook. I could message him."

Rocky smiled. "Would he do you a favor?"

Lexi shook her head. "A favor? No." She grinned. "But he would do anything I asked to make sure his wife doesn't find out about his extra-curricular activities."

Jen groaned in disapproval, but Rocky laughed. "There's my girl. I knew I could count on you. Go ahead and start a message. I have some requests for Officer Greenleaf."

After some back and forth with Brandon Greenleaf, Lexi convinced him to pull together what he could off the list Rocky provided and meet the two of them for lunch the next day. Lexi would get a lunch break during her practicum at the clinic, and she agreed to spend the hour meeting Rocky and blackmailing a jilted lover into forking over some privileged information. They met in the backroom of a downtown pizza joint called Sal's. Rocky arrived first, despite dragging a little from a Moscato hangover. She sat leaned against a wall in a booth with her sunglasses still on. Lexi bounced in as full of life as ever, seemingly unaffected from her half of the bottle. This was the norm since high school. Lexi seemed to be immune to hangovers, always raging until two in the morning and then still hopping up at five to go for a run before school. Officer Greenleaf arrived last. He paused when he saw Rocky, darting his eyes around before slinking into the booth.

He leaned toward Lexi, "Who the fuck is this?"

Lexi grinned. "Nice to see you, too, Officer Friendly."

He rolled his eyes. "Screw you, Lexi. You didn't say anything about another person."

"This other person is my cousin. She knows about us, and the information is for her. So get over it."

Brandon leaned back and sighed toward the ceiling.

Rocky pushed her glasses up into her hair. "Cards on the table, the cousin also perused your Facebook last night and found four other women you wouldn't want me contacting."

Lexi winced. "Ouch, Brandon. She's real good at connecting dots. I should've mentioned that."

Brandon looked back and forth between them with a pained expression. "Can we just get on with this?"

Rocky raised her eyebrows. "Sort of why we're here, yeah. Unless you want to go thirds on a pizza."

Brandon pulled out a thin manila envelope and opened it onto the table. "I couldn't get everything you asked for. I got the occupant of the house on Victoria Street. That part was easy. Her name is Rebecca Margolis. She's lived there for about a year."

Rocky leaned over the papers, staring down at the printout with Rebecca's name and driver's license photo. The girlfriend she and Jen had seen arguing with their mystery man in the brown truck. "She lives there alone?"

Brandon nodded.

"Any known associates or anything?"

He shook his head. "Nope. Not married. Not from here. She works for a maid service part time." He flipped a page. "The rest got harder. Here's a list of houses associated with the break-ins. I got them because the detective working the cases flagged the addresses in case anything came up associated with them again. But I don't have much else. There were some items reported missing from the first houses, but I've seen enough of this type of shit to know a money grab when I see one. I doubt he took anything. They're trying to get insurance to pay out."

Rocky nodded. "And what about the St. Laurent case?"

Brandon shrugged. "Even tougher. They're playing this one super tight. All I know is they are connecting the St. Laurent murder to the break-ins because they put the same lead detective on both cases. He wouldn't work a straight homicide, so it has to be due to the connection."

"Who's the lead detective?"

"Officer Fillmore."

Rocky shot a look at him.

"You know him?"

She smirked. "Yeah. I know him."

Brandon stuttered at the feeble amount of information on the table. "I—I'm sorry there's not more. I tried. I promise. Is this—is this enough to keep you from—"

Rocky and Lexi eyed each other. Lexi shrugged. "Your call. I'm good either way."

Brandon leaned forward, pleadingly. "This is harder than you think. I got the one name though. The first victim. Better than nothing, right?"

Rocky turned back toward him. "The first victim? What?"

Brandon frowned and nodded. "Yeah. Rebecca Margolis. Isn't that why you wanted her name?"

Rocky shook her head. "What do you mean victim? Victim of what?"

Brandon tapped on the list of break-ins. "The first break-in." He studied the paper, "Her house got broken into on Wednesday, the—"

Rocky snatched the list away from him. "Wednesday?"

He nodded. "Yeah. I thought that was weird, too. Only one not on a Tuesday."

Rocky nodded and studied the addresses and dates. "You're dismissed."

Brandon stuttered, "I'm…what? Does this mean—do you mean—am I—"

Lexi leaned toward him. "Dismissed. You heard her. Beat it, crooked dick." He fumed a little but tucked his head into his chest and scuttled out. Lexi turned back to Rocky. "So does this help? I do need to get back to work."

Rocky nodded absently. "It helps, yeah." She snapped back to focus and looked up at Lexi. "What are you doing later?"

Chapter 23

After Lexi finished up at the clinic, as promised, she swung by and picked up Rocky. Rocky, as always, made faces at the peeling upholstery of Lexi's twelve-year-old Honda Accord. They weren't faces of disgust as much as they were of annoyance. Lexi owned a nice car. A very nice car. A Lexus much like Rocky's, but several years newer and a couple of models better. Lexi got the Accord as a high school graduation present. Although already five or six years old when she got the Honda, she drove it all through college and into her first couple of nursing jobs. She put about two hundred thousand miles on the odometer, adding to the fifty the car had when she got it. And while the little coupe held up well, age caught up with parts here and there. Lexi would drive the thing into the ground. When she managed to buy her Lexus, she set up a complex series of rules for when she would allow herself to drive her new car. In the event of rain, she drove the Accord. If traveling any significant distance, Accord. Any trips to questionable neighborhoods, Accord. The Lexus became a special occasions car. Dates, parties, and high school reunions. Those were times when the Lexus came out. Luckily for Rocky, the Accord fit her needs for the afternoon's task.

As Lexi drove, she gave Rocky a side eye. "So what am I doing?"

"We are going to the home of Rebecca Margolis."

Lexi nodded. "The first victim?"

Rocky cocked her head. "Well, I wouldn't call her a victim. Rebecca's house is the house Jen and I followed the guy to."

"What guy?"

"The guy. In the brown truck. The one doing the break-ins."

Lexi nodded. "Right. We need a name for him or something."

"That's the goal. When Officer Crooked Dick brought us the info, I expected to find out Brown Truck's name. He lives there. I sure as fuck didn't think I would find out the house was the first break-in."

Lexi frowned and shook her head. "Yeah, none of this makes any sense."

"I think Rebecca just cashed in on an insurance claim using what she knew her boyfriend was about to start doing." Rocky directed Lexi to park a few streets away from Rebecca Margolis' house. She studied her phone.

"So why do you need me?"

"Because, Lexi, you command a talent for making women jealous. I need you to pretend to be sleeping with Rebecca's boyfriend."

Lexi nodded. "Is he cute?"

Rocky glared up at her. "Focus, Lexi. Focus."

Lexi raised her eyebrows and shrugged. "Why can't you pretend to be sleeping with the boyfriend?"

"Because I need the distraction to look around. There has to be something with the guy's name on it. A bill or something. You can't live in a place and not leave your name somewhere. I need you to work Rebecca up into such a jealous frenzy she won't notice me poking around for her boyfriend's name." Rocky twisted her mouth in thought. "Or, hopefully, she just says it. But she would just say a first name."

"I could just ask him. Guys are always willing to give me their names."

Rocky shook her head. "I'm aware of how this seems like too complex of a plan. But the simplest path means you having to come into direct contact with a guy who may be dangerous. And, of course, he knows what I look like. Rebecca Margolis is harmless. I can tell. The guy? I'm not so sure. He strikes me as the type to be a little more capable of violence. I don't want to take any chances."

"Great. How do we know he won't just show up at his house while we're there?"

Rocky held her phone screen up to face Lexi. "With this. I put a GoPhone in the bed of his truck. This is the trick I used to find out who Chet was fucking. When I used it on Chet, I got about four days of battery life. We should be good. I'll know when he leaves, and we can watch for him to drive far enough away to make us feel safe. Then we go knock on the door."

"And how do I navigate not knowing the name of the guy I'm supposed to be boning?"

"Oh, Lexi. I don't think I have the energy for us to pretend like you haven't navigated this particular territory before."

Lexi smirked and stared back out the window. "Point taken."

Rocky and Lexi sat monitoring the GoPhone for the better part of an hour. They listened to a playlist of songs from their high school days on Lexi's old iPod, which hung permanently connected to the Accord's auxiliary cable outlet due to a jammed cord. She spent a couple of years lamenting the fact she couldn't update the music on the older model mp3 player. But then nostalgia kicked in, and her outlook flipped. Just when they were transitioning from Beyoncé to P!nk, Rocky sat up in her seat and turned the music down.

"He's moving."

Lexi slunk down and peered around. "This way?"

Rocky shook her head. "He's heading out pretty fast. This may be our chance." She kept watch, naming off street names. "Texas Boulevard…State Line…over to 24th." She set the phone down in her lap and looked up at Lexi. "He's at least fifteen minutes away. We need to seize the opportunity."

Lexi didn't hesitate. She eased around the corner and made the two blocks over to Victoria Street. With some guidance from Rocky, she pulled up and parked in front of Rebecca Margolis' mailbox. Lexi hopped out of the car and circled around back with confidence as Rocky climbed out to follow her up the sidewalk. Lexi glanced back. "Look tough. You're supposed to be my backup." She paused. "Unless we're playing like I think he lives here alone. In that case you might be my threesome."

Rocky went full meerkat. "I think I'd rather look tough."

Lexi shrugged. "Suit yourself."

As Lexi powered on toward the door, Rocky scrambled to keep up. "Look slutty."

Lexi smiled. "No, sweetie. Slutty isn't threatening. Slutty can be defeated. Powerful. Commanding. Sexy. And not porn star sexy. CEO sexy. That's the kind of shit people concede to." She pointed back to Rocky. "Take notes. You're single now."

Rocky made a face and flipped Lexi off behind her back. And before Rocky could even set herself, Lexi rang the doorbell with one hand while rapping on the door three times with the other. After a beat and one more series of knocks, Rebecca Margolis came to the door—her face a mixture of anger and curiosity.

Lexi held both of her hands up and swiveled around. "I'm sorry. Who the fuck are you?"

Rebecca went wide-eyed, too shocked to give in fully to anger. "Who the fuck am I? Who the fuck are you?"

Lexi laughed. "I'm here to meet my man. This is where he lives. Why are you answering his door?"

Rebecca veered into anger now. "Your man?" She laughed. "This is my house, you nasty ass whore. Your man don't live here. You've never been here. You've got the wrong house."

Lexi spun around to Rocky. "Am I crazy?"

Rocky shook her head and gave Rebecca a countenance of pure pity. "No, you're not. He lives here, sweetie. I've been in there, too. You've got a brown couch and a glass top coffee table. There's a coat rack by the front door. The kitchen has a small table, but no chairs. There's an island with bar stools. They're black and swivel. And you've got some homemade red cushions on them. There's a big can next to the stove with utensils. Like, a matching set. They're all red."

As Rocky talked, the fight drained from Rebecca's face. Lexi winked at Rocky before turning back around. This wasn't their first time down this road. Rocky had been able to sell a lie with attention to detail since they were five years old. When she faced Rebecca again, the woman hung her head and tried to catch her breath. Lexi softened her tone considerably. "Look, I didn't expect to see you answer the door. And you never expected to see me ringing your doorbell. I think we both got played. Bad. And I don't know about you, but this ain't my first time with an asshole. I learned a long time ago these situations end much better when we girls stick together. If you want me to leave, I'm gone." Lexi motioned to her body. "I've got too many options to fight over a man. But," she ducked her head and toed at the ground, "if you want to compare notes? I'd love to come in and chat, scorned girl to scorned girl."

Rebecca glanced up and cycled through emotions. The request threw her off balance. She backed up and frowned. "Um, sure. Yeah. Yeah, come in. I can," she flailed a hand back toward her kitchen, "I can make some coffee if you want."

Rocky nudged Lexi and nodded frantically at her before Rebecca turned back toward them. Lexi blurted out, "Sure. Yes. Coffee would be great."

Rocky added, "I too love coffee to drink."

Lexi gaped at her, mouthing, "The fuck is wrong with you?"

Rocky tittered and shook her head.

Rebecca pointed toward the couch. "Go ahead and have a seat. I'll start a pot."

Lexi eased toward the couch, keeping an eye on Rebecca's slow walk to the kitchen as Rocky rifled through a stack of mail on a table by the front door.

Rebecca called back from the kitchen, "He told me Tuesdays were his only nights off work. I suppose that was some bullshit, huh?"

Lexi called back, "I'm afraid so. He told me Wednesdays."

"Asshole," Rebecca grumbled while pouring water into the coffee maker. "How long?"

Lexi motioned for Rocky to hurry. "A couple of weeks."

Rocky eased over and sat next to Lexi just as Rebecca rounded the corner and leaned against the wall separating the living room from the kitchen. She wiped her hands on her threadbare yoga pants as the smell of cheap coffee began to fill up the tiny house. "Unbelievable. We've lived together for over a month."

Lexi shook her head. "Did you ever suspect anything?"

Rebecca shrugged. "No more than normal, I guess. I thought he worked all the time." She hung her head and dabbed at an eye with her thumb. When she looked back up, she waved a hand around the living room. "You'd think maybe I'd expect there to be a little more money coming in if he worked so much, wouldn't you?"

Rocky grimaced. "Hey, don't beat yourself up. We've all been screwed over by a guy."

Rebecca cocked her head. "You were fucking him, too?"

Rocky held her hands up and shook her head. "Oh, no. No, no, no. I meant more in a female solidarity way."

Lexi jerked a thumb at Rocky. "Her husband was fucking a pregnant hairdresser."

Rebecca made a pained face and Rocky bobbed her head back and forth. "Well, a waitress, but who's counting."

Rebecca shambled over and sat down on the far end of the couch. "He always talked about coming into some money. Like it was always about to happen. But never did. And he never had two nickels to rub together. He may not even be working five nights a week. There could be two or three other girls out there somewhere."

Rocky shrugged. "Could be. Why was he coming into money?"

Rebecca shook her head. "No clue. He's full of shit. He's been talking about that cash since he moved here from Dallas."

Lexi leaned over closer to Rebecca. "How did the two of you meet?"

Rebecca laughed. "Online. I'd damn near given up on dating sites. But he just moved to town and needed someone to show him around a little. We went out a few times while he lived in a motel over on Seventh Street. Shit hole. Worst I've ever seen. That's why I let him move in after just a handful of dates and a couple of weeks. I should know better."

Rocky rubbed her hands together in front of her face. "And you never saw any of this money he talked about?"

Rebecca laughed and shook her head. "Fuck no. He finally shut up about that bullshit."

Rocky frowned. "When?"

"'Bout a week ago maybe."

Lexi sighed. "What do you think you'll do?"

Rebecca shook her head. "What choice do I have? I ain't no fool. I'm 'bout to kick his ass out as soon as he gets back from the liquor store."

Lexi shot Rocky a look, and Rocky jerked her phone up out of her purse and studied the screen in a panic. She muttered, "Shit," just as a door slammed outside.

Rebecca stood up and puffed out her chest. "Speak of the fucking devil."

Lexi stood and backed up into Rocky who jumped up and clutched her purse to her chest. Lexi whispered over her shoulder, "I thought you were watching the GoPhone."

"I was having a conversation. We should have taken shifts."

Lexi whipped around. "How the hell could we have taken shifts, Rocky?"

Before Rocky could answer, a man stepped through the front door holding a brown paper bag. He wore a black baseball cap and a black t-shirt over greasy jeans. The smell of cigarettes wafted across the living room as soon as the door opened.

Rebecca launched into a litany of curses, throwing a couch cushion at the man. He struggled to duck while not dropping the bag. Taking in the room, he began to take in what she screamed at him—something about fucking the woman standing in his living room. A woman he had never seen before. But the woman behind her …

The man set his bag of liquor on a table and started to shush Rebecca. "Baby, baby, baby. Listen. This woman—not the redhead, the other one—she's full of shit. She came here the other day trying to spy on us."

Rebecca started in again, but the man cut her off by saying, "They don't even know my name. Ask them. Go on. Ask them."

Rebecca did a slow turn toward Lexi and Rocky. They froze, grinning back at her, Lexi nudging Rocky in the hopes she would pull another magic trick out of her ass. But when nothing came, Rebecca shook her head. "You sneaky little bitches. You had me thinking my man cheated on me!"

As Rebecca balled her fists and took a step, Rocky leaned around Lexi and held a hand up. "I know about the break-ins!"

The couple stared at one another. The man shook his head toward Rebecca in dismissal, but Rocky continued, "Every Tuesday. When he was off work. That's where you thought the money was going to come from, right, Rebecca? But did he tell you he never stole anything? Not one thing from one house."

Rebecca paused and cut her eyes toward her boyfriend. He hadn't told her, and it was obvious.

The man pulled a baseball bat out of an umbrella can by the door. Lexi squirmed back into Rocky, but Rocky kept talking. "The only money you saw was the insurance claim you filed when you said this place got broken into, right? Might as well cash in, right, Rebecca?" The man frowned but still moved toward them. Rocky pointed. "Bought yourself a new TV." She looked at the man. "I'm sure she told you she saved up or maybe even won it in some contest, but this house is listed as the first break-in. She reported a robbery so she could file with her insurance. No one would ever doubt her as soon as all the other break-ins started up."

Rebecca bit her lip, and the man cut his eyes toward his girlfriend. This came as new information to him, and the news at least delayed the inevitable. But after a beat, both the man and Rebecca took a step toward Lexi and Rocky—the man gripping the baseball bat and Rebecca picking up a pair of scissors from the coffee table.

Rocky stepped across Lexi while pulling something from her purse. She came out with a pink pistol, pointing the barrel back and forth between Rebecca and her boyfriend. Lexi mumbled into Rocky's back, "Jesus, Rock. What the hell are you doing?"

Rocky growled back, "Getting us out of here."

Rebecca stared Rocky down. "I'll call the cops."

Rocky grinned at her and then turned to the man. "Oh, sweetie. No. You won't." She motioned with the gun for the man to move over toward Rebecca and away from the door. "We are going to walk out of here, and you aren't going to chase us this time. In fact, toss your keys over."

The man complied, but still held the bat. He pulled out his keys and tossed them to Lexi, who caught them and rattled them in front of her face as she scooted behind Rocky toward the door. Rocky nodded to him. "Thank you. We'll drop these in the front yard as we drive off." As they started to back out, Rocky paused. "By the way, what's your name?"

The man swallowed. "Brent Powell."

Rocky caught Rebecca flashing a quick glance at him, but just nodded again. "Thank you. Wasn't so hard, was it?" She glanced back at Lexi. "See? The plan worked after all."

Lexi sighed as they backed out and then sprinted for the car. The Accord's tires squealed on their way down Victoria Street. Rocky threw Brent Powell's keys back toward the house as they pulled away. Lexi looked over at her. "Did you see Rebecca's face when he said his name? I think he lied."

Rocky pulled a piece of mail out of her purse. "Oh, yeah. He did. His real name is Martin Yancy. I found this as soon as we walked in." She paused as she placed her gun back into her purse. Frowning into her lap, she said, "You know, I guess we could have left a long time ago."

Chapter 24

Lexi drove a few blocks, fussing at Rocky the whole way about the dangerous situation they just left before looking up into her rearview mirror and shrieking, "Shit!"

Rocky swiveled her head around. "What?"

"We're getting pulled over."

Rocky frowned, still craning to see the swirling lights. "Were you speeding?"

Lexi eased the car to a stop at the side of the road and cut her eyes at Rocky. "Yes, Rocky. I was speeding. We were running from two people who may want to kill us. Of course I was fucking speeding. But what concerns me a little more is, based on what y'all told me last night, I think there is a bag of weed in your purse. And I know for a fact there's a loaded gun in your purse."

Rocky waved a hand at her. "I have a license for the gun."

"But you don't have a license for the—" A soft rapping at Lexi's window cut her off. She glanced up with a smile, but the smile melted away and she muttered, "You gotta be kidding me."

Rocky smiled and pointed. "Hey look, Lexi. The cop you know."

Lexi lowered the window as Officer Brandon Greenleaf stood there with his arms crossed with an expression of permanent sigh. He shook his head. "Lexi, what the hell is going on?"

Lexi raised her eyebrows. "Was I speeding?"

He shook his head. "No. Well, yes. But that's not the point." He leaned down and whispered, "I told you, they flagged all those houses. So when two girls go running out of one of those houses like it's on fire, and one of those girls is brandishing a firearm? Well, then someone is gonna—"

Rocky leaned across Lexi. "I wasn't brandishing it. I don't even know what brandishing would look like."

Lexi pushed Rocky back, and Brandon craned back over his shoulder and leaned over farther. "Why the hell did you have a gun in the first place? And why did you go to that house? And what were you running from?"

Rocky started and stopped a couple of times. "I'm not sure which one of those you want me to answer. Some of them sounded rhetorical."

Lexi shook her head and mumbled, "Rocky, stop."

"What? Rhetorical?" Rocky frowned at Brandon. "Did I lose you at rhetorical?"

Lexi held a hand up. "She has a concealed carry license for the gun. I've seen it."

Brandon rubbed his eyes. "I know what rhetorical means, and I don't give a good fuck whether you have a license or not. Why were you at that house?" He shook his head. "You know what, no. We don't have time now. Please tell me no one is going to know I gave you the address."

Rocky held up three fingers in a Scout's Honor pose. "Were you ever in the Boy Scouts, Brandon? I was. For eight glorious weeks. I know the meaning of honor, and honor, Brandon, is what I give to you. Scout's Honor."

Brandon sighed and Lexi frowned up at him. "What do you mean we don't have time?"

Before he could answer, they all turned to the sound of a car door. Rondo Singer walked up to the car. He sported his pageboy hat and chewed on a toothpick. His mouth caught between a grimace and a grin, and he called out, "Lord Jesus, save me from these Champagnolle girls. Greenleaf, what the good fuck is going on?"

Rocky leaned over Lexi again and waved at Rondo as he stepped up next to Brandon. "Hey, Uncle Rondo. We were just chatting about my time as a Boy Scout."

Rondo sniffed and nodded. He eyed Brandon. "Took 'em eight weeks to find a rule to kick her out."

Rocky held the signal up toward Brandon again and nodded to her fingers with a wink.

Rondo cocked his head. "You mind telling me what you were doing at Rebecca Margolis' house, Raquel?" He nodded to Lexi. "Lexi. How's your folks? I'm sorry Rocky's dragged you into whatever she's got cooking here."

Lexi smiled. "They're good. Don't worry. I'm used to her."

Rondo laughed into his chest. "I'll bet you are." He looked up at Brandon. "Greenleaf, you can go. I got this from here."

Brandon hesitated, but Rondo gave him a scowl causing him to jump and start away with one last glance at Rocky, who gave him one last Scout's Honor.

Rondo turned back to Rocky and motioned for her to come with him by way of a harsh snap of his fingers. "You mind talking to me at the back of the car, Raquel?"

Rocky nodded. "Of course." She tossed her purse into Lexi's lap. "Can you hold my purse? Thank you."

At the back of the car, Rondo stared down Rocky in silence for a moment. He had a way of standing back and staring at someone in a way to make himself seem taller. Even eye to eye, he could loom over the object of his stare. Rocky held firm, glaring back until he sucked at his teeth to make a smacking sound, followed with, "Rocky, what are you up to?"

Rocky narrowed one eye. "Cards on the table?"

Rondo nodded once. "Cards on the table."

"I want to know why Waverly St. Laurent shot her husband."

Rondo held firm to his hard stare. "She thought he was an intruder."

Rocky shook her head. "I don't think she did. I think she wanted to shoot him. And she wanted everyone to think she thought he was an intruder."

Rondo broke, chuckling and shaking his head. "I think you're thinking too much about what you think she thought we'd think."

Rocky smiled and rolled her eyes. "I'm being serious."

He nodded. "I know you are. But I think you're off the reservation on this one, Rock. I know Waverly pissed you off, but I been knowing Waverly a long damn time, Rocky. Long damn time. The woman ain't no killer. She's an ice-cold bitch. But, honestly, kinda in a good way. In fact, you know what? She kinda—"

Rocky held up a finger. "Don't you dare."

Rondo laughed. "I'm just saying. She ain't bad. And why would she want her husband dead? She got as much money as he does. Maybe more."

Rocky rubbed her hands together. "What if it isn't about money? What if Waverly found out her husband had something to do with Jason's death?"

Rondo started to walk away with a wave of his hand. "Rocky, come on. Let it go."

Rocky grabbed his arm to keep him from walking away. "Just hear me out. Your partner! He thought the same thing, right?"

Rondo stopped and shook his head. "I told you, he got stuck on the dad. It happens. We all do that shit sometimes."

"But why? Why did he get stuck on the dad? What made him suspect him in the first place?"

Rondo shook his head and thought back. "I don't know. A few things. Bo made us take everything through his lawyer. He didn't like getting the lawyer involved so quick. Said lawyers make you seem suspicious."

"Did the lawyer make you suspicious?"

Rondo sighed. "No. They had a family lawyer. Always did. Rich folk use lawyers to wipe they ass. Didn't strike me as weird at all."

Rocky nodded and frowned. "Yeah. Freddy Van Vleck. I met him."

Rondo spun around and frowned. "Freddy Van Vleck? What?"

Rocky nodded. "The family lawyer? Freddy Van Vleck. I met him. Creepy little fucker."

He laughed and nodded. "Yeah, Freddy's creepy as hell." Then he shook his head. "But he ain't the St. Laurent family lawyer. They've had the same lawyer for as long as I remember. Georgia Lee."

Rocky shook her head. "Georgia Lee?"

Rondo frowned at her. "Macon Georgia Lee Jefferson the Fourth. You need to get out more, girl."

"Their lawyer is a woman?"

Rondo laughed hard and shook his head. "No, Rocky. Georgia Lee is a man. A big old six-foot-four man who you wouldn't call a woman to his face. Georgia Lee was the first practicing black lawyer in Texarkana. Been around forever. Started practicing law in the early sixties when he wasn't but twenty-something. Bo St. Laurent sort of helped make his career. Georgia Lee spent ten or fifteen years doing legal work for poor black folk who couldn't pay him for shit. Bo was the first rich white man to hire him. He kept doing the same shit for the poor black folks, too. But Bo St. Laurent kept the man in big and tall suits for the past forty years." He rubbed at his chin. "I got no clue why Waverly would hire Freddy's creepy ass."

Rocky let him stand there and wonder for a moment before leaning in close and saying, "A little suspicious, right?"

Rondo recoiled and shook off his pondering with a smack of his lips. "Rocky, get back in your cousin's car and go home."

Rocky protested a little, but Rondo guided her by the elbow back to her car. She kept turning her head back toward him. "Will you at least look into a name for me?"

"Nope."

"I think Waverly hired him to do those break-ins."

"Nope."

"To make it believable when she shot her husband."

"Nope."

"Run him through AVIS?"

"That's a car rental company."

"Run his prints?"

"You don't have his prints."

"Google him?"

Rondo put her into the car. "Any information about the break-ins you should give to Detective Fillmore." Rocky pouted and slouched in the seat. Rondo leaned over her and said to Lexi, "Take her home, please, Lexi."

Lexi nodded, but Rocky grabbed her purse and grumbled. "I'm not going home. I'm going to go to this witch lady's house and watch her make magic brownies."

Rondo frowned as Lexi laughed and stuttered, "Oh, Rocky. You s—silly girl."

Rondo rubbed at his chin and watched Rocky's dejected pout as Lexi smiled ear to ear and eased away, rolling up the window as she drove. Without moving her mouth, she muttered, "Rocky, you're gonna get me arrested one day."

Rocky swatted at her purse. "It's five ounces."

Lexi laughed. "Five ounces, huh? Of government grade marijuana…in your purse…with a loaded nine millimeter. Rocky, you're like a fucking mobster. I don't have to sit outside this house and keep the car running, do I? Because I need to drive back to Conway tonight."

Rocky shrugged and shook her head, still pouting. "Nah. Jen will be there. She can give me a ride home. You've done your part."

Lexi howled with sardonic laughter. "Oh, thanks. No shit, I've done my part. I should make you walk."

Rocky brightened a notch or two and thanked Lexi for her help, flowing into a little small talk about getting together for something more tame the next time she came in town. When they got to Elaine Maplethorpe's house, Rocky added, "Be safe on your way back, whore."

Lexi grinned. "Yeah. Don't call me to bail you out, you cunt."

With that, Lexi drove off and Rocky spun on her heel to flounce up the steps to Elaine Maplethorpe's wind chime-laden front porch. Jen let her in, the smell of patchouli making Rocky cough as soon as the door opened. Jen's eyes were baggy and her face sagged with annoyance. "You're late."

Rocky held up her purse and shook the contents. "Oh, Jen. Can't be late for the party when you are the party."

Jen chuckled and rolled her eyes. "You still want to go through with this?"

Rocky breezed past her on her way to the kitchen. "Can't stop, won't stop, Jennifer."

The rest of the Junior Leaguers were in the kitchen talking and laughing with Elaine. They all sort of cheered when Rocky walked in, causing Jen to sigh and roll her eyes behind Rocky's back. Elaine had laid out all of the baking equipment, with mixing bowls and bags of brownie mix lining the counters, along with cartons of eggs and gallons of milk and numerous sticks of butter.

The group wasted no time, starting in on the marijuana-infused butter right away. Rocky helped separate the marijuana seeds from the buds, but then bowed out of the culinary responsibilities, opting to sit up on the kitchen island—right in the way—and regale everyone with the story of hers and Lexi's harrowing escape from the clutches of the home invader and their close call with the police.

Jen boiled over. "Rocky, I told you this is going to land you in jail!"

But everyone else marveled at the excitement of Rocky's tale. Elaine put both hands on her face, smearing a little chocolate on a cheek. "Do you think that was the same man who broke in here?"

Rocky nodded. "Oh, I'm positive."

Britney-Brene—from the group who first visited Rocky in her classroom—spoke up. "You know, I hate to be the negative one in the group, but I think I agree with Jennifer on this one."

Jen flailed her hands out. "Thank you!" She stopped and turned. "Wait. Am I the negative one in the group?"

Rocky answered, "Yes," at the same time Britney said, "No, of course not. All I'm saying is we may need to consider getting some legal counsel. You know, just in case. I mean, I now have almost two hundred Adderall hidden in my house."

Another woman spoke up. "No shit. I've got a stash, too. Hidden in a teacup in my linens pantry. That's where I keep all my kids teeth the Tooth Fairy took."

Rocky made a face of disgust. "You keep the teeth?"

The woman shrugged. "Yeah. It felt weird to throw them away."

Another Leaguer nodded and looked back over a shoulder. "I did the same thing."

Rocky shuddered. "Parenthood is so gross." She waved her hands in a calming motion. "But okay, okay. Don't worry. I know a lawyer. I'm going to talk to him tomorrow. I can set something up. Put him on retainer. That's a thing, right?"

Jen nodded. "It's a thing, yes. A thing that costs money, Rocky."

Rocky recoiled. "Oh. Do they take credit cards?"

"What lawyer do you know?" Jen asked.

Rocky studied her nails. "Um, his last name is Jefferson. He's a big lawyer in town."

Elaine gasped. "Not Georgia Lee?"

Rocky frowned and nodded. "Yeah. I think so. Macon Georgia Lee Jefferson the Fourth."

Elaine smiled wide and swooned, putting a hand to her chest and smearing chocolate down into her cleavage. "Oh, Georgia Lee."

Rocky screwed her face up in confusion. "What does that mean? Did you—were you—I thought you were—"

"Oh, it happened so long ago," Elaine said. "But yes. Georgia Lee always knew his way around a woman, if you know what I mean."

Rocky shook her head. "I thought you knew your way around a woman."

Elaine frowned, "What, dear?"

Jen leaned over between them. "I tried to tell her."

Rocky looked back and forth between them. "But you said Beverly." She leaned toward Jen. "She said Beverly, right?"

Jen nodded.

Elaine laughed. "Yes, dear. Beverly is my husband's name. Dr. Beverly Maplethorpe. He's a well-known surgeon in town."

Rocky fluttered her eyelids and shook her head, wrenching her mouth into a sour expression. "Beverly?" She cocked her head. "Beverly is a man's name?"

Jen and Elaine both nodded. Elaine smiled kindly. "The poor man had a very difficult time growing up."

Rocky kept staring off in disbelief, but then changed. Her eyes grew wide and she hopped down off the bar. She grabbed Jen by the shoulders and glared into her eyes. "I know what's going on. I know what's going on, Jen."

Jen shook her head and frowned. "What?"

Rocky let her go and started rubbing her hands together in front of her face. "I need to go hire a lawyer."

Chapter 25

After a couple of phone calls the next morning, Rocky found out Macon Georgia Lee Jefferson, IV, no longer took new clients. By all accounts, Georgia Lee still practiced at a healthy seventy-five or so, but after fifty years or so of accumulating clients, he decided to stop one day around 2013. Rocky, however, pressed on undeterred. She dug around in the corners of the Internet until she found where Georgia Lee rented an office in the third floor of an old building downtown belonging to a small accounting firm, which set up shop on the other two floors. So she packed a light lunch and drove down to the Williams and Johnson Building to camp out in front of Georgia Lee's office.

The Williams and Johnson Building was an old yellow brick building on the corner of Broad and Olive next to the old railroad museum. The sizeable structure housed some sort of department or furniture store back when downtown Texarkana was thriving. One big display window made up the whole front corner of the building. The accounting firm filled the front display with old railroad memorabilia they pilfered from the defunct museum. A receptionist sat at the front desk chewing on a pen. She looked up to question Rocky, but Rocky held up her brown paper bag lunch and called out in a sing-song voice, "Lunch delivery." The receptionist smiled and waved as if to allow passage. Rocky tried to act like she had been there before, spotting an old elevator and making for it. Rocky pulled back an old metal gate before climbing on, and the three buttons made a choice pretty easy once inside.

The third floor turned out to be vacant for the most part. It smelled of an attic—a mixture of mildew and moth balls. Back in the department store days, this had been the offices for managers and the like. There were multiple offices, with doors filled with beveled glass papered off with brown butcher paper. A couple of the doors had old name plates still on the glass, but letters were chipping off or missing. At the end of the hallway stretching out straight from the elevator, one door stood free of paper with a soft glow of a lamp shining through the hazy glass.

A very simple black nameplate on the center of the glass read, "M.G.L. Jefferson, Esq." Rocky tapped on the glass and waited. Tapped again but heard nothing. An old bench—something between a church pew and a shoeshine station—sat outside the door. She took a seat and pulled a book out of her purse, positioning herself to get the light from the door.

After about an hour, Rocky broke down and pulled a sandwich and a juice box out of the paper bag next to her. She nibbled on a couple of bites before she heard the elevator come to life down the hall. Wheels and cables groaned and creaked for an agonizing length of time before opening and depositing a giant man onto her floor. He cut an imposing form. Every bit of the six foot, four inches Rondo advertised. And slim, but solid—built out with broad shoulders and hips. He wore black slacks and a denim shirt, with a pair of black dress shoes with tassels. For the first half of his journey down the hall, Rocky could see nothing but his hair—short cropped but bright white, like a covering of white fur all across his head. As he got nearer, Rocky could make out his features. Georgia Lee was very dark-skinned, and the area around his eyes darkened even more than the rest. His face was broad—square-jawed and handsome. She could see why Elaine might swoon at the memory of a younger Georgia Lee. He smiled at her as he approached, and the smile spread huge. Larger than life. The smile of a man used to smiling, with wrinkles from doing it often in his life, even though his nose betrayed some moments he may not smile about. The bridge was a little crooked, broken and never set. He carried an old briefcase with double clasps and a worn-down handle. He paused in front of her, jingling his keys in one hand while tapping on the handle of the briefcase with the other. "That looks like a peanut butter and jelly sandwich."

Rocky nodded. "It is."

Georgia Lee smiled even wider than before. "I haven't had one of those in over forty years." He shook a key, pointing at her. "You know, there is only one kind of peanut butter and jelly sandwich. One. Anything else is a lie and an imposter."

Rocky took a bite and chewed. "Oh, I know," she managed after a swig of juice.

Georgia Lee raised an eyebrow. "Oh, you do, do you now? And what is that?"

Rocky held the sandwich up and closed one eye to scrutinize the thin slit between slices of bread. "Creamy peanut butter and blackberry jam."

Georgia Lee smiled bigger than at any point before. He laughed to himself as he unlocked his office. "I don't suppose you—"

Rocky pulled another sandwich out of the bag. "Yes, sir, I do."

A minute later, Rocky and Georgia Lee were sitting on either side of his desk, both eating a sandwich and sipping on a juice box. After introductions, Georgia Lee patted the top of his cluttered desk. "Yes, ma'am. I know your family quite well. A Champagnolle gave me this here desk. Before your daddy ran his shop, it was your granddaddy's. Rayford Champagnolle. You wouldn't have known him too well."

Rocky shook her head. "No, sir. I was pretty young when he died."

Georgia Lee nodded. "That you were. He had your daddy and uncle kinda later in life. But Ray was a good man. War vet. World War II, mind you. I ain't that old. A lot of those boys came back with a respect for fellow veterans, regardless of color. Not all of them, mind you. But some of them. Ray was one. He did right by a lot of men and women in the black community. Myself included. I defended a war buddy of his accused of some things he didn't do. When we won the case, the poor fella couldn't pay me a dime. He'd been touched by the war, I think. Fifty-some-odd years old and sacking groceries at the Piggly Wiggly. Didn't always have enough to put food on his own table. So Ray stepped up and paid my bill by furnishing my office. I'd been working on milk crates up until then. I can't tell you how much it meant to sit down at an actual desk and work."

Rocky glanced around the office at framed photos of Georgia Lee with various famous faces—Bill Clinton, Thurgood Marshall, multiple local officials, and countless others. "Rondo Singer told me you were Texarkana's first African-American lawyer."

Georgia Lee smiled and nodded. "So they say. I seemed to remember a man named Preston who tried a case here in the late fifties or early sixties." He cupped a hand around his mouth and whispered, "Before me. But I suppose he didn't live here, so that didn't count. He came out of Fort Worth, I believe. Either way, I'll take it. Nobody still alive to dispute the claim." He leaned back in his chair, rocking and causing the wood to squeak in a steady rhythm. "So I suppose I have Rondo to thank for this visit?"

Rocky grinned. "Sort of. He did tell me about you. He said you were the best lawyer in town."

Georgia Lee chuckled. "Miss Champagnolle, if you're gonna lie to a man who lies for a living, you're gonna need to be a little better at it."

Rocky raised her eyebrows, impressed. "Fair enough, Mr. Jefferson. Fair enough." She smiled at him. "You know what? I'm going to let you call me Rocky."

"From what I hear, everybody calls you Rocky."

She nodded. "They do take that liberty, yes, sir. A select few even get invited."

He guffawed and clapped his hands. "All right, Rocky. I'm gonna let you call me Georgia Lee." He bowed to her. "Invitation reciprocated."

Rocky rubbed her hands together. "Okay, Georgia Lee. I guess now that we're fast friends you're going to want to know what I'm doing here?"

Georgia Lee took a bite and nodded. "Well, I'm betting you're running out of sandwiches, so yeah, I think I would."

Rocky smirked. "Yes, sir. Well, now I know the word is you stopped taking on new clients."

"That is the word."

"Yes. But," Rocky held up a beseeching finger, "hear me out, now. You strike me as the type of man who relishes the opportunity to experience."

Georgia Lee wrinkled his brow and waited. When Rocky didn't continue, he shook his head at her. "Experience what?"

"Something new. Something different. Unique." Rocky waved a hand across the photos on the wall. "The man who has seen everything knows there is always more to see."

He chuckled and rolled his eyes.

"You've been practicing law how long, Mr.—" Rocky caught herself. "Georgia Lee—how many years have you defended clients? Worked cases?"

Georgia Lee raised an eyebrow. "Since 1967."

"What was your first case? Do you remember?"

He nodded. "Defended a girl accused of stealing from her employer."

Rocky leaned across the desk. "And you remember. Because it was special. Different. I'm sure you had countless cases like that since then, right?"

Georgia Lee nodded.

"Of course you did. But the girl accused of stealing was your first. What about your biggest?"

He squinted. "Well, depends on how you define biggest. I helped sue a tobacco company some years back. Made me enough to live comfortable for the rest of about eight lifetimes. Or you could say my biggest was defending the mayor back in the early eighties. He came accused of killing his wife. Made a national paper or two."

Rocky nodded. "Because defending the mayor was unique. And these cases, the unique ones, the ones you remember...when was the last one?"

Georgia Lee scanned a wall of photos and took a sip of his juice box. "I suppose it's been a little while. They kinda run together these last years."

Rocky grinned and nodded. "So even if you didn't know, what you long for is not a new client. We both know you don't need the money. You sure as hell deserve the rest. But what you desire is a new case. Something unique. Something worth remembering."

Georgia Lee laughed. "Goddammit, girl. You got me feeling all despondent. I was gonna help you because I owed your granddaddy. You didn't have to go off making me feel shit."

Rocky scrunched her face up. "Really?"

Georgia Lee held a hand out. "Give me a dollar." When Rocky just stared at him, he shook the hand impatiently. "Give me a dollar. I'll be your damn lawyer. Now, give me a dollar, attorney-client privilege kicks in, and you can tell me what kinda mess you got yourself into."

Rocky rifled through her purse and came out with some cash. "All I have is a twenty."

Georgia Lee snatched the money. "Even better." He folded the bill into his shirt pocket and motioned for her to go on. "All right. Let's hear it. What's so damn unique?"

Rocky crossed her legs and sat up straighter in her chair. "Well, I am in the Junior League."

Georgia Lee cocked his head. "When you're right, you're right. I am blown away."

"Stick with me," Rocky curled a lip. "It gets better."

Georgia Lee finished his sandwich and grumbled. "Hope so."

"This is my first year in the Junior League, in fact. And as a new member, we put together a new member project. And ours, Georgia Lee, is quite a project. We plan to put luggage in the hands of any child taken out of his or her home."

Georgia Lee cut his eyes at her. "Get rid of them goddamn trash bags?"

Rocky nodded and pointed to his words. "You got it."

Georgia Lee nodded once. "Go on."

"Right. So, this project will take quite a bit of money. And it just so happens we found a benefactor with quite a bit of money to offer."

He raised his eyebrows in a question.

Rocky smiled. "Waverly St. Laurent."

Georgia Lee laced his fingers together in front of his face and hung his head. "I see."

"Yes. So, in an effort to keep the project afloat, we decided on a very lucrative fundraiser."

He glanced up. "If you say robbing banks this just got as interesting as promised."

Rocky shook her head. "No. Not robbing banks." She shifted in her seat and recrossed her legs. "We plan on selling pot brownies to elderly people and cancer patients."

Georgia Lee chuckled. "Yeah, that would do it, too. I sure as hell ain't seen nothing like that."

Rocky nodded.

They stared at each other for a beat until Georgia Lee said, "Now, just wait a damn minute. Are you—" He swiveled around, confirming they were alone. "Are you serious?"

Rocky pointed to his shirt pocket and nodded. "It's what the twenty dollars was for."

Georgia Lee slid from shock to laughter and spent a solid two minutes howling in laughter before beginning a line of questions. "You mean to tell me you convinced a bunch of Junior League soccer moms to bake pot brownies to sell to old folk?"

Rocky nodded. "Among other things. We have a line on supplying tired housewives with speed, too. But the brownies are ready to go."

He shook his head. "How the hell did you know how to make them?"

"Elaine Maplethorpe. She says she knew you." Rocky raised her eyebrows.

Georgia Lee nodded. "I guess that part ain't a surprise. And where do you expect to sell these brownies?"

"I'm hoping you can help broker the sale. We realize if we approach anyone directly, we could be putting ourselves at risk. But if our attorney were to set up a meeting and possible transaction without admitting to any wrongdoing on any part, then we may find willing customers without revealing our hand too soon."

Georgia Lee started making notes on a legal pad. "So you want me to find willing buyers without telling them who they're buying from? At least, not until they can convince me they'll play ball?"

Rocky nodded. "Yes, sir. If they act shocked and offended, you never tell them who your client is. If they act interested, you set up a meeting. You know a lot of people. Don't you think there are a few out there who might be willing to bend the rules to make sure those in need can get some much-needed relief?"

Georgia Lee bobbed his head around. "I could ask around. I know a few nursing homes who made a run at medicinal marijuana and got shot down. They may work with us. And the cancer treatment center wing of the rehab clinic. They see people who could benefit the most."

Rocky leaned across the desk and held out a hand. "So? We have a deal?"

Georgia Lee laughed. "You weren't lying about being unique. That's for damn sure." He shook her hand. "All right, Rocky Champagnolle. You got yourself a twenty-dollar lawyer."

Rocky sat for a minute, admiring pictures and letting Georgia Lee chat about some he could tell caught her eye. After a few minutes, she turned back to him. "Can I ask you something about a former client of yours?"

Georgia Lee shrugged. "You can ask, sure. But remember, same privilege you're counting on works for them, too."

Rocky nodded. "Yes, I know. I'm just curious, why did Waverly St. Laurent hire a different lawyer?"

Georgia Lee held out his hands and shook his head. "I don't know, to be honest with you. Bo and I went way back. He gave me a pretty big break back in the day. I suppose Waverly may have surmised my loyalties lay in the ground with him."

Rocky frowned. "Is there any reason Waverly would want Bo dead? Something from the past? Something with Jason?"

Georgia Lee smiled. "Now, Rocky—"

Rocky held her hands up. "I know. I know. But what if she killed your friend on purpose? Wouldn't you want to know?"

He nodded once solemnly. "Of course I would."

"Would it interest you to know Waverly St. Laurent got her creepy ass lawyer to offer me money to stop looking into the break-ins leading up to Mr. St. Laurent's death?"

Georgia Lee frowned. "Freddy offered you money?"

Rocky nodded. "Twenty thousand dollars. Just to stop looking into the break-ins."

"What had you found that bothered them so much?"

Rocky shook her head. "Nothing. I wasn't even looking until after I turned down the money."

Georgia Lee smiled wide. "You know, I kinda like you, Rocky Champagnolle."

"I kinda like you, too, Macon Georgia Lee Jefferson." She tilted her head. "And I'd like you even more if you could tell me a little bit about Waverly St. Laurent. I know your hands are tied when it comes to the old stuff—the stuff with Jason. But you aren't her lawyer now, right? Does privilege extend to a case you aren't even working? Couldn't you at least ask someone in the District Attorney's office about their case? You know people. They would talk to you off the record."

Georgia Lee rubbed the side of his face. "I suppose I could ask. From what I've heard, they plan on striking the shooting up to involuntary manslaughter and letting her off with a slap on the wrist. Odds are whatever they got ain't much and they might be willing to talk."

Rocky held her hands out, palms up. "See? Was that so hard? If you can't do that much for your favorite client, then what am I even paying you for?"

He stared at her. "You're paying me to keep you out of jail on drug trafficking."

Rocky nodded. "Oh yeah." She stood up, leaning over the desk and patting his shirt pocket. "Money well spent." She started for the door. "Thank you, Georgia Lee. Good to meet you."

Georgia Lee stood, but bent over his desk to write something on a scrap of paper. "Pleasure meeting you, Rocky. Now, I'm pretty certain I can work out a meeting with a lady over at Whispering Pines retirement home tomorrow. Should be your first sale. I know the people there, and I can talk to them. I'll call you with a time and a contact. But here." He handed her the slip of paper. "When you get there, you should take a minute to visit someone. She is a lovely lady who I am sure would love to talk to you for a few minutes."

Rocky studied the name on the torn scrap of paper. "Who is she?"

Georgia Lee stepped around his desk and put a hand on Rocky's shoulder to see her out. He tapped the sheet of paper in her hand. "She worked as a maid for many, many years. Most of those years for the St. Laurents."

Rocky jerked her eyes up to meet Georgia Lee's.

He smiled back at her. "You see, Rocky. There is no maid-client privilege."

Chapter 26

As soon as she left Georgia Lee's office, Rocky sent out a group text to inform the brownie crew that their first delivery would happen before the end of day. She expected confirmation from Georgia Lee within the hour. She, of course, removed herself from the group text. Rocky enjoyed starting them but hated participating in them. Too many notifications.

With an hour to kill downtown, Rocky wondered if Patterson "Face" Fillmore would be in the same coffee shop. Within walking distance, worst case scenario, she'd get a donut out of the deal. Downtown Texarkana turned into a ghost town during the day. Nights lit up with patrons of several restaurants. A couple even hosted live music, and all offered active bars. All of downtown fell within ten or twelve blocks, so the nighttime crowd would sometimes walk from one spot to the next. A downtown rejuvenation group hosted occasional pub crawls and progressive dinners. But where downtown struggled was with entertainment and daytime businesses. A movie theater tried and failed. As did a couple of nightclubs. And nothing had sprung up to get foot traffic during the day—no boutiques or bookstores or bakeries. All of those things felt close, but they never quite materialized. So when Rocky walked down to Patterson Fillmore's favorite coffee shop, she did so alone until she neared the Bi-State Justice Building.

Bi-State was one of the larger buildings downtown. The square block of glass sat in front of the partially deserted train station and beside the completely deserted McCartney Hotel. Amidst the barren landscape of downtown, the Bi-State Building buzzed as the most bustling hub. Police, lawyers, and alleged criminals came and went through revolving doors non-stop. Although the crowd didn't spread out too far, the two bail bonds places, the lonely bar, a greasy spoon diner, and Bi-State Coffee and Donuts all stayed pretty busy from 8:00 to 5:00 or so. And, as hoped, one of the patrons of Bi-State Coffee, sitting in the same back corner booth, was Patterson "Face" Fillmore.

He noticed Rocky as soon as she walked in. A curvy brunette with a killer smile and a flowy summer dress would never fail to catch his eye. But this curvy brunette made him hang his head and sigh into his coffee. "What are you doing here, Champagnolle?"

Rocky looked around. "A girl can't get a donut and some chocolate milk without a reason?"

Face rolled his eyes and took a flask out of his jacket pocket. "I gotta feeling you can't." He poured a shot of brown liquid into his coffee and held the flask up toward Rocky.

Rocky scrunched her face up and shook her head. "No, thank you. Frank Sinatra hasn't lowered the flag quite yet." She pointed at the empty booth across from him. "But do you mind if I sit?"

He smiled. "Does it matter?"

Rocky sat down and crossed her legs. "I wanted to follow up with you on a couple of questions."

Face tapped on the table. "You know, I feel like I was very polite with you last time. But you should know, cops don't much like digging around in the past."

A waitress came over to the table and smiled at Rocky. "Can I get you anything, dear?" She was either older or more world-worn than Rocky, but she was petite, blonde, and super cute. Her name tag read, "Jackie."

"Why, thank you so much," Rocky responded. "I would love a chocolate covered donut and a glass of chocolate milk." Jackie grinned at her and Rocky closed one eye. "I know. Like a child, right?"

Jackie laughed. "Same thing my daughter always gets."

Rocky shook her head. "Me and three-year-olds."

Face leaned forward. "She'll take hers to go, Jackie."

Jackie swatted him with her notepad. "Hush, Patterson. Or I'll make yours to go."

Face grinned at her. "If you'll go with me."

The waitress blushed and rolled her eyes. As she left to get Rocky's order, Rocky eyed Face and said, "What if I didn't want to talk about the past? What if my questions are about the present?"

Face frowned. "What present?"

"I am told you are the lead detective on the Junior League break-ins and the St. Laurent murder."

He drummed his finger on a file folder in the seat next to him. "I wouldn't say murder."

Rocky raised her eyebrows. "I would."

Jackie returned with a donut and a bottle of chocolate milk. "Here you go, sweetie. Take all the time you need. Don't mind this old man."

Face slid a business card into Jackie's apron pocket. "I keep telling you, I'm not old. Just experienced. You should give me a chance."

Rocky laughed. "How many business cards do you think it'll take to get her to call you?"

Jackie laughed hard and walked away. Face stared at Rocky. "What's your interest in the St. Laurents?"

She shook her head. "Curiosity."

He smirked. "I think it's more than curiosity. You've been snooping around, haven't you, Nancy Drew?"

Rocky shrugged. "Not snooping. But I heard a thing or two."

Face drummed his fingers faster on the file folder. "How'd you know I've given her more than one business card?"

Rocky nodded in the direction of Jackie. The waitress had tucked one of the detective's cards into the pages of her notepad, to which Rocky pointed with one eye closed. "I suppose you could take as a sign of some possibility. But, to be fair, she also has a rewards card from a gelato place next to it."

He poked out his lips, impressed. "And how'd you know she has a three-year-old?"

"She has some crayon scribblings in the notepad. There are some attempts at letters. I teach five and six-year-olds, and those are a couple years off what I'm used to seeing. She also has her phone in a pocket where she can feel it vibrate in case she gets a call. Most likely going to be a babysitter, not a daycare. At four, she could get her into a summer program of some sort. At two, she's not getting anywhere close to forming those letters. I guessed three. I'm more impressed you know she has a three-year-old."

Face topped off his coffee with one more tiny shot of liquor. He waggled the flask before he put it back in his pocket. "As a person, I'm suspect at best. But I'm a decent cop. So what do you know about my case?"

Rocky shook her head. "Nope. This is an exchange. You answer a question of mine, and I give you some information."

"I don't think it works—"

Rocky twisted off the cap to her chocolate milk. "It does if you want to know what I know." She took a bite of donut and waited him out.

After a contemplative scan of the ceiling, Face sighed, "All right. Ask a damn question."

"Do you have a suspect in the break-ins?"

Face shook his head. "Now you."

Rocky nodded, taking another bite. "Waverly St. Laurent called me to her home, where Freddy Van Vleck offered me twenty thousand dollars to stop looking into the break-ins."

Face frowned at her.

Rocky raised her eyebrows. "Do you think Waverly hired someone to break into houses?"

He nodded. "Your turn."

"A man in a brown truck followed me from the site of the first break-in."

Face hesitated, but pulled out a notepad and pen, writing down what she said. "What kind of brown truck?"

Rocky shook her head. "Do you think Waverly wanted her husband dead?"

Face sighed. "Come on, Rocky. This is serious."

Rocky nodded. "Do you think Waverly—"

"Yes," Face grunted. "Yeah, I do."

"Do you think she killed him herself? Or paid someone?"

Face shook a finger back and forth at her. "Nope. Your rules."

Rocky nodded and took a bite. "Okay," she said with her mouth full. "I have two names. One real. One fake. I'll give you the fake one, but if you let me look at that case file, I'll give you the real one."

Face laughed. "There's no way in hell I let you look at this file. And you owe me something, remember?"

"Fair enough," Rocky said. "Brent Powell."

He leaned back into his seat. "The fake one? Means nothing to me. Give me the real one."

"Tell me if you think Waverly wanted her husband dead because of Jason."

Face frowned. "What? No. Why would she want him dead because of Jason?"

"You suspected Bo for Jason's murder."

Face shook his head. "I didn't. Bo was an asshole, not a murderer. Damn sure not a serial killer." He took a sip of coffee. "I think I'm done playing now. Finish your donut and go back to shopping or whatever the hell it is you do."

Rocky took a last bite of the donut and patted at her mouth with a napkin. She pressed her fingers together. "Fine. Where's the ladies' room? My fingers are all sticky."

Face pointed to the far end of the lunch counter. "Around the corner."

Rocky hopped up and flounced away. Jackie put an order in at the counter. As Rocky got even with her, Jackie turned to head back to tend to a table and ran right into Rocky. They got tangled up for a second and came away both apologizing.

A Rocky Divorce

As soon as Rocky got into the restroom, she shut herself into a stall and pulled out Jackie's phone Rocky lifted from the waitress' apron when they collided. She hit the home button and found the screen locked with a four-digit code. She whipped out her own phone and went to Facebook. Face had been hot for Jackie for a while, so he would have friended her on Facebook. A quick search of his friends yielded two Jackies, but Jackie Miseldine's profile picture showed her with a cute little three-year-old girl. Jumping onto her page, Rocky scrolled until she found photos of the little girl's birthday party. November. Either the eleventh or twelfth. She punched in one-one-one-one and got nothing. Then one-one-one-two and the phone sprang open. Face left a few business cards strewn about the table, and Rocky palmed one before leaving for the restroom. She opened Jackie's text strands and started a new message to Face. She typed, "How about you show me some of your experience during my break. Meet me out back?" The idea of someone buying this made her laugh. But a man like Face was so full of himself, he would see her offer as a logical outcome of his advances. Rocky waited on his eager reply of, "On my way." She shot back a quick, "Okay, wait for me…give me two mins." She then blocked his number and deleted the strand. She deposited Jackie's phone next to the sink, where she would hurry to search once she noticed it missing. And then Rocky hurried back to her booth.

As expected, Face was gone, making a horny beeline for the back alley. Rocky leaned across the booth and scooped up the case file. She figured on having about five minutes.

The first pages were all about the robberies close to Rebecca Margolis' house. Those didn't matter. The next break-ins were all she cared about. She flipped through, speed reading as much as possible. All of the houses were names she recognized as Junior League women. All of the men were doctors. At one point, Rocky found a note about a surgeons' meeting on Tuesday nights. They were all surgeons in the same group, so the Tuesday night target could connect to when the men would be out more than when Martin Yancy took off from work. The reports confirmed the only thing taken was from the final break-in before Waverly—Dot Dingledowd's bottle of Adderall taken from her purse. But the report also confirmed the pill bottle held just one or two pills when taken.

Finally, she came to a series of documents related to the death of Bo St. Laurent. Rocky knew Face would come storming back in soon, so she skipped straight to the photos of the crime scene. There were plenty of them. Many showed almost candid shots of Waverly being led out and processed. She pulled closed her bathrobe and tiptoed on bare feet. Squinting into flashing lights, Waverly carried the unmistakable frazzle of shock. A photo of the shotgun at the top of the stairs had been annotated with a note stating this is where they found Waverly, shotgun in hand. The photos of Bo St. Laurent were gruesome. He lay at the foot of the stairs. As found, he stretched out on his stomach with a grapefruit-sized hole in his back. His legs were pretzeled into a sort of cursive letter *k*. And his arms splayed out, reaching up the first step of the staircase. A huge spray of blood spread up the wall of the staircase and all across the first few steps. Bright red splattered out in a diminishing pattern of tiny dots. Blood pooled all around the body, forming a large puddle at the base of the stairs. The stairs popped off the page as pristine white carpet and clear save for one rounded imprint on the third step, just outside the splatter. Rocky whipped out her phone and turned on the camera, zooming in as close as she could on the imprint. It was a footprint—a rounded footprint.

Rocky shoved all the documents back into the folder and set the packet back onto the seat. She stood up and started for the door, pausing to grab Jackie by the elbow. "I think someone left her phone in the women's restroom." Jackie reached a panicked hand to her apron. Rocky added, "Oh, and Officer Fillmore said he would take care of my ticket. Thanks." She hurried out the door.

When she stepped out onto the sidewalk and looked up, Face stood there, arms crossed. Rocky smiled and jerked a thumb back toward the coffee shop. "I stuck you with the bill. Figured you owed me."

As she started around him, Face stepped in front of her. "Not yet, I don't. You owe me a real name."

Rocky cocked her head. "I said I would give you a real name if you—"

Face groaned and hung his head. "Rocky. Please don't insult my pride twice in one day."

Rocky grinned. "Fair enough. Martin Yancy."

His head shot up and he leaned toward her. "What?"

"Martin."

Face shook his head. "No, no. The last name. What was the last name?"

Rocky nodded. She figured as much. "Yancy. Does that mean something to you?"

He stared off and started past her in a hurry. "I used to know someone named Yancy is all."

Rocky smiled and hurried for her car, pulling up Jen's number as she went. "Rocky!"

She turned back, and Face hung out of the coffee shop door.

He swallowed. "Look, Freddy Van Vleck, he—" Face paused and thought about his words. "The money was just a first attempt. The carrot. There's a stick somewhere. Trust me."

Rocky nodded. "Oh, I know. I've met him."

Face frowned. "I mean it, Rocky. Freddy Van Vleck will do whatever it takes to eliminate all threats from his client. He will tie up every loose end."

Rocky frowned and nodded. "Okay. Thanks."

Jen shouted, "Hello" in Rocky's hand.

Rocky pulled the phone up. "Jen? After our delivery to Whispering Pines, I need you to take me somewhere. We need to find Martin Yancy. Fast. I think his life's in danger."

Chapter 27

When Rocky met Jen at Elaine Maplethorpe's house, both cousins were buzzing around at top speed. Jen wore her bright red Junior League apron and ran back and forth between the house and an SUV carrying elaborate trays of brownies. Rocky nipped at her heels all the way into the house and back.

Rocky bounced back and forth on either side of Jen. "Jen, I think they're going to kill him."

Jen shoved a red apron at Rocky. "Kill who?" She shook her head. "Who? Who is killing and who is being killed? What are you talking about, Rocky?"

Rocky struggled to put on her apron. "Martin Yancy. The guy in the brown truck."

Jen's eyes grew wide. "The guy who tried to kill us?"

Rocky held up a finger. "He chased us."

"With intent to kill."

"That's beside the point here, Jen. Freddy Van Vleck is going to send his more muscular and scary clone to kill this man."

Jen frowned. "So Waverly hired him to break into houses and then hired her lawyer to kill him? This all sounds a little far-fetched."

Rocky shook her head. "Yes and no. I just need your help. Will you help me?"

Jen looked around. Numerous women in red aprons were rushing around, loading brownies. Others were placing them on plates and wrapping them in cellophane ordained with ribbons. Elaine hovered and stuttered out attempts at directions. "Rocky, this is your doing. This is happening. We are delivering pot brownies. Pot brownies, Rocky. Because of your idea. Stay focused."

Rocky heaved a sigh. "We deliver the brownies and then you take me to find Martin Yancy. Deal?"

Jen shook her head. "Sure. Whatever, Rocky. Just help. Please."

Rocky spun around in Elaine Maplethorpe's entryway and surveyed herself in the mirror. She fussed with her hair for a moment, shaking out a few curls and placing a strand behind her ear. She pulled out her phone and opened up a text strand from Georgia Lee. "Okay, girls. I've got the address. Let's do this," she called out and started for Jen's car.

Jen hung her head and called after her, "I meant, like, carry something or—" She sighed. "Never mind."

On the way to the nursing home, Jen drove in front of a caravan of Junior Leaguers. Rocky had already told her about the adventure with Lexi the night before, so she chattered about Georgia Lee and crime scene photos while Jen barked at her for directions. "Are you watching for where I'm supposed to turn, Rocky?"

"Yes! Chill out. I can multitask."

"Yeah, when you are interested in both tasks. And I can't chill out. There are drugs in my car right now, Rocky. If I get pulled over, what am I supposed to do?"

Rocky shook her head. "I don't know. Don't offer them a brownie? Why would they assume there's marijuana in the plates of brownies we are delivering to old people? They won't. Relax."

Most metrics ranked Whispering Pines as the nicest retirement home in Texarkana. The facility was set up in levels. As Jen first turned in, they passed a series of small cookie cutter houses where the more independent retirees could live and receive minimal assistance—dinners, laundry service, cleaning every other week, and the like. Straight in front of them, a five-story apartment complex stretched to their left on either side of the turn in the road. The residents were similar to those in the houses, but they could get a few more services, like regular medical checks or dialysis—anything of that nature. Georgia Lee told Rocky to take the Junior Leaguers all the way around to the back of the complex. Back there they would find the intensive care unit. The patients with the most needs lived there. They were not as helpless as the name made them seem. Although some were bedridden or eaten up by Alzheimer's or dementia, many could function with round-the-clock care. As Georgia Lee put it, these people needed the most relief from the pain of living a long life. He told Rocky to pull up into a circle drive and watch for a white woman around mid-forties. He said she would be dressed in sharp business attire. Thin, brown hair, attractive features. Natasha Kiser was the manager of community relations for Whispering Pines. And she would serve as liaison between the retirement home and the Junior League's "outreach effort."

As promised, an attractive, petite woman in a blazer and dressy gaucho pants stood in the circle drive waiting on them. She laced her fingers together in front of her and twiddled them in a display of nervous impatience. Jen pulled up close to her and turned to Rocky. Rocky jumped out smiling, "Ms. Kiser?"

Natasha nodded and stepped forward, extending a hand. "Rocky? Natasha Kiser. So nice to meet you."

Rocky shook her hand. "Likewise. Thank you so much for letting us come help out."

Natasha nodded through her nerves. "Can we talk outside for a moment? Before we go in."

"Of course."

Natasha guided her to a bench just outside the door and they sat down. "For obvious reasons, my bosses are not comfortable drawing up anything in writing."

Rocky nodded and shrugged. "We understand."

Natasha nodded. "We did, however, discuss some terms with your attorney. And we came to an agreement he said you would be fine with. Did you need to discuss our agreement any further?"

Rocky shook her head. "No. We trust our attorney's judgement."

"Good. So, from this point forward, we don't plan to have any need to discuss the contents of the brownies. Our patients—many of them—are in need of pain management and relief we have no way of giving them. We talked with Mr. Jefferson about obtaining a license to dispense medical marijuana legally. But those efforts never panned out. This, however controversial it may be, is viewed by the management of Whispering Pines as a godsend."

Rocky squinted and smiled, patting Natasha's hand. "We are so happy to be able to help."

"But we do not see a need to call any undue attention to our partnership."

"Nor do we. Obviously."

Natasha smiled. "Perfect. So we have an arrangement?"

Rocky shrugged. "Um, sure."

"Will this time work out for you each week?"

Rocky cocked her head. "Each…week?"

Natasha frowned. "Yes. Weekly deliveries. Mr. Jefferson said that wouldn't be a problem."

Rocky shook her head. "No. No problem. This time should work just fine."

The smile returned to Natasha's face. "Great. So what do you say we deliver some brownies?"

Rocky rubbed her hands together. "Sounds good to me." As they walked back toward the car Rocky pulled from her pocket the slip of paper Georgia Lee gave her. "Natasha? Would it be okay if I visited a patient while I'm here? Mr. Jefferson told me she and I share a friend in common."

Natasha brightened. "Of course. All visitors are always welcome. It makes their day when they get visitors of any kind. Who did you want to see?"

"Daisy Brooks."

"Oh, sure. Miss Daisy is great. And she's feeling pretty good today, too. Let's get your girls rolling and I can take you right to her room."

Rocky thanked Natasha and walked around to Jen's window. "Okay. Everything's all worked out. Tell everyone these are just brownies. Nothing more. No reason to talk about anything else from here on out. Whispering Pines is on board, and they are working all the business side of this through our attorney."

Jen breathed a sigh of relief and hopped out of the car. "Thank God. So we're just bringing brownies to old people?"

Rocky patted her shoulder and nodded. "Yes, Jen. That's all"

Jen smiled and nodded. "I can do that. I'll go tell everyone."

Rocky smiled back and started to walk inside with Natasha. She looked back over her shoulder and whispered to Jen, "Once a week."

Jen did a double take. "Once a—" she grabbed for Rocky but missed. "Did you say once a week? Rocky!" But Rocky was gone.

As Jen ran up and down the line of cars prompting Junior Leaguers into action, Natasha took Rocky on a ten-cent tour of the facility. Two sets of automatic sliding doors opened into a foyer with a reception desk. Beyond the desk were two sitting rooms with big screen TVs and multiple spaces for cards and games of Scrabble. There were shelves upon shelves filled with paperback books, detective novels with a few romances mixed in. Rocky chuckled. "How old do you have to be to move in?"

Natasha laughed and said, "I get asked that all the time. Doesn't seem too bad, does it?"

They walked past a small cafeteria, empty at the moment. Three hallways led in separate directions to patient rooms. Natasha took Rocky down one to the last room on the hallway. It was almost remote, with a large window overlooking woods at the back of the property. With the door open, Rocky could see a short, squat lady in a wheelchair admiring the view. She had two quilts wrapped around her shoulders and she wore slippers with wool socks pulled up to mid-calf. Her hair was thinning, but fixed. Rocky could see her reflection in the window, and the old woman smiled at the sight of birds playing in a birdbath at the edge of the woods. Her eyes betrayed some wrinkles at her eye lines. Otherwise, her skin was smooth and the color of cinnamon with countless ruddy freckles all over her plump cheeks.

Natasha called out, "Miss Daisy? You have a visitor."

Daisy reached out and patted a chair next to her and laughed back, "Oh yeah? Well, tell her to come on over here and watch these birds."

Natasha smiled at Rocky and held a hand out toward the chair. "I'll leave you two and go check on the girls."

Rocky returned the smile and thanked her, and then walked over to the chair. "What am I watching?"

Daisy laughed as the birds bounced off one another. "I got no clue. They either fighting or fucking, but it's the funniest damn thing I ever seen."

Rocky watched with her for a moment, both ladies laughing until one bird flew away. Daisy harrumphed. "I guess he got his fill of whatever her was doing."

"I guess so. My name is Rocky Champagnolle, Miss Daisy."

Daisy nodded. "Frank's daughter?"

"Yes, ma'am. Georgia Lee Jefferson gave me your name."

She almost spat. "Rascal. He ain't been up here to visit in three days." She frowned at Rocky. "He send you in his place?"

Rocky laughed. "Oh, no, ma'am. He said you might be able to fill in some gaps for me in some research I'm doing."

Daisy scratched at her head and closed an eye. "Research? Into what?"

Rocky donned a somber face. "It isn't pleasant, I'm afraid. But I'm beginning to think it may be very, very important."

Daisy followed Rocky's gaze over to a framed photograph on the woman's bedside table. The photograph showed a younger Daisy with a younger, happier Waverly St. Laurent—with jet black hair, giant sunglasses, and resembling Jackie O. A dirty-faced boy with a wild smile and messy platinum blond hair hung from each of their arms. Daisy didn't turn away from the photo, but said, "You want to ask about Jason. I figured somebody'd get around to talking to me one day."

Rocky frowned. "No one ever talked to you about Jason's murder?"

Daisy kept staring at the photo. "Oh, the police talked to me a little bit. The Singer boy knew me a little, so he asked a few questions. Early on. After they found him, nobody asked much of anything."

"What did Rondo ask you? When Jason went missing."

"Oh, we brought in a girl to do some cleaning a little while before. I did a little of everything—maid, nanny, cook. So Miss Waverly would let me bring in some help now and again."

Rocky shook her head. "Why did he ask about her?"

Daisy gave Rocky side eye. "Miss Waverly let her go right before Jason went missing. You see, oftentimes the girls who came to help were young. And oftentimes they were pretty."

Rocky nodded along. "Bo St. Laurent?"

"Mm hm," Daisy confirmed. "The man couldn't keep his little dick in his pants."

"What did you think about Dr. and Mrs. St. Laurent?"

"Bo was a right asshole. He bullied everyone in his life. I could always stand up for myself all right, but Miss Waverly ain't as tough as she seems. And Jason," Daisy trailed off.

Rocky leaned toward her. "Did Bo abuse Jason?"

Daisy sniffed. "There was a time I might say no. Times is different, you know? People went a little harder on they kids at one time. I know I did. We all did. But looking back? I can see. Wasn't just a hard whoopin now and again. Turned emotional. He belittled the boy. Always trying to make him tougher than he knew how to be. Jason was a little delicate as a kid. He would've turned out just fine, but Bo couldn't stand it." There were tears in her voice, but she didn't break. "I should've stood up for him more."

Rocky gave her a beat to collect herself before asking, "What about Waverly?"

Daisy shot her a frown. "No, ma'am. Waverly St. Laurent never laid a hand on that boy."

Rocky waved off the answer apologetically. "Oh, no. I just mean, what did you think about Waverly?"

Daisy gazed back at the picture. "Me and Miss Waverly were best friends when Jason was little. Before he came along, too." She turned back to Rocky. "I stood right there by her side when they first brought that baby home, you know? Not Bo. Me. We were raising Jason together, me and Miss Waverly."

"But after he died?"

Daisy shook her head and squinted out the window. "We couldn't talk to each other much afterwards. I think we both felt responsible. Like we didn't do enough. Too scared of blaming each other. So we just kept a distance. She's still family. She put me in here. Pays the bill every month. Don't visit, but she sends things now and again."

They both glanced back at the photo for a minute. Rocky smiled. "You know, I had no idea Jason was blond."

Daisy grinned and nodded. "Oh, yeah. Shiny blond hair since he was a baby. Damn near white. Just like his momma."

Rocky frowned at Daisy. "His momma? You knew his birth mother?"

Daisy snorted. "Hell, yes. One of those little nurses working for Bo. Little blonde nursing student when he got her pregnant. A damn student. Girl wasn't but nineteen years old, Lord save her."

Rocky shook her head. "Jason was Bo's biological son?"

Daisy nodded. "Yes, ma'am. They don't talk about it, but he was. Bo got the little girl pregnant and tried to make her get an abortion. And bless it if she stood her ground. Georgia Lee ended up having to tell Miss Waverly. Bo was too much of a coward, so he sent his damn lawyer. Miss Waverly always knew about the women, but the pregnancy still gave her a shock. Of course, Miss Waverly couldn't have no kid of her own. She'd had a hysterectomy a few years before. So she agreed to raise Jason. Georgia Lee worked things out with the girl to make sure nothing blew back. Wasn't hard. Poor girl couldn't raise no kid." She shook her head. "Nineteen years old. A damn student."

"What became of the girl?"

Daisy snorted again. "Oh, she kept working for the man for a while. Craziest damn thing I ever did see. She drifted off somewhere sometime, but not soon enough. Could you imagine? Having to see pictures of the boy you gave up sitting on your boss' desk. Lord God."

Rocky scrunched up her face and rubbed her hands together. "Do you remember her name?"

Daisy shook her head. "No, girl. I'm sorry. Can't remember my own damn name some days. Cute little blonde thing. I can still see her, but I can't place her name."

Rocky leaned over and took the old woman by the hands. "Thank you, Miss Daisy. Would it be okay if I come see you again? I think we'll be making weekly deliveries for a while."

Daisy smiled. "Of course, sweetheart. You come see me any time."

Chapter 28

Once all the brownies were delivered and the Junior League Baking Team had spent some time exchanging pleasantries with the Whispering Pines staff and residents, Jen found Rocky sitting in the front seat rubbing her hands together, lost in thought. Jen plopped down in the driver's seat. "What are you doing, Rocky?"

"Thinking."

Jen snorted. "Thinking? Thinking? Are you thinking about how you didn't help at all in there? Or are you maybe thinking about how in the good fuck we are going to be able to deliver a batch of brownies once a week?"

Rocky held up her phone. "Georgia Lee texted. He said they deposited the money into our designated account. They paid us twenty dollars per brownie. Which is two forty per batch. We brought them eight batches today, and we have eight left at Elaine's, which Georgia Lee is working on selling to the rehab clinic for cancer patients. I paid nine hundred for the pot. And Georgia Lee takes fifteen percent. So, if the price holds, we are netting about twenty-five hundred a week. Our project will be fully funded in a month, not factoring in the Adderall."

Jen stared at the calculator screen on Rocky's phone, which displayed a readout of $9,996. Jen nodded. "Oh. Well…good. I didn't know it would be…okay."

Rocky put her phone away. "Jen, I need to find Martin Yancy. I know what this is all about. And he is in real danger."

Jen frowned and shook her head. "I don't understand why this is our problem, Rocky. Martin Yancy tried to kill us."

Rocky shook her head. "We don't know he would have killed us. He chased us. But this is our problem because I'm the one person who even knows about him." She cocked his head. "Well, other than Freddy Van Vleck. And he's trying to have him killed, I think."

Jen narrowed one eye. "So…what? We find him and warn him? And leave?"

Rocky curled her lip, frowned, and nodded. "Sure."

"Then just track him on your phone thing."

Rocky flopped a hand toward her purse where she put her phone. "I tried. The damn thing shuts itself off after a while to save battery."

"Then how do we find him?"

Rocky closed her eyes and put her fingers to her temples. "I need to think. There has to be something. It's not Tuesday, so, by all accounts, he would be at work right now. Think about the house. What did you see? What did you hear? What did you smell?"

Jen shrugged. "I don't know. It smelled good. Kind of—"

Rocky nodded. "Caramel spice. They had one of those wax cube burners. Vanilla Caramel Spice. I used that in my classroom for a while. Good. Keep going."

"The furniture looked okay. Good, but cheap. The kind you'd buy at—"

Rocky opened her eyes and turned to Jen. "Walmart?"

Jen shrugged. "Sure. Someplace like that."

"The coat rack. Do you remember it?"

Jen nodded. "Kind of. Where you saw the military green jacket and black hat, right? How you figured out he was for sure the guy. I remember you pointing the jacket out, yeah."

Rocky closed her eyes again. "Something hung there under the jacket, right?"

"I...think so, yeah."

"What color was it? It poked out a little bit." Jen didn't reply, so Rocky promoted, "Close your eyes. Think."

Jen closed her eyes. "Blue. Bright blue and—"

"Yellow," they said at the same time and looked at each other. Rocky smiled. "Like a Walmart employee vest."

Jen laughed. "Holy shit. He works at Walmart." She nodded and started the car. "Okay. There's a Supercenter on the Arkansas side, one out toward Nash, and two or three of those neighborhood markets. Which one do I try first?"

Rocky shook her head. "Neighborhood market employees wear those tan vests, I think. It's a Supercenter."

Jen pulled out and started winding her way back out of the Whispering Pines campus. "We're closer to Nash. Try Texas side first?"

Rocky frowned and shook her head. "No. When I used those wax cubes I always had trouble finding them. I finally found them at the Arkansas side Walmart. Start there."

Jen pulled out in the direction of the Arkansas side of town. "Why do you think Waverly wants Martin Yancy dead?"

"I don't. Not Waverly. I think Freddy Van Vleck is cleaning up a mess Waverly created. Detective Fillmore said Freddy would do anything to keep things from blowing back on his client."

"But they offered us money to stay away from Martin. Why would Freddy go along with paying us if he planned on killing him?"

Rocky shook her head. "Freddy didn't want to pay us. You could tell. And I'm not sure he knew where Martin Yancy was. I'm afraid we may have led Freddy to Martin ourselves."

"This doesn't make any sense."

Rocky nodded. "It will." When they pulled into the Walmart parking lot, Rocky directed Jen to pull around to the far side and to the back—close to the loading docks in a side parking lot. "This is where the employees park. Watch for the brown truck."

After easing up and down the aisles, Jen quick-swerved into a spot and parked, ducking down and swearing, "Shit."

Rocky followed suit, ducking down herself, but trying to peer over the dash for whatever Jen had seen. "What? Did you see the truck?"

Jen pointed. "Not just the truck but look who found it first."

Rocky eased up. Two rows over, Martin Yancy's truck sat backed into a parking spot. Freddy Van Vleck's henchman circled the front bumper, peeking into the windows and checking to see if the doors were locked. After a moment, they watched his shiny bald head bob through the cars on his way toward the building. "This is okay," Rocky reassured. "We need everyone."

Jen folded herself down into the driver's seat with her knees up and curled around the steering wheel. She turned to Rocky. "What? Everyone together? You didn't say everyone together. You said find him, warn him, and leave."

Rocky shrugged. "Yeah. We're sort of doing that."

"Everyone together doesn't sound like sort of doing that. It sounds like some kind of fucked up Rocky plan. I don't like fucked up Rocky plans."

Rocky winced. "Well, then you aren't going to like what I'm about to ask you to do."

Jen started shaking her head. "No. Whatever it is, no."

Rocky held her hands out to ease her. "Now, just hold on. Hear me out. One of us has to, Jen."

Jen squinted at Rocky. "Has to what?"

Rocky nodded toward the building. "Go in there."

Jen's eyes bugged out. "Go in there? With two men who both want us dead? Are you kidding me?"

Rocky tilted her head. "One of them wants us dead. But the other one wants him dead. It's like a—" She snapped her fingers, "What do they call it?"

"I don't care what they call it! Why would I go in there?"

Rocky frowned at her like the answer was obvious. "To pull the fire alarm."

"What? What the fuck are you talking about, Rocky? I'm supposed to walk into a crowded Walmart with two killers inside and pull the fire alarm? What in the good fuck are you going to be doing while I'm committing a felony while surrounded by murderers?"

Rocky held her phone up. "I'm calling in a bomb threat."

Jen nodded. "So I am getting out of the car, walking into the store where we know two criminals are, and pulling a fire alarm, while you sit in the car and make a phone call?"

Rocky pointed at her. "And watch for them to come out. See, we need to get them out of the store before they see each other. And we need Martin to see us before Freddy's guy sees him. But then we need Freddy's guy to see both of us. To be sure to get them out here together, we need to empty out the store. And I will be out here to meet them. All you do is pull the alarm and run."

"Run where, Rocky?"

"Back to the car. I'll need you to drive when they start chasing us." She patted Jen on the leg. "You're so good at driving in chases."

Jen screamed, "Chasing us? Since when are they going to chase us?"

Rocky frowned. "That's the whole goal of this. I told you. Warn him, then leave."

"You didn't say he would be chasing us when we left."

"I didn't? I'm pretty sure I did." Rocky looked at her phone. "Do you know Walmart's number?"

"Rocky!"

"Chill out. I'm Googling it." Rocky raised eyebrows at her. "You better go. There's a fire alarm right when you walk in next to the buggy return."

"Why do you know where the fire alarms are?" Jen fumed, but started out of the car. "I can't believe I let you drag me into this shit."

As Jen stamped off to pull the fire alarm, Rocky found the number and dialed. After a beat and a couple of automated keypad choices, she got a voice just before Jen reached the doors. Rocky smiled and said into the phone. "Hi! Yes, I'm calling to report a bomb. ... Yes, ma'am. I said a bomb. ... Yes, ma'am. An actual bomb. There is a bomb in Walmart right now. You need to get everyone out. ... No, this is not a joke. I'm sure you are wondering whether or not to believe me, but in a moment like this you must ask yourself, do I want to be the person who received a warning and chose to ignore it? Do I want to be the person talked about on all the news shows a week from now? The person who could have saved lives instead of allowing countless deaths. What's your name? ... Well, Cindy, this is your moment. This is your opportunity to be one of two things. Today, you will either be the hero. Or you will be the person who sat on privileged information and chose to do nothing." Rocky hung up and nodded at her own approach.

Rocky climbed out of the car and walked toward Martin Yancy's truck. She fished around in the bed of the truck until she found the GoPhone. Fiddling with buttons for a moment, she got the screen to come on—the phone had shut itself off, but still held a tiny bit of battery life. She set the cell on the ground and kicked it across under a car one row over. The back of Martin's truck faced the store, so Rocky sat on the tailgate and waited. Within seconds, confused shoppers started wandering out into the parking lot. Seconds later, alarms started a shrill wail from inside. The flow of foot traffic picked up into a herd. Rocky's phone rang in her hand. The screen showed a picture of Jen. "Good job, Jen. I'm very proud."

"I don't think anyone saw me. People were too busy telling everyone to get out."

Rocky watched Jen swift-walk from the store. "Hey, circle around the parking lot a little. Don't come straight to the car."

Jen paused and nodded, changing direction. "Good idea." She kept walking but slowed down. "Wait, why am I doing this?"

Rocky kept watching the crowd pour out. Most people shuffled out toward the main lot, but one shiny bald head broke from the herd and started her way. "Hey, Jen? Can you look this way and wave your arms around?"

Jen frowned and wedged the phone between her ear and shoulder. She started waving her arms back and forth in Rocky's direction. "Why am I doing this? Can you not see me?"

Rocky nodded. "I see you. Keep doing that." She watched back and forth between Jen and Baldy until she could tell Baldy also noticed Jen. He squinted and then reddened with anger. Rocky said into the phone. "Okay. He sees you. Good job."

Jen dropped her arms and looked around. "Who sees me? Rocky? Who sees me? Who sees me?"

"Don't just stand there, Jen. You need to move faster. He's headed your way."

Jen started to trot. "Who is headed my way?"

"Bald guy. Just circle around to the car and come pick me up at Martin's truck."

Jen screamed and panted into the phone. "Rocky, what did you do? I can't believe you—"

"Ooh. Gotta go." Rocky hung up. Martin Yancy strolled out of the doors toward the back of the big crowd. He walked with his hands in his pockets, bored with the panic. He started toward his truck, pulling a cigarette from an apron pocket and lighting it. Another employee said something to him and they both laughed.

When Martin got about ten yards from his truck he stopped. The other employee veered off in another direction. Martin stood and stared at Rocky, who sat on the tailgate of his truck swinging her legs. He took a drag of his cigarette and jerked a thumb back toward the store. "This your doing?"

Rocky donned an innocent pout. "Me? I've been right here." She cocked her head at him. "What have you been doing?"

Martin took another drag. "Why are you here?"

"I'm here to warn you, Martin."

He glowered at her.

Rocky rolled her eyes. "Don't look shocked. Your name is about the easiest thing I've figured out in the past few days."

Martin frowned.

"That's right, Martin." Rocky nodded. "I know everything. I know you broke into those houses. And I know you didn't steal anything. You weren't trying to steal anything. You broke into a few around Rebecca's neighborhood first, just to get the hang of it. And to check police response time. Then you targeted doctor's houses. Doctors with Junior League wives, specifically. And I know what you were looking for, Martin."

He took a step toward her and flicked his cigarette to the ground. "Shut up."

Rocky raised her eyebrows. "I know *who* you were looking for."

Martin broke for her with his hands extended. Rocky hit the send button on her phone tucked behind her back. The GoPhone sprang to life, chirping behind Martin. He paused and turned for just a second, giving Rocky enough time to hop off the tailgate and scramble around the truck.

Jen squealed to a stop and reached over to fling open the passenger side door. Rocky jumped in and Jen tore off, leaving the bald man and Martin staring at one another across the empty space. They both darted toward their cars—Martin to chase Jen and Rocky, Baldy to chase Martin. Rocky twisted in her seat to see the dance play out and then flopped back around and pumped a fist. "Perfect! What timing, Jen. Top notch detective work on your—"

"You almost got me killed!"

Rocky frowned. "That's a little hyperbole, isn't it?"

"No! A killer chased me through a parking lot! I rolled under a van to get away from him!"

Rocky nodded, impressed. "Rolling under a van. Wow. Good work, Jen."

"Shut up, Rocky! I could have died! We need to call the police!"

Rocky pulled her phone up. "Excellent idea. I'm calling Rondo and Georgia Lee. They both need to meet us there." She started dialing.

Jen shook her head incredulously. "Meet us where?"

Rocky spoke into the phone. "Rondo? Hey, it's Rocky. We're headed to Waverly St. Laurent's house. I think you should meet us there."

Chapter 29

"Waverly St. Laurent's house?" Jen screamed at Rocky as they barreled around corners.

Rocky nodded. "Yes. And slow down a little. We need them to catch up."

"Rocky, you have lost your mind. They are chasing us to kill us. And Waverly St. Laurent hired them both to do it!"

"No. She didn't. Waverly is a massive cunt, but the only person she hired was Freddy Van Vleck."

Jen frowned as she checked the rearview to find the brown truck gaining on them. "Then why did Martin Yancy break into those houses?"

"He was looking for Waverly and Bo St. Laurent."

"Why?"

Instead of answering, Rocky pointed to the circle drive in front of Waverly St. Laurent's giant red brick house. "Pull in right there."

Jen shook her head, mumbling, "This is insane." But she pulled in and slammed the gear shift into park.

The brown truck rumbled up past them and whipped into the circle drive the opposite direction, jackknifing and blocking their path. Jen reached to put the gear shift in reverse, but Rocky jumped out of the car. "Rocky! Rocky, what the hell are you doing?"

Martin Yancy climbed out of his truck to meet her, both of them walking to where the front of the vehicles almost touched. Martin licked his lips and swallowed down a ball of nerves. "Get in the truck. We're leaving."

Rocky shrugged. "Why, Martin? Wasn't this the plan all along? Confront Bo? Confront Waverly? Well," she held her hands out wide, "here we are. Let's do it. What do you say?"

Martin reached for her, but Rocky dodged back. He waved for her to come. "This isn't your business. Now, come on. Get in the truck. Both of you." Jen made her way around to Rocky's elbow.

Before Rocky could say any more, a car door slammed behind them. The bald henchman had pulled up, blocking Jen's SUV on both sides now. He walked toward them, holding a gun at his side like a sack lunch. He sighed. "I think we all just go inside and hash this out in private."

Rocky clapped. "Great idea."

Jen punched her in the side. "No. Horrible idea. He's going to kill us."

Rocky shook her head and motioned toward Martin. "No, he wants to kill him."

Martin held his hands up and moved toward the door. "Thanks."

The man used his gun to guide the three of them toward the door. Rocky rang the doorbell without having to be told to do so. A cleaning lady answered, confused, then shrieked and scampered back toward the kitchen as soon as she saw the gun. The kitchen sat off to the left, through a living room across from the parlor where Rocky and Jen met with Waverly. In the middle of the house, a large staircase curved up to a landing filled with towering shelves of decorative items—framed photos of a young Jason and vases filled with glass marbles and ornate fake flowers—before leading up to the second floor. Rocky recognized the white carpeted stairs as the same ones where Bo St. Laurent had been shot. Waverly came down and stopped at the landing—the same place police found her on the night of her husband's murder. She shouted down, "Jeffrey! What is going on here?"

Rocky cut her eyes toward the bald man. "Jeffrey? Really? I would never guess Jeffrey."

Jeffrey scowled at her. "Shut up." He called out to the cleaning lady, waving the gun in the direction of the kitchen. "Get back in here! I want everyone where I can see them."

Waverly started barking more questions at Jeffrey, while he continued to urge the cleaning woman back and to quiet her sobbing screams. Martin used all the commotion to reach into Rocky's purse and extract her pink pistol. He grabbed Rocky around the neck and backed toward the parlor, knocking Jen onto the ground. Jen rolled into the parlor and cowered at Rocky's ankles, while Martin held the gun to Rocky's head, the other arm wrapped around her neck. "Drop your gun!"

Jeffrey turned and smiled. He eased into the living room. "This is a bad play, Martin. You think I care if you shoot her?" He held his own gun up, leveled at Martin's head.

Martin sneered, "I think you want this as clean as possible. Not a bloodbath in your client's entryway." He readjusted and gripped Rocky around the neck. "Now we're going to walk out of here real slow. And no one is going to shoot anybody."

"Sounds like a damn fine idea." The front door had eased open without anyone noticing. Rondo Singer and Face Fillmore stood shoulder to shoulder, guns drawn. Face locked in on Jeffrey, and Rondo crooked the barrel of his sidearm around trying to get an angle on Martin.

Rocky reached down and slapped Jen's arm. "A Mexican standoff! I knew it would come to me."

No one lowered a gun. Rondo's eyes were darting all over the room. "Rocky, who the hell are these people?"

"Well, I think you know Waverly. Jen is down here on the floor."

Rondo smacked his lips. "The people with guns, Rocky."

"Oh. One of them is named Jeffrey. I'll bet you never guess which one."

"Rocky!"

Rocky pulled at Martin's arm to get some breathing room. "The one holding me goes by Martin Yancy."

Rondo glanced over at Face.

"Yes," Rocky added. "You do know that name. Detective Fillmore had a similar reaction. Trying to place it. I'll help you out. Yancy was the name of the cute blonde nurse who worked for Bo St. Laurent. The same one who, as a student, got pregnant with Bo's baby, Jason St. Laurent. And the same one who got pulled in to do an eye check on Jason at school. And the same one who lived in Trailer Pines, where Jason had been going after school. He had been going to see his birth mother."

Face frowned. "I picked up on the name, but who are you saying this guy is? Her other son? And why come here now? Did Debbie Yancy kill Jason?"

Rocky held up a finger, pointing back at Martin. "Nope. She raised him."

Waverly called out from the stairs. "Stop! Stop talking!"

"Martin is Jason St. Laurent," Rocky stated with a smirk.

Rondo shook his head. "Can't be. I was there. We found his remains."

"Found what exactly?" Rocky asked. "This was mid-eighties? Pre-DNA, right? You found a pile of ash and a few charred bones. The type of remains someone could come by if she owned a funeral home."

Rondo raised an eyebrow. "We identified him. We found Jason's—"

Rocky held a hand up. "Let me guess. Teeth?"

Both of the detectives paused but nodded.

Rocky continued, "Teeth like the ones a mother might save after every visit from the Tooth Fairy?"

Rondo looked up at Waverly. "But why?"

Rocky waved to get their attention. "Could I just," she struggled to get a little more breathing room. "I'm kind of having a moment, here." She cleared her throat. "You see, Bo St. Laurent was an asshole. An abusive asshole. And Waverly might be an asshole, too, but not on the same level. So, to save her son, she worked it out for him to go away with his birth mother. She used the whole Rye Mother—" She winced toward Rondo. "Sorry. She used the serial killings to cover their tracks. Jason was young enough to forget a lot of his early life. But he didn't forget enough. Did he, Waverly?"

Waverly began to cry. "I…I wanted him to have a good life."

Jason jerked the gun up toward Waverly. "You sent me off to have a life somewhere else! I was your son!"

Rocky waved. "Well, adopted son, to be fair." That got the gun back to her head, but she continued, undeterred. "Debbie Yancy did her part. She moved, she loved her biological son, and she managed to wipe most of the memories clean. But Jason remembered a few things. Bits and pieces." She jerked a thumb back toward the parlor. "He remembered Bo St. Laurent's gun cabinet in his office."

Jason's eyes glazed over. "He used to sit in there and drink a glass of scotch and clean those guns almost every night."

Rocky kept going. "And he remembered his dad was a doctor, with a Junior League wife. That's why he targeted these houses. He looked at photos and ruled out anyone who didn't fit the bill. He even made the same mistake I did about Elaine Maplethorpe."

Jason shook his head. "Beverly is not a man's name."

Rocky peered up at him. "Right? In no culture is Beverly a—"

Rondo sighed. "Rocky, can we wrap this up?"

"Oh, sorry," Rocky fluttered. "When he found the prescription bottle in Dottie Dingledowd's purse, he saw the name: St. Laurent. It came back to him. And he knew who to confront about the one thing he remembered most. The abuse. Whatever it was or wasn't, I have no idea. But it left a mark on a young Jason St. Laurent in a way he could never—"

Jason pointed the gun back at Waverly. "You could have stopped him!"

Rocky sighed. "Are you kidding me? I practiced this part in my head. I had a whole thing. Come on, man."

Waverly cried back at Jason, pleading with her arms outstretched. "I did stop him. I did the one thing I knew how to do!"

Rocky strained to leer up at Jason again. "She tried to take the fall for you." She eyed Face Fillmore. "Jason shot Bo St. Laurent. Take a look at the crime scene photos. You found Waverly up the stairs and barefoot. She couldn't have shot Bo in the back and walked back up the stairs without leaving footprints. But there was one footprint. The one Jason left when he stepped up to hand Waverly the shotgun. After, I'm assuming, she begged him to let her take the blame."

Waverly moaned. "I wanted to help you, Jason."

Jason cried, screaming back at her and pointing the gun as he spoke. "Why didn't you want to help me when I was little? I was a kid! I was your kid!"

Rondo used the moment of distraction to make eye contact with Jen. He telegraphed his glare back and forth from her to Rocky's purse strap looped around her neck and over a shoulder. Rondo made a sharp movement down with his eyes.

Jen nodded, swallowed hard, and took a deep breath. She reached up and grabbed onto Rocky's purse strap with both hands. With everything in her, Jen jerked Rocky down out of Jason's grip and rolled with her into the parlor. Rondo fired one shot into Jason's shoulder, sending him down onto the ground in a crumpled heap.

Gunfire erupted in the entryway, echoing off the high ceilings and sending up the smell of gunpowder. Rocky and Jen slid back into the parlor, but they could still watch as Rondo and Face exchanged a quick round of fire with Jeffrey. The shots all went wild, fired off as all three men dove for cover. Rondo and Face ducked behind a couch, but one of them hit Jeffrey. He slunk into the kitchen and leaned against a counter with his gun up and ready for either detective to show his face. Jeffrey kept his eyes locked on the back of the couch, never noticing Rocky and Jen in his clear line of sight through the parlor doors.

Jen pulled on Rocky. "Let's go out a window."

Rocky peeked around the parlor door. "We can't." She pointed to Jason, who struggled to his feet and scooped up Rocky's gun. He stalked up the steps toward Waverly, who froze in fear. Rocky looked at Jen. "He's going to kill her."

Jen gave Rocky the wide eyes of utter shock. "Three hours ago you wanted to kill her."

Rocky shook her head. "I wanted to kill her reputation and rob her of the will to live. There's a huge difference."

"Is there?"

Rocky ran to the gun cabinet and found a Ruger twenty-two caliber rifle. She dug through the bottom of the cabinet until she found a clip fit for the gun. Jen ran up behind her. From the other room, shouts rang out from everyone in an unintelligible cacophony. As Rocky loaded the clip into the gun, she mumbled, "This is just like the rifle Daddy used to teach me to shoot squirrels."

Jen shook her head. "Rocky, you never shot any squirrels."

Rocky winked at her. "Missed on purpose, Jen. Those squirrels never did anything to me." She ran back over and took a position at the parlor doors where she could see Jeffrey and Jason. Jason crept closer and closer to Waverly.

"Rocky, you can't shoot a person! What the hell are you doing?"

Rocky surveyed the scene, holding a finger out and closing one eye, first toward Jeffrey and the kitchen, and then toward Jason, ascending toward Waverly on the mid floor landing of the stairs. "Oh, Jen. Such a bleeding heart. Fine. I won't shoot any people. Happy?"

Jen steamed. "No! No, I'm not happy. Do you know what you're doing?"

Rocky turned and looked at her. "Yes, Jen. Of course I know what I'm doing. I took a firearms safety course. Best shot in class."

"Rocky, that doesn't mean you are capable of—"

Rocky put a finger on Jen's lips and lowered herself into a shooting stance. She moved the sights back and forth between Jason and Jeffrey, Jeffrey and Jason. Jeffrey screamed at the police, shaking the gun, but held a wound at his side. Jason pulled within four steps of Waverly, forcing himself up one laborious step at a time. "The question is do I help Rondo or save Waverly?"

Jen put her face in her hands. "Neither! I want to go home."

Rocky nodded. "Both. Great idea, Jen."

Rocky moved the sights over to Jeffrey but raised them up to the counter over his head. A carafe rested right above his head. She took aim and fired. Jeffrey jerked the gun toward the noise, but the carafe exploded, sending hot coffee and glass showering down onto his head. He recoiled and screamed.

Rocky swiveled up to set her sights past Jason's shoulder and onto Waverly. She shifted to her right until she found the shelf with a vase full of glass marbles. One shot and marbles burst out all over the steps. Jason ducked, but raised his gun and tried to continue on, but his first step found several of the tiny glass balls. Jason went tumbling down the steps.

While Face ran to secure Jeffrey, who writhed on the floor with a gut wound and a face full of coffee, Rondo placed cuffs on Jason and kicked Rocky's gun to the side. Rocky stood up and walked over to pick up her gun. Rondo smacked his lips at her. "Rocky. Leave the damn gun."

Rocky frowned at him. "But it's mine."

With both Jason and Jeffrey in cuffs, Face walked over next to Rondo. "Yeah, it's yours. And it got taken from you and almost used in the murder of a police officer! Not to mention you just fired off a rifle and almost hit an innocent woman!"

Rocky twisted her mouth up and mumbled. "I don't know about all that. I wouldn't call her innocent."

Jen moved in next to Rocky and shook her head, answering out of the side of her mouth as well, "She did try to cover up the murder of her husband."

Rocky nodded. "And fake the murder of her son."

"Who she technically kidnapped."

Rondo closed his eyes and shook his head, waving his arms. "Stop it! Just stop it. You're both coming down to the station. We gonna sort all this shit out right."

"I'm afraid I'm going to insist my clients be released to come with me, Officer Singer." Macon Georgia Lee Jefferson the Fourth stepped into the threshold of Waverly's home, filling up the entire doorway with his frame. He wore the same denim shirt and dark pants, with a tan blazer on over the shirt. He held a leather briefcase and adjusted small reading glasses on his nose.

Rondo spun around. "Detective Singer."

Georgia Lee smiled broadly, flashing those big white teeth and the hint of one dimple. "My apologies, Detective. I still see you as a young pup. I forget you're all grown."

Rondo ruffled and motioned to Rocky and Jen. "We need to talk to them."

Georgia Lee nodded. "And you can make an appointment to do so."

Rocky held up a finger. "Afternoons are best for me."

Jen added, "But I work two to five."

They faced one another and babbled: "So, one?" "One-ish." "Yeah, not on the dot or anything. Just in the—" "Ballpark, right."

Face waved an arm to cut them off. "Enough. Look around. They helped destroy this woman's home!"

Georgia Lee raised his eyebrows. "And so did you, Detective." He rolled his eyes up at Waverly. "And if Ms. St. Laurent cares to press charges, then my clients will be more than happy to accompany you so we can work everything out. But I got a feeling she won't." He nodded once. "Waverly."

Waverly stood frozen, shaking and in shock. But she grinned and nodded back. "Georgia Lee." She turned her whole body to Rondo and Face, waving a hand like swatting a fly. "Let those girls go. You got what you came for. And if Raquel hadn't done your job for you, you wouldn't have anything more than your dicks in one hand and a thumb up your asses."

Rondo sighed into his chest. "Fine. Go."

Rocky stooped to pick up her gun.

"Rocky! Leave the gun!" Rondo closed his eyes. "Please?"

Rocky nodded. "Oh. Okay. Yeah. You can bring it back to me when you're done, I guess."

Georgia Lee motioned for the girls to follow him to his car. "Let me drive you home, ladies."

Rocky paused and looked up at Waverly. She smiled. "You can call me Rocky."

Chapter 30

A month and a half later, news broke of the tragic death and life of Jason St. Laurent. At the behest of Frank Champagnolle, Rondo kept Rocky out of the official report, but rumors spread. Primarily because, while she may never admit it to Rocky's face, Darrelene Champagnolle was nothing if not a proud mother.

Freddy Van Vleck distanced himself from Jeffrey Baumgardner (the last name even more surprising to Rocky than the first), so he skated on all possible charges. But Waverly fired him and talked Georgia Lee into representing Jason. From what Rocky heard, Georgia Lee worked out a plea deal which would allow Jason to see freedom again in his life.

Before the buzz about the case built into too much fury, Hi Hallmark wrote a piece about what these new revelations meant for the Rye Mother. The mere mention of the salacious cold serial killer case all but eradicated thoughts of Jason St. Laurent. Rocky was thrilled to get a little reprieve before the quarterly Junior League meeting.

Waverly went home free from all charges or suspicion. Statute of limitations protected her from any wrongdoing in Jason's fake murder. And, in all honesty, everyone in town felt too sorry for her to stand for any further persecution. Rocky could get behind a charge of some kind, but she was a minority of one. Still, Waverly had yet to leave her house after the news hit the public, which meant she did not attend the quarterly meeting when Brittney Binet Bridges announced the reinstated offer of full funding of the new member project by Waverly St. Laurent.

"Girls," Brittney crooned. "You are not going to believe this!" She paused for dramatic effect.

Rocky leaned over to Jen and whispered, "God, I hope she pulls off a mask like on *Scooby-Doo*."

Jen elbowed her.

Brittney raised both hands over her head in triumph. "The new member project is triple funded!"

Everyone cheered. Rocky frowned. "Triple funded? She said that like it's a thing. No one uses triple funded as a normal term."

Brittney waved for quiet. "In addition to Waverly St. Laurent," she put her hands to her chest in respect, "following through with her original offer of full funding, the new member fundraiser brought in over twenty thousand dollars!"

Everyone cheered again. Rocky called out, "Minus legal expenses," but her words got lost in the noise.

Brittney hushed everyone again. "With this type of funding, we will be able to provide luggage for each and every displaced child in Texarkana for the next three years. Wonderful work, girls."

After a little more self-congratulation and shrill cheering, the group broke to mingle and sip wine with recruits for next year's new member class. Rocky tried to hang back in a corner, but blonde girls all named Brittney kept finding her and saying things like, "Girl, I heard you're a regular Nancy Drew."

Rocky managed to dodge going into details. Offering comments like, "I prefer Miss Marple, but with an ass that won't quit. More like a mix between Olivia Benson, Veronica Mars, and Kim Kardashian. Like if Rizzoli and Isles raised the love child of Peter Dinklage and Jennifer Lopez."

Most Brittneys would try and fail to chuckle and then walk away to leave Rocky with her wine. She sidled off to a table at the side of the room where she could sit alone with three different bottles of sweet white wine and three glasses. She poured them out into each a different glass when Jen ran up to her. "Rocky, what are you doing?"

Rocky eyed the level in her glasses to see if they were even. "I am performing an experiment, Jen. We're going to see which wine makes me take my top off first."

"Well, straighten up and come meet someone."

Rocky shook her head, still studying her wine. "Nope. I've met two people already. Any more and I start to get confused. Like a baby wolf in a stuffed animal factory. Poor thing would never know its mother's love, Jen."

"Rocky, this is serious. I met a girl who needs our help."

"I don't do help. I do sardonic wit and insults and revenge capers where we steal back her grandmother's engagement ring from her lesbian lover." Rocky looked at Jen. "Does her lesbian lover own a safe? I'd really love to crack a safe."

Jen shook her head. "There is no lesbian lover."

Rocky clucked her tongue. "Too bad. I wanted to serve as a helpmeet to my fellow—"

"Her sister is missing, Rocky."

Rocky sighed. "Jen. I can't go running to help every—"

"She disappeared from a locked room without a trace."

Rocky paused. "Locked room?"

Jen nodded. "Locked room. And this girl is super sweet. She would be a great person to—"

Rocky waved a hand. "You're ruining it, Jen. Locked room. Stop at locked room." Rocky grabbed a wine glass. "Just let me finish my experiment real quick."

Before she could take a drink, someone behind her walked by and bumped Rocky's shoulder with her purse. Rocky's hand jerked, spilling wine all over the table. Rocky mumbled, "Motherfucker." She stood up and turned around to find four women grouped up behind her like a parliament of magpies. The woman who bumped her was oblivious to the fact.

Rocky and Jen lingered until one of the four—Christina from the baking group—looked past the three strangers and said, "Oh! Jen! Rocky! Let me introduce you!" The three strangers turned to face them. Christina pointed to them one by one, the first two were probably named Brittney. Rocky stopped paying attention. The third was the one she was waiting on.

She stood a good six feet tall, towering over Rocky. She was lean, not too skinny, but thin and fit. Like someone who cycled. Or at least did a fucking spin class. Her blonde hair fell down past her shoulders, with a few dark hints mingled in. Maybe someone gave her bad highlights. Rocky seemed to remember knowing a shitty hairdresser once. Christina motioned toward the towering woman and said, "And this is Cordelia Cornet."

When Christina spoke the name, Cordelia held out her hand and smiled in the most peculiar way. Her mouth twisted a little, staying closed. The smile of someone with bad teeth. But a deliberate approach, like she took too many selfies.

Christina patted Cordelia's shoulder and added, "Cordelia was Miss Teen Texarkana. Can you believe that?"

Rocky shook her head. "No." She never shook Cordelia's hand, but rather turned to Jen. "Did you know a group of magpies is called a parliament, Jen?"

Jen frowned and shook her head. Christina just laughed and said, "Oh, Rocky. You are so funny." She led her parliament off to meet other people.

As they started away, Cordelia paused and turned back. "Wonderful job on your new member project, by the way." She narrowed her eyes into a repeat of that horrible smile along with something one could mistake for a laugh.

When they walked off, Jen made a slight gagging sound and grabbed Rocky's arm. "Okay. Now, let's go meet—"

Rocky stared off after the tall blonde and squinted, rubbing her hands in front of her face. She muttered, "What the hell do you suppose she meant by that?" Rocky's lip snarled up in a soured expression of disdain. She whispered, "Cordelia Cornet."

Jen hung her head and sighed. "Jesus, Rocky."

End

Rocky's Mountain High Brownies

Cannabutter:

4 sticks of butter for each ounce of pot

1. Preheat oven to 245
2. Heat * cannabis buds for 40 minutes
3. Finely grind buds to a powder
4. Melt butter in saucepan on low heat
5. Add cannabis powder and simmer for 1 hour (45 minutes if using half the butter/cannabis)
6. Strain butter into a glass jar (using a spoon to press ground cannabis until all butter is strained into the jar)
7. Refrigerate butter until it sets up

Brownies:

8 tablespoons of unsalted butter

1 tablespoon of cannabutter

1 cup of sugar

2 eggs

1 teaspoon of vanilla extract

⅓ cup of Guittard Rouge Unsweetened cocoa powder

½ cup of all-purpose flour

¼ teaspoon of salt

¼ teaspoon of baking powder

1. Preheat oven to 350 degrees
2. Grease and flour an 8-inch square pan
3. Melt butter and cannabutter over low heat
4. Remove from heat and stir in sugar, eggs, and vanilla extract
5. Beat in cocoa powder, flour, salt, and baking powder
6. Spread powder in pan
7. Bake for 25 minutes (or until a toothpick doesn't come out with batter on it)

*Publisher and Author Disclaimer: Do not use this recipe if you live in jurisdictions that do not permit use of some of the above ingredients.

Acknowledgments

This book, more than any other I have written, is loosely based on a lot of very real people. So I have to start by thanking all the people who stroll through my life never realizing they might be becoming a character. I took plenty of liberties and changed enough to probably make some happy and piss others off. Just know you all made an impression on me, and that's more than can be said for so many people not in the book. Those who are friends and family, I love you more than you know. I wouldn't write about you otherwise. And for those I haven't gotten to yet, your time is coming.

Writing is a hard gig, man. And none of us get anywhere in this business alone. I may not have forced this manuscript on everyone like I usually do, but I still depended on the support of so many writers and friends to get it over the finish line. Matt Lyle, as always. My Pandamoon family: Zara, Allan, and Don Kramer; Elgon Williams; Christine Gabriel; Meg Bonney; Laura Ellen Scott; and my editor … Jessica Reino, you do not have an easy job, and I thank you. I also thank my family of writers: John Vercher, Amina Akhtar, PJ Vernon, Kelly Ford (and Sarah!!), Penni Jones, Stephanie Gayle, Emily Ross, and Shawn Cosby. You people are my tribe, and I love all of you. Also, Gabino Iglesias, Sara Lippmann, David Joy, Angel Colon, Cheryl Head, David Nemeth, Alex Segura, Neil White, Ted Flanagan, Kellye Garrett, and a ton of people I'm forgetting. You've all lifted me up in some way. For that, I thank you. And don't think I'm forgetting the AWDC: Eli Cranor, Travis Simpson, David Tromblay, John Post, Josh Wilson, and Mike Sutton … I see you, fellas.

But this book is really a love letter. It's a love letter to a person who completely changed my life for the better. I made it through some dark times in the past several years. I learned to be a single dad to two wonderful kids. But it was tough. And lonely. Sam, you have made me a better person. And this book is for you. I started it as a present that no one else was meant to see. But when you marry a writer … there's always that chance. And so here we are. Your book is out there. But it's still your book. It always will be. I wrote it about you. For you. Turning it into a series of mysteries doesn't change that. I swear. I love you more than I can ever write, no matter how many Rocky books there may be. I even changed my writer photo for you to something where I'm smiling. With flowers. Because you make me feel like I should never be embarrassed to smile in front of some flowers. I love you.

About the Author

Matt Coleman is a writer of mystery and comedy. *A Rocky Divorce* is his third novel. His debut, *Juggling Kittens*, was recently optioned for a feature film. His second book, *Graffiti Creek*, was not. Matt's comedic writings have included *Raptured: A Sex Farce at the End of the World*, co-written with Matt Lyle, and a three-year stint writing for the comedy podcast, *The City Life Supplement*. Shorter fiction can be found between the pages of *Ellery Queen Mystery Magazine*, online at *Shotgun Honey*, or at Book Riot, where Matt is a regular contributor. He is the father of two girls, who are growing up too fast. Matt lives in Texarkana, Arkansas, with a beautiful wife who is way out of his league.

Thank you for purchasing this copy of *A Rocky Divorce*, Book 1 in <u>A Rocky Series of Mysteries</u>. If you enjoyed this book, please let the author know by posting a review.

Growing good ideas into great reads…one book at a time.

Visit http://www.pandamoonpublishing.com to learn about other works by our talented authors.

Mystery/Thriller/Suspense

- *A Rocky Series of Mysteries Book 1: A Rocky Divorce* by Matt Coleman
- *A Flash of Red* by Sarah K. Stephens
- *Ballpark Mysteries Book 1: Murder at First Pitch* by Nicole Asselin
- *Code Gray* by Benny Sims
- *Evening in the Yellow Wood* by Laura Kemp
- *Fate's Past* by Jason Huebinger
- *Graffiti Creek* by Matt Coleman
- *Juggling Kittens* by Matt Coleman
- *Killer Secrets* by Sherrie Orvik
- *Knights of the Shield* by Jeff Messick
- *Kricket* by Penni Jones
- *Looking into the Sun* by Todd Tavolazzi
- *On the Bricks Series Book 1: On the Bricks* by Penni Jones
- *Project 137* by Seth Augenstein
- *Rogue Alliance* by Michelle Bellon
- *Southbound* by Jason Beem
- *The Juliet* by Laura Ellen Scott
- *The Last Detective* by Brian Cohn
- *The Moses Winter Mysteries Book 1: Made Safe* by Francis Sparks
- *The New Royal Mysteries Book 1: The Mean Bone in Her Body* by Laura Ellen Scott
- *The New Royal Mysteries Book 2: Crybaby Lane* by Laura Ellen Scott
- *The Ramadan Drummer* by Randolph Splitter
- *The Teratologist Series Book 1: The Teratologist* by Ward Parker
- *The Unraveling of Brendan Meeks* by Brian Cohn
- *The Zeke Adams Series Book 1: Pariah* by Ward Parker
- *This Darkness Got to Give* by Dave Housley

Science Fiction/Fantasy

- *Children of Colonodona Book 1: The Wizard's Apprentice* by Alisse Lee Goldenberg
- *Children of Colonodona Book 2: The Island of Mystics* by Alisse Lee Goldenberg
- *Dybbuk Scrolls Trilogy Book 1: The Song of Hadariah* by Alisse Lee Goldenberg
- *Dybbuk Scrolls Trilogy Book 2: The Song of Vengeance* by Alisse Lee Goldenberg
- *Dybbuk Scrolls Trilogy Book 3: The Song of War* by Alisse Lee Goldenberg
- *Everly Series Book 1: Everly* by Meg Bonney
- *Hello World* by Alexandra Tauber and Tiffany Rose
- *Finder Series Book 1: Chimera Catalyst* by Susan Kuchinskas
- *Fried Windows (In a Light White Sauce)* by Elgon Williams
- *Magehunter Saga Book 1: Magehunter* by Jeff Messick
- *Revengers* by David Valdes Greenwood
- *The Bath Salts Journals: Volume One* by Alisse Lee Goldenberg and An Tran
- *The Crimson Chronicles Book 1: Crimson Forest* by Christine Gabriel
- *The Crimson Chronicles Book 2: Crimson Moon* by Christine Gabriel
- *The Phaethon Series Book 1: Phaethon* by Rachel Sharp
- *The Phaethon Series Book 2: Pharos* by Rachel Sharp
- *The Sitnalta Series Book 1: Sitnalta* by Alisse Lee Goldenberg
- *The Sitnalta Series Book 2: The Kingdom Thief* by Alisse Lee Goldenberg
- *The Sitnalta Series Book 3: The City of Arches* by Alisse Lee Goldenberg
- *The Sitnalta Series Book 4: The Hedgewitch's Charm* by Alisse Lee Goldenberg
- *The Sitnalta Series Book 5: The False Princess* by Alisse Lee Goldenberg
- *The Thuperman Trilogy Book 1: Becoming Thuperman* by Elgon Williams
- *The Thuperman Trilogy Book 2: Homer Underby* by Elgon Williams
- *The Wolfcat Chronicles Book 1: Dammerwald* by Elgon Williams

Women's Fiction

- *Beautiful Secret* by Dana Faletti
- *Find Me in Florence* by Jule Selbo
- *The Long Way Home* by Regina West
- *The Mason Siblings Series Book 1: Love's Misadventure* by Cheri Champagne
- *The Mason Siblings Series Book 2: The Trouble with Love* by Cheri Champagne
- *The Mason Siblings Series Book 3: Love and Deceit* by Cheri Champagne
- *The Mason Siblings Series Book 4: Final Battle for Love* by Cheri Champagne
- *The Seductive Spies Series Book 1: The Thespian Spy* by Cheri Champagne
- *The Seductive Spy Series Book 2: The Seamstress and the Spy* by Cheri Champagne
- *The Shape of the Atmosphere* by Jessica Dainty
- *The To-Hell-And-Back Club Book 1: The To-Hell-And-Back Club* by Jill Hannah Anderson
- *The To-Hell-And-Back Club Book 2: Crazy Little Town Called Love* by Jill Hannah Anderson

Made in the USA
Las Vegas, NV
02 September 2021

29504797R00118